GIFTED

J.A. George

To Hanawi

CHAPTER ONE

Someone was watching me.

I turned the corner onto Dulscent Street, normally busy at five in the evening, but always deserted when it was raining. I looked back and caught the tail of a long black coat. Or it could have been a long black skirt. Trying to open my eyes wider was pointless because whatever I'd seen had already gone and I only saw what I'd squinted my eyes to avoid – flying strands of my brown hair and stray rain droplets.

A woman stepped out of the dental practice on the other side of the road, her heels clicking on the pavement as she ran to her car, climbed inside and drove off. Only a few other shops were open out of the many lining the street since most owners decided to close early on a Saturday. The dull, cloud-heavy sky drowned the entire town in grey, so I supposed shopping wasn't what people had in mind.

That's probably who was watching me, someone on their way home. Why were they staring at me? Well, I did the same thing when it was only me and another person and they couldn't see me. That's all it was. I shook off the *the call is coming from inside the house* feeling and carried on up the hill. The wind blustered downwards, coercing my umbrella and me in opposite directions. My boyfriend jacket released itself from my one-handed grip, the zip scratching my palm as it did so and flapped behind me. My fault for thinking a jacket one size down from my actual size would fit.

I felt my phone vibrate in my pocket, but didn't answer it. I knew it would be Toni as she always grows slightly piqued whenever I'm late and whenever I'm late, she calls. The restaurant was at least ten minutes away and I was currently fighting against the wind, and losing, so it would take me even longer to get there. A fact I didn't want to have to explain to a hungry friend.

As soon as my phone stopped buzzing, the wind became too strong a match for my umbrella and snapped its rusted hinges, leaving shredded holes in the multi-coloured nylon. *Balls. That had been my favourite umbrella.* I shoved it into a nearby bin and carried on up the road. As if wrecking my umbrella hadn't been enough, the wind suddenly steeled its breath before blowing it out with fervour, almost throwing me back down the hill. 'This isn't normal!' Whether I was talking to myself or to the wind, I was too cold and wet to decide.

It almost always rained here in Huxton and in winter the temperature never reached above ten degrees Celsius, but this was England – you could only ask for so much. But the wind and rain had never been this strong before or appeared so suddenly; it had been cold sunshine when I'd left my student flat

A storm must be coming.

Funny how it came when I had no umbrella, a coat I couldn't zip up and shoes with open tops.

With my head down to shield against the fierce air, I pushed against the burgeoning storm. The shorter strands of my layered hair wrapped across my face, my jacket flapped around my shoulders, and my feet slapped shallow puddles. With every step I took, my breathing grew laboured and I soon had to stop to catch my breath. When I looked up again, I was standing outside a familiar alleyway. My friend Jamie once told me that going through this alley and straight down the road would lead to the very edge of the street where I needed to be now. I'd also overheard a girl in one of my lectures say she'd been robbed going through the same alleyway at night. It wasn't exactly *Sophie's Choice*, but it wasn't chicken or fish either.

I continued to loiter at the entrance. It was the long tunnel and arch-shaped top obscuring any natural light that put me off. And the unshakable feeling that somebody was *still* watching me. I looked back and again saw the flying end of a black coat or skirt disappear around another corner. This street was filled with corners, filled with places for people to hide.

I pulled my jacket in as tight as it would go and walked through the empty alleyway. I stepped out onto a pathway with trees lined up on the left side and various shops dotted beside each other on the right. All of the shops were closed and the street was completely empty. The wind was calmer on this side of the road and I took the time to push back all the hair stuck to my forehead and cheeks that had come loose from my ponytail. I checked my watch and then considered the likelihood of me running to the opposite side of the street without tripping over thin air, when I heard a scream.

I whipped my head around and the wind returned with a vengeance. It cried and echoed over the treetops, pushing and pulling me in different directions. My heart kicked repeatedly against my ribcage as I regained my balance. I scanned the area to see if any form of danger was heading my way, but it had grown too dark to see if anyone was around. If I got robbed now, I'd never forgive myself. My body remained frozen, until a gust of wind, seemingly separate from that which was already blowing, swept by.

Something wasn't right.

I had the undeniable feeling that I was not alone, and it was with this thought that iced fingers pinched the nape of my neck before melting, dripping down my back in one steady stream. There had been something strange about that gust of wind – it seemed to signal the end of something. And where had that scream come from?

I wrestled my jacket to fit back around me. 'Hello?' I said. Even if somebody was around, they wouldn't be able to hear me amidst the howling gales.

My phone vibrated against my thigh and I came to, biting the inside of my lip on the way. I didn't check to see who it might be but instead decided to walk forward. I made it a few feet before a loud crashing sound came next, an amalgam of broken glass, heavy books hitting the floor, and upheaved tables. I halted where a bookshop was located on my right; a big, grey marble building, artistically decorated in black and silver. Three quarters of the bookshop's face was taken up by a large window, leaving the remaining quarter for double doors with silver handles. The top of the building bore the words *Hayven Books*. The sign in the window said *Closed*.

I hesitated before embracing whatever it was that compelled me to walk closer to the doors, the fight part of my fight or flight instinct maybe, despite knowing deep down that it would probably be best to turn and walk the other way. I continued to take small steps forward until my hand reached the handle because I knew even deeper down that I couldn't just walk away. Not if somebody was in trouble, hurt, or...

Dying.

Every muscle in my body tightened. I continued to grip the side of the door I'd opened before slowly edging closer, until I found myself on my knees beside an old woman lying on the floor in the midst of scattered and battered books. Her body lay lifeless and she was leaking blood from her back, as if she'd been punctured. The old woman's hair must have been in a bun that had come loose during whatever struggle she'd been involved in, as silver tendrils spiralled out from within her hair band. Her eyes were hidden under blue, vein-lined lids, and her extended arms were limp. *Who would do this to a defenceless old woman?* I looked around the room but it was only us here. The perpetrators had gone. Probably with all the money from the upended till.

Suddenly the woman's right leg twitched and I flinched away until she became still. I waited a few moments to see if she would move again, the only sound being my shallow breathing and the rain as it attacked the windows. She didn't. I studied the woman's pale, soft face before deciding I couldn't just wait for something to happen. I rolled up my jacket sleeves and placed the palms of my hands against her chest to check for signs of breathing. My hands grew wet. I withdrew them and found that they were covered with red, *glistening* blood.

I dropped back on my heels and felt the world stop. I opened my mouth to breathe and my shortness of breath came out in puffs of silence. I turned to notice that closer up the trail of blood that flowed from the woman's back matched the blood on my hands, blood that looked like it had

11

been doused in glitter. It shined and sparkled even in the dimly lit room. It was almost...*beautiful*. The stream of blood continued to travel downwards, slashing a line across the floor, almost reaching the door and decorating the cream-and-coffee-coloured marble swirls with red.

Then it stopped flowing and began to *disappear*, retreating up the route it had travelled down, as if being sucked back into the woman. The blood on my hands also began to slowly fade. The woman's eyes flickered open. She grabbed my exposed arm at the wrist. I started at her sudden, cold touch and looked down at her. Trapped inside her dark blue eyes was the reflected image of my own brown eyes, dilated and fearful. The woman opened her mouth to speak, her stare unwavering as she said, 'The Cliders have returned...growing each day in strength and numbers...Madrina...Hayven...you must lead as I once did...you must fight...you must win...or...*terrible* darkness.'

The woman's breathing became dangerously erratic, her voice weak and hoarse towards the end. Her grip on my arm tightened with a strength I never thought possible in such a frail and dying woman. I went to pry her hand from my wrist, to unlock her fierce grip, but ended up gasping at the sight. The hand holding onto my wrist had become almost transparent, the woman's blue veins more prominent, and as I watched, her veins turned purple, then blue, then silver, and back to blue again. One look at my arm showed the numerous lines of veins beneath my pale skin doing the same. I stared, transfixed and horrified. My mind grew foggy and my gaze hazy. The blood in my body was flowing fast and the room began to spin. Soon, darkness clouded my vision. I could only hear the sorrowful song that the wind made the trees sing, the sound of the rain pummelling the empty street and the loud drumming in my ears. Images flickered by in the darkness. A random city. A dark sky. A burning park. A house on fire. A woman on the top of a cliff, watching it all with a smile on her face. A Muslim girl. A boy wearing glasses. When my sight finally cleared, the silver-haired woman smiled softly up at me as she released her grip, letting her hand fall back to her side.

'You will do well, Ava,' she said before she took her final breath, closed her eyes peacefully and died.

It was at that moment I lost consciousness.

CHAPTER TWO

I woke up in a hospital bed, my eyes victim to a harsh light.

'Oh! Thank goodness you're up!'

I turned to my right, where to my surprise, Toni was standing. Her dark blonde hair had been thrown into a bun, her hazel eyes, wide and filled with apprehension, were fixed on me, and her slim face was taut and looked even paler due to the moonlight streaming in through the window. Once my eyes properly adjusted, I found that the bright light came from a small table lamp on my left. The rest of the room was shrouded in shadows created by that lamp, the glow from the moon, and the light coming in from the hospital window where a nurse sat at her desk in the hallway.

'What's going on?' I asked. My tongue felt heavy in my mouth, causing my words to slide into one another. I tried to lift my head, but was rewarded only with dizziness. 'What happened?'

Toni stepped forward to explain but before she could, a doctor walked in.

'Hello, Avery,' she said. 'I'm Doctor Matthews. How are you feeling?'

I felt disorientated and actually quite disgruntled, as if I'd been shoved awake before I was ready. 'Urm…Fine, thank you?'

'Good. Now, do you remember why you're here?'

Doctor Matthews had kind brown eyes and a mass of curly hair that looked impossible to constrain and it suddenly all came rushing back. The bookshop, the old, silver-haired woman, the sparkling blood that had disappeared and our veins changing colour. I stared silently down at my arm, rubbing my skin and forgetting to answer the doctor's question. When I finally looked up again, two policemen were standing outside my door, staring back at me through the window. I sat up.

'You're not in any trouble, Avery. They just want to ask you a few questions about the event,' Doctor Mathews assured. 'Is that okay?'

I nodded again. It seemed to be the only thing I could do. What did the police want with me? What had happened to that woman? The silver-haired woman who had taken hold of my arm and changed the colour of my veins? The woman who had shown me things, had said I'd do well. The woman who had known my name.

The two policemen took Doctor Matthews's nod of consent to mean they could come in. They came to stand at the foot of my bed and I noticed that the two policemen were in fact, one policeman and one policewoman.

'Hello, Miss Gray,' the policewoman said. She had blonde hair pulled back into a low ponytail and a round face that made her look approachable. 'I'm Officer Roberts and this is Officer Madden.' She gestured to the taller, more stern-looking policeman. 'How are you feeling tonight?' she asked.

'Fine, I suppose.' I rubbed the back of my neck whilst looking warily at both officers. I've watched enough TV shows to know that the police rarely delivered good news.

'Good,' said Officer Madden, clearly more interested in getting to the point of their visit. He on the other hand looked much less friendlier than his partner. He kept a straight face, his brow was wrinkled in a constant state of suspicion and his chin jutted out impatiently. 'We want to ask you a few questions concerning the events that occurred in *Hayven Books* several hours ago.'

Several hours ago? I turned to see the clock above Toni announce the day was nearing an end.

'You've been unconscious for six hours,' Toni whispered to me, spotting the look of confusion on my face.

'*Six* hours?' I repeated. 'Really?'

Toni nodded, the apprehension flooding her eyes understandable to me now.

'Oh.' I turned back to face the police officers and nodded. Again.

'Did you know, or have any relation to, Sidra Calix?' Officer Roberts asked.

I looked towards each officer. 'I'm sorry, who?'

'The elderly woman you were found lying beside in the bookshop,' Officer Madden clarified.

'Oh. No, I didn't know her,' I answered truthfully. I didn't even know her name was Sidra, having never met her before. Yet, she had known me. My gaze went back to my arm.

'Can you tell us in your own words exactly what happened?' Officer Roberts asked. By the way she already had her pen poised to write on her pad, I knew this wasn't so much a question but an order.

So I told them everything that had happened, right up to finding Sidra lying on the floor, blood flowing from —

'Blood?' Officer Madden interrupted. 'There was no blood on the scene or anywhere on the victim's body.'

Then I remembered how the blood had disappeared from the floor and from my hands.

'*Oh*...really?' I cleared my throat to hide the tremor. 'It must have been the shock...or a trick of the light.'

Both officers nodded, convinced.

'Please, go on,' Officer Roberts prompted, but I didn't continue. I couldn't tell anyone in the room what had happened from that point onwards; how Sidra had woken up, grabbed my arm and...had done whatever she had done. With no proof, nobody in the room would believe me, not even Toni. They'd all think I was mad and it was too early in the game to say they'd be wrong.

'Do you remember anything else, Miss Gray?' Officer Roberts asked.

'No.'

'Right,' Officer Madden said, straightening his jacket, 'it's likely Mrs Calix died from something age-related; a natural cause no one could help.' He turned from Officer Roberts who closed her notepad. 'The doctors believe you passed out from the shock, can't say I blame you, seeing something like that at such a young age. Nothing helps prepare you for death,' he said before giving me a small, sympathetic smile, but for some reason, I didn't believe it. 'Well, that's all for now. We'll leave you to recuperate and if we need anything else, we'll be in touch. Thank you for your cooperation.' With a final smile from both officers, they left the room. My eyes followed the back of Office Madden.

'Your blood work has come back and your vitals are normal, so you're free to go,' Doctor Matthews said, bringing my attention back. 'Unless you'd like to stay in overnight, just to make sure?'

'No, thank you,' I replied. 'I'd like to go home.' Hospitals were not my favourite place to visit, minor injury or not.

Doctor Matthews nodded and with a soft smile that reached her eyes, she left the room.

I turned to Toni whose static facial expression almost made me chuckle.

'Honestly, Toni, I'm fine.' And I was. 'Just a little tired.'

'You were unconscious for six hours,' Toni replied, stressing each word. 'How can you be fine? Or tired?'

I rolled my eyes and gingerly swung my legs off the bed and was surprised to find that I was relatively stable on my feet. My legs felt a bit weak, like they were sore, but I was able to walk out of the hospital and to Toni's car without assistance.

'I know I should be calmer now that you're fine and everything, but you really scared me, Ava,' Toni said once we'd gotten into her car. 'I thought you were dead!'

'How did you even find me?' I asked, plugging in my seatbelt.

'I'd been ringing your mobile phone non-stop, but you weren't answering my calls,' Toni explained, putting her key into the ignition. 'I thought you were just ignoring them; I had no idea it was because you were passed out on a bookshop floor!'

I shifted in my seat. There was clearly no need to tell her that I had been ignoring her calls and that the incident hadn't happened until after she'd stopped trying to call. No harm done.

'Anyway,' Toni continued, 'I got tired of waiting and was on my way back to your room. Thankfully, I always take that short-cut Jamie told us about and when I passed by, the bookshop door was wide open and there you were! Lying right next to that Sidra woman, completely knocked out.'

To think, if Toni had been the one running late, it might have been me standing beside her hospital bed. I was glad she'd been on time; I wouldn't have wanted her to have experienced… *that* or to feel so unsettled, too scared and nervous to admit how I truly felt right now.

Looking out of the car window to the cloudless, calm sky, something suddenly occurred to me. 'Hey, Tone, was it raining and like, ridiculously windy when you found me?'

'What? No,' she replied, backing out of the car park. 'It was a little cold, but the sun was out. Why?'

'No reason.' I stared down to where Sidra had held my wrist hours ago.

'You okay?' Toni asked, her eyebrows joining in the middle.

'Yeah,' I said. 'I'm fine.'

It took a while before everyone would believe that I was fine, leaving me on my own after heading off to their own student flats on the university campus. Toni had called the entire gang when we left the hospital, starting with Jamie, who had then called Alfie and Susie, and I was met at the university car-park with even more taut, concerned faces. It was nice to know they cared about me, but I didn't like being the centre of a big fuss, especially when there was nothing to worry about. I *was* absolutely fine, in the sense that I was still

19

breathing, but for some reason, to my friends, I must have looked all set to embrace the angel of death. Susie's anxious blue eyes watched me continuously as if she thought I would faint at any moment, and Alfie kept one protective hand on my arm as we all climbed my building's three flights of stairs. Jamie even offered to carry me up, but I declined. Not because it would be a lot of effort on Jamie's part. I was heavier than Toni and Susie, but he was quite muscular so I imagined I wouldn't weigh too much for him, but because, again, it wasn't necessary.

It was now past two in the morning and I'd just finished listening to all the messages on my phone. Five were from Toni asking where I was, her tone in each message sounding more peeved off than in the last. Somewhere along the line my parents had been informed about the incident as there was also a message from my mum, telling me that despite being assured by both Toni and Doctor Matthews, herself and my dad were coming down at noon to make sure I was okay. As it was now early morning, that meant *this* afternoon, which happened to be less than ten hours away. I sat cross-armed at my desk and stared out of the window. The night was black, but the university street lamps were on and beacons of light illuminated the grassy grounds and the gold and burnt orange beech trees.

It had been a spur of the moment decision to move from London to Huxton for university, but I've never regretted it. Huxton University was only an hour away from London by train, yet it was so different from England's capital. It was a small town, with cool afternoon breezes and old houses. The quiet and normalcy, that's what I've always liked most about it here. The ease of fitting in. Tonight was the first time I'd looked at Huxton in a new way. It wasn't my safety I worried about, dangerous things happen in every town in the world, but Sidra managing to change the colour of my veins hadn't been a magic trick. I didn't believe in hobgoblins or bugbears. I didn't believe in the impossible. Yet, I couldn't help but consider that perhaps Huxton wasn't as normal a town as I had once thought. The disappearing blood I could blame on shock – if I tried hard enough – but the sudden change of weather coinciding with Sidra's scream? The feeling that something significant had ended before I found Sidra? The feeling that something was just beginning? The person watching me? Those were occurrences I couldn't blame on anything plausible.

I switched off my phone and placed it on my bed side table. I got into bed, prepared for the lack of sleep I would endure, expecting to stay awake for the rest of the morning, haunted by earlier events. But as soon as my head touched my pillow, I was out quicker than a dwindling candle flame in the midst of a brewing storm.

I woke up nine hours later feeling oddly refreshed, almost as if last night hadn't happened. I found myself looking down at my arm again; I didn't know why I kept doing that, but it was quickly becoming a reflex. Nothing had changed on my arm; there was no rash, no bruising, no change of colour, and my veins were gently staring up at me beneath the surface of my skin, their usual pale blue. There had been an irritating and itchy spot on my arm a few days ago, but I couldn't be certain *when* that had disappeared.

21

In the shower, I thought about last night's dream. I'd dreamt of a blank canvas and occasionally a burst of coloured light would shoot out of nowhere and streak across the blackness only to disappear off into the dark distance, somewhere I couldn't see. I chose not to dwell on it, as it wasn't the first weird dream I'd had and thanks to the events of last night, I doubted it would be my last.

At least I'd gotten some sleep. I'd imagined that as soon as I'd closed my eyes, images of Sidra Calix lying in a pool of sparkling blood would creep up, but there had been no dreams of Sidra Calix, *Hayven Books*, or any of last night's happenings. I had witnessed someone die and it didn't seem to be affecting me in the kind of way I'd have expected it to. For some strange reason, it was as if I couldn't accept that Sidra had died, even though I'd watched her take her last breath. I couldn't shake the feeling that she was still alive.

I left my flat and headed in the direction of the restaurant I'd convinced Mum to meet me at for lunch, located in the middle of Dulscent Street. It was just past twelve in the afternoon on a Sunday, meaning almost no students were awake, let alone outside and because a rather cold wind floated around the town, not many people were on the streets either.

I reached the town centre a lot quicker than yesterday and as I passed the alleyway entrance, an unnerving tingle made its way down my back. All the horror movies had it right, no good came from alleyways. I took one last look before hastening my steps towards the restaurant.

'Oh! Hello, sweetheart! My poor darling!' My mum enveloped me in a warm perfume-scented hug as soon as I'd stepped through the restaurant's front doors. 'How are you feeling?' she asked, placing a hand on my forehead.

My mum meant a lot to me, I loved her more than anyone. She may not have saved me from a burning building, or risked her life for mine – that I knew of – but she'd lovingly nurtured me for nineteen years. Nobody would ever care for me the way she did. I smiled for the first time today.

'I'm fine, Mum, I feel just... fine.' I kissed her forehead and she smiled. 'I'm the mum, not you,' she used to say whenever I did that when I was younger. 'Hey, Dad,' I greeted, gently edging past to reach my dad who was waiting with his arms outstretched beside our table. My dad was a tall man, standing at a towering six-feet, four-inches. He was where I got my five-feet, eight-inch height from, as well as my brown hair, brown, near-sighted eyes and appetite for food. Unlike Mum, he looked more composed. Although my dad did have a tendency to worry, he would only seriously fret if the situation were dire. I guessed that after he spoke and confirmed with Doctor Matthews that I wasn't lying at Death's Door patiently waiting to be answered, he had been able to relax.

'Hello, Ava,' he said as we took our seats. 'You look well, thank goodness. Better than your mother thought you would anyway.'

'What happened last night, sweetheart?' Mum asked as soon as she'd sat on her wooden seat. Although my mum's short, blonde hair was neatly combed and her make-up immaculate; her blouse buttoned correctly and her linen trousers pressed to perfection, I noticed the small, dark areas under her eyes due to the lack of sleep I knew she would suffer. Her blue eyes watched me nervously, like she was waiting for me to flip out at any moment. 'We want to know the full story. Toni assured us we had nothing to worry about, but your father and I thought it best to visit and make sure. Hear the events of last night for ourselves.' *She does seem okay; I don't think she's pretending. They must have taken wonderful care of her at the hospital. I must remember to write that lovely Doctor Matthews a Thank-You card...*

I jerked backwards and my chair scraped across the wooden floor. 'Mum?'

'Yes, dear?'

'How did you do that?'

'Do what?' she asked.

'What you just did. Speak without moving your lips...'

My parents exchanged puzzled looks with one another before my mum asked, 'Darling, what are you talking about?'

Good question. What am I talking about? What was that voice I'd just heard? I looked behind me to see if I'd been unintentionally eavesdropping on somebody else's conversation, but we were the only people seated at a table. Anyway, it couldn't have been someone else because it had been my mother's voice I'd heard. Hadn't it?

'Ava?'

'What was the last thing you just said?' I asked.

'I said your father and I just wanted to make sure you were alright,' my mum answered.

So where had the rest come from? Had I just imagined it? That must be it, I had just imagined it. Or, predicted it. I could usually tell what my mum was going to say just by looking at her and this had been one of those moments, that's all. To be on the safe side I shook my head vigorously from side to side, just to clear my head of any more stray thoughts.

I looked up to find my dad's thick eyebrows fiercely furrowed, his fingers anxiously tapping his round belly and my mum's mouth slackened.

Perhaps she's not so okay after all...must be the trauma...

I flicked my head to my dad. His lips hadn't moved either.

'What's wrong?' he asked.

'What did you just say?'

'Ava! I didn't say anything.'

I turned my gaze back to my mum, then to my dad, then to my mum again.

'Sweetheart,' Mum whispered, 'are you hearing...*voices*?' The last word came out as a shrill squeak.

'No? I mean, no! Of course not,' I said. I wasn't crazy! 'My ears...they're...just blocked. I took a shower this morning, and a lot of water got into them so...I can't hear you properly, that's all.'

Somehow, my parents were mollified by this rather weak explanation, obviously as desperate as I was to believe me. My mum placed her hand on her chest as a gesture of relief and the fear in my dad's eyes fled as he removed his glasses momentarily to subtly dab at his forehead. I on the other hand, repeatedly brushed my jeans with my palms and watched my trembling right hand bounce up and down as I restlessly tapped my foot. *What's going on? Where were these voices coming from? What's happening to me?*

'Perhaps you should come home with us, Ava. Just for a few days so that I can look after you,' Mum suggested. *She's really not alright. Just look at her, pale as a ghost, eyes as wide as saucers and her mouth gaping open.*

I pressed my lips into a thin line and clenched my jaw. There it was again. Her voice but without her saying anything. So if I could hear her but she wasn't speaking...

'Mum...what are you...thinking?'

'I'm sorry?' she said.

'What are you thinking?' I repeated with a casual shrug. 'Right now, what's going through your head?'

'Well, the truth be told, I was thinking maybe you're not alright after all,' she confessed. 'Your eyes have grown twice their size and you've turned extremely pale in the last few minutes.'

I could hear my parents' thoughts. That was what was happening? *How could I possibly —*

'Ava?' my dad started.

'I'm fine! I promise. I'm fine,' I said, perhaps a little too hysterically for it to be deemed realistic. 'I'm not in shock and I'm not traumatised. Believe me, I really am...fine. Never been better.'

My parents didn't look too convinced this time, but luckily for me a waitress came to take our order before they had a chance to analyse my symptoms of insanity any further. As they conversed aloud as to what to order, sneaking furtive glances at me every so often, I stared down at my menu, aware that the words were beginning to swim and beads of sweat were starting to form on the bridge of my nose. Hearing voices? Wasn't that a myth?

I like her jumper. I wonder where she got it.

I slowly looked up to find the waitress staring at my navy turtle-neck.

I looked away and inhaled deeply. *Okay, organise yourself.* I just had to stay calm for the time being, finish lunch, convince my parents that I was okay, go home and lay down for a few hours. A nap could fix anything.

When our food reached the table, I looked down at the bowl of pasta I'd hurriedly ordered. As soon as the steam wafting off my three cheese pasta hit my nose, saliva started to build in the corners of my mouth – I was going to be sick. I pushed the bowl away from me before hastily dragging it back. If I didn't at least try to start my meal, my parents were going to get suspicious again and I didn't want to risk any questions that I would undoubtedly struggle to answer. I picked up my fork, stabbed a piece of pasta and put it into my mouth. I couldn't pick up any taste or texture and concentrated on keeping the food down.

My parents proceeded to ask me this, that, and the other about university and life in Huxton and I was able to give satisfactory answers, even managing to laugh convincingly at Dad's terrible jokes.

About an hour later, the waitress returned to clear away our bowls.

'Any dessert for you today?' she asked.

I was in the middle of shaking my head when Mum said, 'Of course, Ava always has dessert!'

The normal conversation we'd been having for the past hour had ironed out the anxiety-filled lines on my mother's forehead and any talk about silent voices was forgotten. I always ordered dessert when out with my parents and if I turned down the option of something sweet, the lines would return. *That's what you get for always eating so much.* Appreciation for food is what my mother calls it. Karma is what I'd now call it. I nodded at the waitress to answer her question and took the dessert menu she offered me.

After struggling through my cheesecake slice, my dad repositioned his glasses, ready to study the coffee menu. I feigned a long yawn and hoped for the right, concerned reaction from my parents.

'Oh, Ava, you must be exhausted. No coffee, thank you, just the bill please,' my dad told our waitress.

A few minutes later, we gathered outside the restaurant where Dad had parked the car. The breeze familiar to Huxton was colder than usual, with a distinctive bitter edge to it. I wrapped my cardigan tightly around myself, folding my arms across my chest to keep it in place.

'Now, you will call us if you need anything, won't you?' Mum asked.

'Of course,' I reassured. *A straitjacket, if you have one.*

'She's fine, Mandy,' Dad said, giving me one last hug that squashed my cheek against his woolly jumper, before making to get into the car. 'Look at her, all she needed was some good food and a visit from her old man!'

'Yes,' I agreed with a genuine smile, 'I hadn't eaten since yesterday afternoon.'

'Alright. Okay. But are you sure you don't want us to drop you off in front of your campus?' Mum asked for the third time.

'Yes, I'm sure. I want to walk back so I don't feel too lazy when I get home.'

Mum reluctantly nodded. *I'm sure she'll be fine.* Then she gave me a kiss on the cheek and got into the car. I waved them off and watched as they drove further and further away.

Once they were out of sight, I spun on my heels and walked with new purpose to the alleyway entrance. I didn't know what was going on, or why, but one thing I could no longer deny was that *something* happened to me last night at that bookshop. And it was time I found out what.

CHAPTER THREE

I stood in front of the double doors. The windows showed the inside of *Hayven Books* to be in complete darkness. All I could see was my own reflection. My brown, thick hair in its usual ponytail, the shorter strands framing my face, my brown almond-shaped eyes, my heart-shaped face, my pink lips, and although I couldn't see it through the dark glass, I knew the odd number of freckles on my cheeks were still there. *Hayven Books* was closed for the day.

I attempted to open the door all the same but as expected, it remained shut. With both hands on my hips, my reflection scowled back at me. I paced outside the bookshop, not wanting to return home without any answers. Then I banged on the door three times with the palm of my right hand before noticing a laminated sheet hanging from the inside of the door announcing the bookshop's hours. *Monday-Friday: 9am-6pm, Saturday: 10am-4pm, Sunday: closed.* Fine. I had to accept that short of breaking in, there was nothing I could do today. I kicked at an innocent passing leaf when a soft beeping sound came from the pocket of my cardigan. A message from Toni:

We're at the library for a study session if you feel like joining. X

They must be at the university library on campus. I decided to join them. The best thing to do would be to keep myself busy until tomorrow when I would visit *Hayven Books* again.

Toni, Susie, Alfie and Jamie were on the third floor, sat at a long table in the corner of the library. The area was one of the few spaces in the building where silence was mandatory, so I mouthed my hellos and sat next to Toni, opposite Susie. I took out my books and the various coloured pens used for making notes and settled in for what I'd hoped would be a productive couple of hours. But as soon as I'd opened my textbook onto the right page, people began to talk.

I looked up to find who the voices belonged to, but there were so many and I couldn't pinpoint any because nobody's lips were moving. I continued to search fruitlessly for a source until I felt a hand on my wrist and flinched, only to see it was Toni's. She slowly withdrew, her eyes wide but her forehead scrunched tight. I couldn't think of a way to explain my reaction to her innocent touch, so just gave a small smile that hopefully said: *Sorry, I'm fine*, before staring back down at my textbook. I attempted to ignore my friends' questioning looks that I could see from the corner of my eye, but it was difficult when it was not only them staring. Students I didn't know who were also seated around the table threw me fleeting glances.

I desperately wanted to escape, but I couldn't just pack my things, get up and leave when I'd just sat down. That sudden action would surely arouse unwanted suspicion and after lunch with my parents, I was out of false answers to difficult questions. The best thing to do was remain where I was.

It took eight minutes for the students I didn't know to grow disinterested and a little while longer for my friends' thoughts to go from *What's wrong with her?* to *She seems fine now*, and slowly but surely, their minds grew relatively silent. All but Alfie's.

She looks pretty today, but then again she always does… she still seems a bit off though…maybe I should wait awhile before asking her to dinner.

Oh.

Give her some time to adjust after the incident.

Alfie's thoughts shouldn't have been that much of a surprise to me because the girls – Toni and Susie – have always reckoned that Alfie *likes* me. Toni brings up the idea of Alfie and me 'together' often. She thinks it's unreasonable to be nineteen and not have had a proper boyfriend. Even Jamie reckons they could be right. Nonetheless, I didn't think it was true. Why would it be? I wasn't fat or ugly but when sat beside Toni and Susie, I wasn't the prettiest and my curves were a lot more *noticeable*. There was no competition. Or maybe I was being too hard on myself, like my mum always says I am and was just secretly hoping it wasn't true. Alfie's great; he's funny, laid-back and cute too, with sun-bleached blond hair and blue eyes that were always warm, but we've known each other for almost two years now.

Toni and I met in our last year of college when she first moved from Bath. Her and her family moved into the house next to my family home in London and we've been best friends ever since. We met Susie, Alfie and Jamie during our first year of university.

Susie used to be on the same International Business course as Toni and me, and one day, when Toni had been sick with the flu and confined to her bedroom for two weeks, Susie had sat in Toni's chair and introduced herself to me. 'Everyone calls me Suse,' she'd said, tucking a strand of long, blonde, wavy hair behind her ear. Three minutes into the lesson we had started bonding over how the course wasn't what we had expected. I'd decided to complete the year, just in case I changed my mind, but a month later, Susie changed her course to Creative Writing because she said the one thing she never got tired of was her imagination. Alfie and Jamie came from Susie's old school. Alfie studies English Literature and Jamie studies Sport Management; both of their department buildings are located at the furthest end of campus, so I'd never seen them before, but with Susie, came Alfie and Jamie. Within six months of starting at Huxton University, we had become quite a close-knit group of five. Alfie and Jamie were like brothers to me now.

She might still be in shock. I don't want it to seem as if I'm preying on her vulnerability.

I continued to look down, gripped my book tighter and waited for it to end.

I'll ask her later. Or should I ask her sooner? Toni did say that there's a high chance she'll say yes.

Damn you, Toni.

I'll think more on it later.

Then there was silence. I surreptitiously wiped my forehead with the sleeve of my jumper and waited for my heart to simmer down. I would never get used to hearing sudden voices; hearing people's thoughts wasn't normal, but I was, relatively, and I intended to stay that way.

After the study session, everyone headed to our favourite restaurant on campus, *The Sandwich Bar*, for lunch – except

33

for me. I returned to my room and spent the rest of the afternoon on my bed. With my back resting against the wall and my knees pulled to my chest, I stared at the twinkling, multi-coloured fairy lights Susie had draped around my bookshelf once she'd declared my bedroom too bland. I've always liked being in my room simply because it reminded me so much of my bedroom at home. I'd been excited to leave for university at first, but homesickness had struck three days in. I missed breakfast with my parents and the bark of our neighbour's dog. I missed the routine on the weekdays and the freedom of the weekends. As the months went on, I began to replicate my bedroom at home here, so that it almost felt as if I was still there. The notice-board fastened above my desk helped significantly with that. It was as large and as wide as my desk and stuck on it were silly pictures of me and my uni friends, holiday snaps with my parents, photos of me as a baby and shots of special occasions. It's what I usually found myself staring at whenever I started to daydream.

But my room was fast becoming something other than a reminder of home, it was a reminder of normality too. In here, with nobody's thoughts to intrude upon, I could almost fool myself into believing that yesterday night had never happened. However, it didn't help that I usually took these moments of solitude to think about what was happening to me. I could read people's minds – that I could no longer deny – but now that I'd thought about it, I hadn't heard the thoughts of those passing by, only those sitting at my table in the library. People didn't ever stop thinking to themselves, did they? So what was different? Distance? Could I only hear the thoughts of those physically close to me? How far did someone need to be for me *not* to hear what was running through their heads? What about the images or scenes they played in their minds? Why couldn't I see those?

I changed position so that I was lying on my back. Was I *psychic*? No, I couldn't be. Psychics were those women who wore silver shawls wrapped around their shoulders, read Tarot cards and rubbed crystal balls in dimly lit rooms filled with glass jars with eyes and dolls heads floating inside them. They were not slightly chubby university students whose biggest decision of every day was whether to struggle with contact lenses or to just wear the glasses she's buried in the back of her sock drawer.

I would have to find a definitive answer at the bookshop tomorrow. Ask around to find out who that Sidra woman was, whilst conspicuously trying to figure out what she had done to me. And most importantly, *why*?

***

On Mondays, I finish all my classes by noon, meaning I was always free for the rest of the day. This particular Monday, I was going back to *Hayven Books* – alone. Trouble was, on the days we all finished early, my friends loved to make afternoon plans. We were currently having lunch, which I'd decided to tag along to, hoping it would give the illusion that everything was back to normal, and after yesterday, my friends needed convincing. I figured, if I appeared to always be around it wouldn't be so odd when I chose to be alone, which was my plan for today. Until Toni suggested we all go see an afternoon movie.

'Sorry, but you're going to have to count me out,' Alfie apologised, piercing his milkshake cap with a straw. 'I've got two essays due that make up fifty per cent of my final grade, one of which is due tomorrow. I have a group study session in ten minutes.'

'Count me out too,' Susie added, plucking away a strand of hair that had stuck to her lip gloss. 'I have an eight thousand word essay due at midnight and I'm not even half-way through.'

I couldn't help but be silently thrilled about my friends' non-existent social lives. Not because Susie and Alfie would have nothing but books and papers for company later on tonight, but because despite them not knowing it, Susie and Alfie had just given me a way out.

Unfortunately, I couldn't use the same essay excuse because Toni and I were on the same course, so any essays I got, she got too. So in order to keep my afternoon free, I had to come up with something else.

'I shouldn't come either; I'm getting a headache and I don't want to make it worse.' I squinted shamelessly and massaged my temples for effect.

'Toni told me the doctor warned that you might have a lot of those because it's likely you hit your head on the ground when you passed out,' Jamie sympathised.

I felt a pinch in my chest and swiftly avoided his sad eyes. I hated lying to Jamie. He believed that he was to blame for the entire incident, because he thought that if it weren't for him, I'd never had gone through the alleyway because I wouldn't have known where it would take me. Yesterday, he'd bought me a tub of vanilla ice cream and a giant slab of my favourite apple pie from the bakery at the end of the high

36

street, half of which I'm not ashamed to say is already gone. He'd even gotten me a *Get Well Soon* card the night of my brief hospital-stay and every now and again he'd reach down and give me a bear hug, which Toni, Susie, and I didn't get very often.

Jamie has this unspoken rule – he keeps girlfriends and friends who are girls, firmly apart. So if you're lucky enough to become a friend of Jamie's, be prepared to stay that way. I was glad this rule was in place because even though Jamie was an undeniable flirt with us girls, he'd never take it any further. Not to mention that with his colouring and face shape, from a distance, you'd probably think we were related.

'Yes,' I agreed, bowing my head lower and technically speaking to the table. 'So, I think it would be best if I just lie down for a bit and take it easy for the rest of the day.'

'That leaves just you and me, Jamie,' said Toni and she gave him a playful punch. Which I would have thought nothing of until I heard what I did next: *Finally, some alone time with Jamie.*

I'd been tucking my chair under the table when I'd stopped to stare at her.

'What?' Toni asked me, confused by my sudden change in countenance.

'Nothing,' I said quickly. 'I...I thought I saw a...bee. But...it's gone now.'

It was the weakest excuse I'd given in the past three days, yet Toni shuddered and began swatting the air around her just to make sure.

'I'll leave you guys to it,' I said with a nod. 'Have fun at the cinema.'

Jamie looked at his watch. 'Yeah, we'd better leave now if we're going to make it in time.'

I nodded sagely in agreement and before I could be stopped, casually made my way out of the restaurant and back to my room, ignoring the thoughts of students who passed close by.

I had been planning to head down to the bookshop straight after dropping my bag off in my room, but decided to wait twenty minutes in order to reduce the risk of running into Jamie and Toni near the town centre where the cinema was located. I'd been quick at making up excuses on the spot so far, but I doubted I'd be able to come up with a convincing enough justification as to why I was walking down that particular alleyway when I'd told them I'd be taking it easy in bed for the rest of the day.

Once thirty minutes had passed (just to be on the safe side), I made my way to *Hayven Books*. On my way there, what I'd heard in Toni's head sprung to mind. Who would have thought it? Toni had a thing for Jamie? I was suddenly disheartened that Toni hadn't told me this when she usually told me everything. Maybe that was because she knew I'd point out what was likely to happen to the dynamic of our group if anything did happen between them. Jamie was known for being Huxton's own lothario and I knew Toni was as good at sharing her love interests as she was at sharing a blueberry muffin on a particularly hungry day. In other words, she'd bite your hand off.

Perhaps I should broach the subject myself? But that was as far as that thought went once I found myself stood outside *Hayven Books* for the third time in the past three days. Although I was more confident than ever to find some

38

answers today, I couldn't help but just stand and stare at the entrance. The door sign said they were open and I could see people moving around inside. Various books and numerous items of attractive stationery were displayed neatly behind the window to lure people inside: giant information packed academic books, glossy teen romances, smooth, leather journals of various colours and old fashioned fountain pens. I loved bookshops and if this bookshop had been located on the other side of the alleyway, I'd most likely be a regular customer; there was just a...*magical* feel surrounding the place.

I heard a sudden noise and started so violently my knees almost gave way, but it wasn't the sound of a scream or a crash; it was a much friendlier sound, it was a giggle. Somebody was laughing. I turned my head to see three teenage girls with linked arms, walking towards the bookshop just as two women were leaving, chatting to one another. Each party walked straight passed me, the girls on my left and the women on my right, as calm as day. *That was unexpected.* Each time I had been on this street it had been absolutely deserted. However, *Hayven Books* had been closed both times.

I looked to the right of the bookshop where an antiques shop stood, bereft of customers. On the left, a white wall stood, half the width of the bookshop and beyond that wall was a park with grass, concrete pathways and low-branched trees. The grey and weathered iron gates at the entrance of the park were open, but only an old man in a tweed hat could be seen, sitting on a bench, puffing heavily on a brown pipe. It was beginning to dawn on me that *Hayven Books* may be the life of this street.

A man with a pushchair followed closely behind the three giggling girls, also making his way to the bookshop. I held the door open for him so he could easily manoeuvre the buggy inside. Then he turned back and returned the favour, expecting me to follow, which was a reasonable enough assumption. Because who just stands outside bookshops opening the door for strangers? So I stepped inside.

The room I walked into was big and full of bookshelves, bookstands and bookstalls that I hadn't noticed the first time. There were a lot more people than I'd thought there was when looking in through the window and the queue to pay had a long tail with no end in sight. There were only two cashiers in the room, a young man and a young woman. She had rosy cheeks, looked about eighteen-years-old and wore her sandy blonde hair plaited into two pigtails. The young man had his back to me, but something about him made me stay where I stood and stare.

I stared for a little while longer, trying to figure out what it was about him that had required me to stop in the first place. Then my nose picked up the strong aroma of freshly ground coffee beans. I may not enjoy the taste of coffee but I loved the bitter, roasted smell more than anything – it soothed me. I breathed in deeply and as I did so, my senses were met with another smell. The smell of melting sugar, buttery pastry and freshly baked bread.

Carefully edging around customers, I followed the smell into another room. The ground floor of *Hayven Books* was much bigger than the first floor because it was two rooms combined. An arch at the far edge of the cashier desk separated the rooms so that when you stepped through it, you walked onto the rest of the ground floor. This part of the bookshop was very different to the section beyond the archway where the entrance into *Hayven Books* was, but both rooms were absolutely beautiful. The first room was decorated in violet, silver and natural daylight; this room had a grand staircase and seemed to exude pure, golden light. Not the brash, harsh, in-your-face kind of gold, but rather the subtle, mellow, shiny yellow type of gold. Pendant lights hung from the high ceiling, the windows were stained glass and the walls were painted in soft shades of gold, causing the room to *glow*. There was an enormous range of books on the ground floor, with comfy chairs and scattered sofas positioned all over the place and whilst the huge, airy room was full of people, plenty of space remained for those just arriving.

I climbed the staircase steadily but eagerly, pausing every now and again to look over the edge to everybody down below. I loved a good bookshop.

I was already unable to grasp the world I had just walked into, just to reach the end of the stairs and be given even more of a surprise. The first floor was guarded by a golden railing and was split into two sections. The further half was a cafe. A counter, another man and woman were serving behind, was situated at one end, laden with cakes in glass domes, biscuits on silver trays and pastries in woven baskets. An open fridge softly hummed beside it, full of drinks, snacks and sandwiches. At the other end, were polished, pastel-coloured wooden tables for people to use. The pastel pink wall at the back, opposite the staircase, had a large italic quote by an unknown author, printed in black: *Never interrupt someone who is reading because they're no longer in your world.* I smiled, knowing from experience how true those words were.

The other half, where the staircase opened up to, was a miniature version of downstairs.

There were teenagers sat giggling uncontrollably in the corner, all four of them huddled over one book that looked suspiciously meant for women much older, even though they were doing their best to conceal the jacket. Mothers were chatting, drinking teas and feeding their toddlers bits of cake and biscuit. Old men wearing glasses sat solitarily with a hardback and children sat cross-legged on the floor reading large picture books, their small mouths moving as they read quietly.

This wasn't your average bookshop. *Hayven Books* had the atmosphere all bookshops wished to create, but none quite managed to achieve. It was bustling, full of life and laughter, yet still remained quiet enough to read and study in. With strenuous effort, I resisted the urge to grab any book at random, purchase a hot chocolate and a slice of lemon cake and sit in the hazelnut-brown chair down at the far end. I needed to return home as soon as possible to avoid bumping into Toni and Jamie *and* to make sure I was in my room in case Susie or Alfie decided to check up on me.

It was at that moment I realised, I had no idea what I was doing. I had come in search of answers, but hadn't thought to think any further. There were a few booksellers walking around, talking with customers, answering queries, and tidying shelves and tables, but I immediately felt too nervous. What was I going to say once I'd asked them if they knew Sidra? If they said no, I could leave it at that, but if they said yes, then there would be an awkward silence whilst they waited to hear what else I had to say. Did I even want people to know I had been here when Sidra had died? They'd most likely start asking questions, or they might even assume I had something to do with her death. What would I do then? Running away would be my go-to move, but nothing screamed *guilty* more than that.

I kept my head low, avoiding eye contact with anyone and walked over to the furthest bookshelf in the back and read the header: *Spiritual/New Age*. Surely if there was a book on psychics or reading minds in this bookshop, it would be here.

It was wonderfully warm and I shrugged my jacket off. *Don't get too comfortable.* I couldn't stay any longer than ten minutes. After a thorough search, I found a beautiful, small, hardback book. The binding was strong and supple, the jacket was a deep shade of purple and it gave off that wonderful shine new books often did. The spine read, *The Secrets & Teachings of a Psychic*. Couldn't get any more straightforward than that. I headed down the staircase, wistfully looking back once, vowing to return another day when I'd be free to just mill around and maybe sit down with a book and a slice of something sweet.

I hadn't thought to check if I could pay in the next room. It was likely I could but there was no need to turn back. The queue in the entrance room had disappeared, yet there were still people browsing on the shop floor, so I stood in front of the cashier desk before the queue had a chance to form again. Both cashiers had their backs to me, sorting through a stack of books. The young man was no longer standing in the same position he had been when I'd first entered the shop, but it was still there. What I hadn't been able to identify when I'd first seen him. Yet now that I was up close, it was much more

43

discernible. Surrounding him was a soft but unmistakable *aura*. I knew of someone that also glowed like that but couldn't seem to remember who. You'd think I would since it was such a strange thing for a person to be doing – glowing. I was jogged out of my reverie when I heard the female cashier announce she was going for lunch. I watched the back of the boy's head nod before she made her way to the back room, only accessible to staff. It wasn't until I heard her think of the salami sandwich waiting in the fridge that the inner thoughts of the people in the room returned, loud and clear. It wasn't until then that I realised that I hadn't heard anybody's thoughts since Toni's earlier today. Time to leave.

I placed my book on the cashier table, noisily enough to indicate that I was there but not so loud so it seemed as if I was purposely interrupting him and he turned round.

'Sorry about that,' he apologised and once he caught sight of me his prepared smile fell slightly. He masked his surprise swiftly enough but continued to stare at me questioningly, subtly looking me up and down with a preoccupied expression. He was rather nice to look at. I took in his chestnut brown, tousled hair, his light brown eyes that were almost hazel and his defining jawline. My gaze returned to his eyes and became trapped there. His eyes smouldered, telling me something, screaming at me, until he blinked and the look was gone.

'Are you alright, ma'am?' he asked me.

'Yes,' I answered quickly, aware that I'd been staring.

He picked up the book and proceeded to scan it, looking up at me with searching eyes every now and again, as if he had seen me somewhere before but was struggling to remember where and when. Whilst he completed the transaction, the midnight blue leather bracelet encircling his wrist caught my attention. I wasn't really into jewellery, but I liked leather bracelets and this one was faultless. It was very simple, with a criss-cross detailing and a silver clasp in the middle.

'You're into psychics?' he questioned with a smile.

'What?' I looked up from typing my pin into the card machine to glance at the book he was now putting into a navy blue paper bag. 'Oh! Well…not exactly. It's just…become a recent…interest.'

He smiled at me again, unable to hide the amused look dancing in his eyes. I stared down at my shoes as I felt an uncomfortable heat rise from my neck and flood my face. Since when had it become too difficult for me to verbalise one flowing sentence? Once the machine had accepted my card, I yanked it out and stuffed it into my coat pocket, aware that I was now blushing wildly. I couldn't remember the last time a guy had made me blush.

As he handed me the bag, my hand accidentally brushed against his. The name *Theo* flashed into the forefront of my mind.

'There you go,' he said kindly.

'Thank you, Theo,' I replied absent-mindedly. I felt the air still.

'How did you know my name?' he asked. Despite his face remaining perfectly composed, the previous look in his eyes returned. He was begging me to tell him something.

'I'm sorry?'

'You called me Theo,' he said. 'How did you know that was my name?'

I searched vainly for a name-tag or a sticker plastered onto his chest with *Theo* written in black block capitals, but there was none about his person. How *did* I know his name?

'I...I... I don't know," I stammered truthfully. 'I...I have to go.'

'What's *your* name?' he asked just as I turned to leave. I turned back to see he wasn't asking out of common interest. I caught the way he curiously regarded me, the way his thick, dark eyebrows almost caught in the middle. He was trying to piece something together.

'Avery,' I answered. 'Or Ava.' I reached for the door.

'Avery? Avery Gray?' he asked, making his way from behind the counter and closer to me. 'You were the girl who was found in here when Sidra died?'

He was coming even closer.

'Yes,' I reluctantly acknowledged, 'but I had nothing to do with it.'

Then, I plead guilty. I ran.

'Wait! Please! Wait!' I heard him shout from behind me, but I didn't turn back. I didn't stop running or even dare slow down, not until I was safely back in my bedroom.

CHAPTER FOUR

Describe myself in one word? Crazy.

Four weeks ago I might have said geeky, chubby, sarcastic, or even pushed for funny. Four weeks ago, any of those words would have been suitable, in fact they still were, but no word suited me more than crazy. Because I had to be. Hearing voices equalled crazy.

It's been three weeks since my last visit to *Hayven Books* and the temptation to return grows stronger every day. It's fair to say I haven't led the eventful life of, say, an undercover pimp; I've been painting the town beige rather than red, so it's easy for me to pinpoint the fact that both of my life's strangest moments have occurred at that bookshop, and that couldn't just be a coincidence.

The Secrets & Teachings of a Psychic proved to be a complete waste of time and money. I'd read it seven times already, but every time I picked it up and opened at page one, I hoped to find something I might have missed. I never did; the book was completely useless. Its main focus was something called "the third eye" and how to decipher a person's emotions through their actions and facial tics. It even had a chapter titled: Speaking with Spirits and that was when I decided to end my re-reading for good. If I *could* speak to spirits somehow, I'd rather not know.

However, reading that book proved one thing, I wasn't psychic, not by the book's definition anyway. But maybe I was something similar, something that wasn't written down in any book because hardly anyone knows about it? *Theo would know*. I pushed that thought firmly out of my head. He wouldn't know; how could he? He was just an ordinary guy who worked in a bookshop.

But even I couldn't convince myself of that. *How had I known his name?* Something about Theo was niggling away at me, interrupting any other thought I had that wasn't to do with him. The more I thought about everything that had happened to me ever since I came across that bookshop, the more likely it seemed there was something peculiar about *Hayven Books*, and that something peculiar kept pointing to Theo.

I'd spent the first two weeks since the latest incident at *Hayven Books* trying to convince myself that I was over-thinking things. That having this ability wasn't the worst thing that could have happened to me. I mean, you read about this kind of thing happening to people all over the world. Mainly in comic books, and normally a spider or a crazy scientist was involved, but that's not the point. Most people would be thrilled with the ability to read minds, to see what was going on in other people's heads. If someone had asked me four weeks ago what superpower I wanted, after invisibility, I'd probably have said mind-reading. But there are dangers that come with wanting certain things you've never had because you don't know what it entails until it's too late. I couldn't turn this thing off, I couldn't control it and so by default it was controlling me. People's voices drowned out my own, meaning I couldn't hear myself think, and that alone was enough to drive me insane. Whenever too many people thought at the same time, it became a jumble of monotonous sound and I had to bite the inside of my lip just to stop from screaming aloud, from begging everyone in the room to be quiet for just a *few* seconds. Was that too much to ask? A *few* seconds? I had no peace, no repose, no time to myself, unless I locked myself away from the outside world. Not to mention I was involuntarily breaking some sort of moral code. Whenever a person came near, I always heard what they were thinking. People thought silently for a reason, because they didn't want others to know what was buzzing around in their heads and during the following weeks, there were a lot of things I'd heard that I shouldn't have. Like what teachers really thought of their students and how Alfie was still pursuing the idea of asking me to dinner, which meant I had to continuously keep excusing myself from the group whenever that moment felt near. There were only so many times I could pass off my sudden absence as the result of a headache. According to Toni's thoughts, I was traumatised and afraid of the outside world because of what happened to me at *Hayven Books*. I didn't mind her thinking that, regardless of whether it was the truth or not. I'd take any excuse available to me that I didn't have to come up with myself.

That had to be the worst thing about it all, having to hear my friend's private thoughts. I'd hate it if they had unauthorised access into my head. Listening to a stranger's silent musings felt like intrusion, listening to the things my friends didn't want me to know, felt like betrayal. Especially Toni's, since many of her thoughts consisted of Jamie and mainly because not all were PG rated. It turns out she had really enjoyed their cinema "date", but she hadn't made a move yet. She was in big trouble when she did because according to *his* thoughts, *the red-head with the massive boobs* in his class was more to his liking.

***

'What do you think?' Toni asked.

'What do I think of what?'

'My tattoo idea! Ava! Are you even listening to me? Is anyone even in there anymore?' She waved her hand over my glazed eyes.

'Sorry. Sorry,' I said, focusing back to the present. 'Of course I'm listening, just…remind me.'

Toni rolled her eyes before launching into the beginning of whatever it was she had been saying before.

We were currently sat in the kitchen of Toni's building which she shared with five other girls, but today it seemed they either had classes or preferred the comfort of their rooms, as Toni and I had the moderately large kitchen all to ourselves. I preferred Toni's student kitchen over mine as it was more homely, with wooden cupboards and tables and soft colours on the walls. Mine, being one of the newer buildings, was decorated mainly in silver, black and marble. Despite usually spending most of my time in Toni's flat, I couldn't quite comprehend how I had gotten here today, but that is usually how my days went; they sort of just passed me by.

'Urm, Toni,' I interrupted, 'is the chicken meant to be doing that?'

Toni turned her attention back to the stove and the wok of burning chicken, and colourfully swore. I took that as a no. However, the burning chicken answered how I'd gotten here.

Toni must have offered to cook dinner for the two of us, which was odd because it was common knowledge to anyone who knew her that Toni was a terrible cook. I was the chef in our friendship. My mum's the author of a collection of family recipe books and over the years she's taught me a thing or eight about cooking. I had once tried to show Toni the basics, simple things like pasta and rice, but honestly, she could burn water, which she did when she'd forgotten to add the pasta. So our one-on-one cooking lessons had ended soon after they had started.

'Oh, forget it,' Toni muttered, upending the wok of blackened chicken and charcoaled egg noodles into the bin. 'We'll just order pizza,' she decided, turning to me. 'Anyway, I was talking about my very first tattoo!'

Ah, of course. Toni had been very excited about turning eighteen because that meant she could legally get a tattoo. However, her choice of tattoo design changed at least once every month and it was now fourteen months after her eighteenth birthday. As expected, she had again thought of a new tattoo design she was sure was the one. I smiled fondly.

'What is it this time?' I asked. 'Last month had been a dolphin on your back, the month before was a snowflake behind your ear, before that was a heart on your finger and before that was an anchor on your wrist. Let me guess, this month is…a flower?'

'So you were listening!' She smiled and pulled a seat out from under the dining table. 'But not just any flower. I want a really long one, like, loads of flowers on a winding stem. It'll start here…' She pointed to the bottom of her hip. '…and end here,' she said, tracing a trail from the bottom of her hip right up to the back of her right shoulder.

'I see.'

'Well?' Toni persisted, finally taking a seat after her demonstration.

'It's nice,' I said with a nod, 'very nice and…long.'

'I know!' she squealed. 'I cannot wait to get a detailed design drawn up! Right, okay. Pizza?'

Some days were good, others weren't. For example, that was one of the better days. I'd spent the morning and a large portion of the afternoon in bed, willing away the hours by thinking meaningless thoughts and falling in and out of soft clouds filled with empty dreams. I'd reluctantly gotten up in the late afternoon to attend the only lecture I had that day. I sat through Professor Garold's talk concerning market strategies and the strengths and weaknesses of new products in a consumer market until sixty minutes had passed.

Toni's and my building were close to each other, so we'd usually walk home together after a lecture if we didn't have anything else planned for the day. We walked down the same stone path until the trail split at the far end, sprouting off into two separate pathways that took us to our individual buildings. This particular pathway was usually quiet and secluded, surrounded by greenery and tall trees with full, swinging branches that submerged the pathway in shade. I used to enjoy the two minute walk Toni and I would usually fill with mindless conversation. But things had changed now.

As I'd been doing for the past few weeks, I stayed relatively silent on the walk back, but as I'd then made my way to my flat, Toni had grabbed my arm, mumbling, 'Oh no you don't!' and dragged me off to her building, where after burning dinner, we ordered pizza and watched a movie of my choice.

I could handle days like that. In class, most people's thoughts were about what was being taught and I discovered that when Toni was preoccupied or distracted by something, she thought less. I dreaded the not-so-good days – days when I had no classes to attend and declined invitations from friends. This led to a lot of free time on my hands and my refusal to leave my room meant I was confined; trapped. But going outside was never an option I felt I had. Outside, there wasn't one place I knew of that would be completely empty of people and most importantly, their thoughts.

I'd often pace my room restlessly, stopping every now and again to sit and take a bite out of a sandwich I'd made an hour ago, but after the third bite or so, I couldn't eat any more. Nevertheless, I welcomed the restlessness because it guaranteed some sleep later on. Whether I was going to sleep for the night or just taking an afternoon nap, I would get into bed and allow the darkness to cloud my mind and before I knew it, it was morning or a few hours later. It was a grim way to live, I know, but I'd rather a dreamless sleep than a nightmare.

This afternoon was a different story; a different dream.

I dreamt of the evening I had found Sidra, but parts were missing, as if my subconscious wanted to get to a certain point. I started in my room and then I was stood in front of *Hayven Books*, then right after, I was kneeling beside Sidra and she had woken up after I'd thought she was dead, exactly like she had on the actual night. She even said the same words, 'The Cliders have returned…growing each day in strength and numbers…Madrina…Hayven…you must lead as I once did…you must fight…you must win…or…*terrible* darkness.'

The same images flickered beneath my eyes. The dark night, the house on fire, the brown-haired boy, the Muslim girl. But the old woman with the rotting teeth was new.

Then the scene went to my brief conversation with Theo.

'You were the girl who was found in here when Sidra died? …Wait! Please! Wait!'

Sidra returned. 'You will do well, Ava.'

The picture disappeared in a cloud of smoke and I woke up, drenched in sweat, my vision cloudy, hair plastered to my face and my heart thumping manically. My phone buzzed with a notification, reminding me of the dinner plans I'd made. I showered, dressed and brushed my hair into its usual ponytail. There was one thing I needed to do before.

Despite knowing it was 6:18 p.m. on a Thursday and that meant that the bookshop would be closed, I went on regardless, just in case *he* might be locking up or doing some late night inventory. I smoothed the top of my hair back and checked my reflection in the antiques shop window. I don't know why, I wasn't expecting anything to have changed and it hadn't. The only differences being the faint flush in my cheeks from the brisk walk, and my square rimmed glasses I'd put on because I couldn't wait the six minutes it usually took for me to insert my contacts in. When I reached the bookshop doors, the sign was turned to *Closed*. I tugged fiercely on the handles so that the silver bolts rattled noisily, but I was still not permitted entry. I heaved a heavy, audible sigh and made to turn away. Then I heard the unmistakable sound of keys and a male voice.

'I was wondering when you'd come back.'

CHAPTER FIVE

It was a beautiful night. The sky was slowly darkening, turning from powder blue, to cobalt blue, to the indigo blue it was now. Silver stars popped out of nowhere and hung like sparkling dew drops on invisible lines. The breeze was soft and warm on my skin and the rustle of the tree branches swaying and their leaves kissing, melodious.

Then there was Theo.

He'd opened the door to me fifteen minutes ago, led me up to the roof of *Hayven Books* where a cream rug had been placed in the middle, then proceeded to lay down on it, gently patting the area beside him – enough space for another person. He hadn't said anything since. He didn't need to speak. His presence seemed to fill the entire space, rendering words redundant. So we remained in silence. He didn't speak and he didn't think. I didn't speak, but I did think. And of all the things a regular person should be thinking in a situation like this, I decided to focus on the one thing that was bothering me the most: *Why had I put my glasses on today?*

I looked like a class A geek with my glasses on.

'Who are you?' he finally asked without taking his gaze off the evening sky. He had one arm positioned under his head for comfort, the other laying leisurely over his toned stomach, which I could see from his T-shirt riding up slightly. I focused my eyes firmly back on the sky.

'Avery Gray,' I answered. 'Everyone calls me Ava. Who are you?'

'Theodore-James Connors, only some people call me Theo.'

'Some?'

'Well, I don't know "everyone", so not "everyone" calls me Theo.'

Despite it making perfect sense, it was an unconventional response to give. Then again, this guy didn't exactly strike me as "normal". He was currently lying on the roof of a bookshop with a person he didn't know, but who was I to judge? I was doing the same thing.

'What are you doing in Huxton?' he asked.

'You make it sound as if there's somewhere else I should be,' I replied, to which he simply shrugged and waited.

'I go to Huxton University,' I answered, 'but used to live in London,' I added quickly. 'Where do you go?'

'I dropped out of university,' he responded. 'I couldn't find a subject I was truly passionate about.'

I considered telling him that's how I felt about university, but I hadn't told anyone that, not my parents, not even Toni. I hadn't even admitted to myself yet – that during my last year of college, whilst everyone was picking their university courses with fervent decisiveness, I had hit a wall. I didn't know what I wanted to do in the future and so I didn't know what to pick. The only thing I was relatively certain of was that I wanted to attend Huxton University because of all the positive reviews and recommendations it'd received, not to mention the truly beautiful campus I'd visited and fallen in love with.

One afternoon, Toni suggested that I do a four-year International Business course with her, because apparently you could do a lot of things with a business degree. At the time, I'd thought this a good idea because this option then gave me four years to try to figure out what I really wanted to do. Now I was slowly trudging through the sticky beginning of my second year and I was no closer to discovering my true passion than I was when I'd started. All I knew for certain about the future was that I wanted a job I'd love so much, I'd never have to work a day in my life.

It didn't matter now anyway, I'd stayed silent for too long to add to his comment. I turned to look at the guy I'd only met once before, not easy to do when the arm of your glasses was pressing into your skin. He was still as handsome as I'd been secretly picturing and the glow was still there, made even more prominent by the still and soft darkness. I shifted on my side slightly so I could focus on it. From a distance, the glow had seemed more natural, so natural I could have blamed it on a trick of the light. Now, up close, it didn't seem...*right*. It was natural in the fact that it suited Theo, as if the glow was a part of him. What I couldn't put my finger on was *how* he was doing it. It was as if he wore a full body suit of golden armour, and then the armour itself had been stripped away and all that remained was the golden, glowing outline.

I was very tempted to touch him.

Only to see if I *could* touch him, of course. Would my finger go through his armour, or would it stop right before it, acting as an impenetrable shield?

Glowing wasn't a natural occurrence. And I'd known as soon as I'd seen him the first time, without having to look at his face, that there was something about him. Theo was obviously different, but everyone was different; no two people are alike in every aspect of their being. I liked different, except when different meant dangerous. What I needed to know was *how* different was Theo.

'How old are you?' he asked, pulling me away from my thoughts. I shifted again so that the back of my head rested on the rug.

'Nineteen,' I answered. 'How old are you?'

'Twenty.'

Then there was more silence, which I first took to be a thoughtful pause on his part before he asked his next question, but it went on for a considerably long time. Theo remained perfectly still, but it was proving difficult for me to do likewise. I'd twist into a more comfortable position every few minutes, cross and uncross my fidgeting fingers and soundlessly tap the heels of my trainers together. I couldn't seem to keep still, so I tried to think of random things to distract me. Counting stars. My dinner plans. If I'd be late to dinner. Whether I would tell Toni any of this. Theo's breathing…The rhythm of his breathing, so soft and measured, gave me something to focus on. At least eight minutes had passed before he spoke again.

'Would you like me to continue asking you questions or do you have some questions for me?' he asked.

This was it, my golden opportunity. My chance to ask all the questions I had kept stored up in my head for the past few weeks.

'Who was Sidra Calix?' I asked, attempting to prioritise the questions in my head.

'She was an old woman,' he answered slowly yet instantly, as if he had anticipated the question and so rehearsed the answer. 'She owned *Hayven Books* but kept to herself; she was a very private person. The bookshop is now in her husband's name, but we hardly see him around. She had no children, nieces or nephews. She and her husband lived a quiet life...elsewhere.'

I'd noticed that Theo had managed to answer my question without really answering it; he'd given me a summary when I'd wanted a report. I chose to ignore that.

'So who is your boss?' I asked next.

'Andrew Dillon. A man hired by Gaige to tend to business whenever he's away.'

'Gaige?'

'Gaige Calix, Sidra's husband,' Theo clarified.

'And where does he live?' I asked.

I was surprised by what happened next. Theo turned to balance on his side and for the first time since he'd opened the entrance door, he looked at me. His mahogany coloured eyes sparkled despite his serious expression.

'Elsewhere.'

That was the answer he gave me before resuming his previous position, but I continued to stare at his side profile. The straightness of his nose and fullness of his lips were accentuated by the dark night, and the curve his jaw made under his ear seemed to cut through the darkness entirely. Why did he keep saying "elsewhere"?

This guy is seriously weird. I think I like him.

More silence passed before his next question.

'What happened when you found Sidra?'

My heart skipped a few beats, but Theo was not the only one who had been preparing his answers.

'Nothing,' I said flatly. 'I found her in the bookshop and then fainted from the shock.'

'Yes, that's what the police told me you said when they came by to explain what had happened the next day. The doctors said Sidra likely died from "natural causes".' He fixed me with an intense stare. 'But we both know that isn't true,' he whispered. 'Don't we?'

My pulse accelerated and I was unable to tear away from his gaze. I clenched my jaw and pressed my nails into my palms, but it did nothing to subdue the trepidation building in my chest. *Don't admit to anything.*

'Don't we?' he repeated. His voice remained a harmless whisper, his gaze still entirely frozen.

I nodded and he slowly turned his gaze back to the ink-blue sky.

'So, why don't you tell me the truth about what happened and maybe we can clear some things up?'

I said nothing.

'Whenever you're ready,' he said gently. 'We've got a lot more time than you think.'

Ignoring his last comment and the minute smile that played on his lips, I told him everything before I lost my nerve. I told him how after walking down the other side of the road for the first time, I'd heard a scream followed by a crashing sound. How I'd gone in to see what had happened and found Sidra lying on the floor, unconscious, with no one else around. I confessed that there had been blood on her chest and blood flowing from her back; blood that sparkled like diamond jewels had been liberally scattered in its puddle. I told him how the blood had then disappeared. I explained how she had woken up, taken hold of my wrist and turned my arm transparent before making my veins change colour. I recited what she had said to me, how she had died straight

61

after and how I had passed out and woken up in the hospital hours later. By the time I had finished, my chest was heaving.

Theo listened patiently throughout, his expression stilled. Only once did it change and I'd caught the look before it disappeared, but it hadn't stayed long enough for me to analyse it. Or maybe I was just seeing things. Theo nodded to himself before saying, 'Everything that happened has a reason behind it.'

As we lay in silence, I could feel my body unwind, like a ball of yarn with a loose thread, for the first time in over a month. It was as if a huge weight I hadn't known I'd been carrying had been lifted off my shoulders. To truly share everything, especially the vanishing blood and not be declared insane, made me feel normal again. I knew better than anyone that I wasn't, but it was nice to at least *feel*, if only for a brief moment, as though I was, as though I had my old life back.

'I know what you are,' Theo said. He spoke to the dark heavens.

'That's impossible,' I replied. '*I* don't even know what I am.'

He sat up abruptly to face me.

'But *I* do,' he insisted, a sudden fire igniting in his brown eyes so that they pierced through the darkness.

I sat up and found my face very close to his. His cool breath made my skin tingle and the heat from his body wrapped around mine. He leaned in closer still…and then grabbed the same wrist Sidra had.

And it happened again.

Theo's hand and arm become transparent and his blue veins turned purple, then blue, then silver and then back to

62

blue again. One look at my arm confirmed that my veins were doing the same, just like they had with Sidra. I gasped and looked back up at Theo.

He smiled and said, 'You're gifted.'

CHAPTER SIX

That's all he left me with. Can you believe that?

After saying that, Theo simply stood up and made his way downstairs, and for fear of being locked out on the roof overnight, I hastily followed. Once down the stairway, out of the roof entrance door located in the cafe section on the first floor and back downstairs, he gently pushed me out the front door and said, 'I have something to do before I can tell you more, so come by on Saturday at 5 p.m. Just knock; I'll be here.' Then he shut the door on my bewildered face.

After staring at the closed door for a few seconds, I gave up and walked away. *What had just happened there?* I readjusted my glasses and decided to answer my own question. *No idea.* The only small comfort provided to me was the fact that I at least had an answer. A poor and unacceptable answer, but beggars can't be choosers. It was an answer that proved I wasn't going insane, unless Theo was also insane and judging by recent events, that didn't seem such an implausible possibility. At least I'd have someone to be insane with.

But enough about him. I had a dinner date at a Mexican restaurant and after what had happened the last time I'd been running late to dinner, I was determined to get there on time.

'Look at you, Ava! You're outside of your room for more than an hour, acting like a normal person again!'

'What do you mean by that?' I asked Toni.

I knew exactly what she meant, but engaging with Toni when she was like this was fun. She was slightly drunk from the three strong cocktails she'd had, and when Toni was tipsy, it was quite a charming sight to behold. She often got what I've uniquely branded "the uncontrollable giggles" and loved to suffer these spontaneous attacks whilst swaying in her seat in time to whatever song was playing in her head. Tipsy Toni was the *preferred* stage before drunken Toni. I subtly pulled the half-filled glass of her fourth cocktail away from her, silently hoping tipsy Toni was the one who'd be staying with us for the rest of the evening.

'Well, you come out to lunch a few times but other than that, we hardly see you!' Toni answered.

'Toni's right,' Susie added. 'You've preferred your own company so much lately; all you do is stay in your room. What is it you do all day?'

I hesitated for a moment. 'I catch up on school work. And...I do other things...'

'Like?' Alfie jibed playfully.

I think about the fact that I can hear minds and whether that means I'm destined for something beyond my present understanding. 'I draw?'

I was constantly surprised to find how much I could get away with. The mere mention of my favourite pastime was enough to sway them into believing that instead of going on lonely walks in the most sequestered areas I could find, hearing people's thoughts when I couldn't find such areas, and visiting *Hayven Books*, I was alone in my room doing something semi-productive.

Drawing was something I loved to do and was quite good at; I use to fill any spare time I had with drawing and even time I didn't have to spare, and I'd hand out my finished pieces to my friends and they'd happily accept. In fact, my ideal day would be spent walking around an art supplies shop, silently convincing myself to buy things I already had a similar version of at home. I had been close to picking Art to study at university, but I didn't like being told what to draw. It was a hobby for a reason and I indulged in drawing whatever I liked in whatever time frame I chose. But I hadn't drawn a single thing in the past three months. One more white lie fed to my friends couldn't possibly do much harm, right?

'How you spend all day just drawing is beyond me,' Jamie voiced, beer in hand. 'Drawing has to be the world's most boring hobby in existence.'

'You're only saying that because you can't draw,' Susie said with a smile.

'I know the basics,' Jamie replied, a hint of a slur mixed in with his words.

'The basics?' Toni questioned.

'Yeah, you know. Like the typical square house, a tree, a sun —'

'A sun?' Toni repeated. 'You know how to draw the sun? The circle with lines sticking out of it? However did you manage to gain such artistic knowledge?'

Whilst the others laughed, I narrowed my eyes in Toni's direction, fully aware that the position of her chair had gone from facing me, to facing Jamie, and any time she looked in my direction, I could see her eyes were twinkling hazel gems.

Either she was openly flirting with Jamie, or was drunker than I'd thought.

'Like I said,' Jamie said, interrupting the laughter, 'the basics. That's all you really need to know in the art world. As long as you've got those basic skills, you're set.'

'I believe Picasso and Warhol would highly disagree,' Alfie said.

'Who?'

Susie sighed, burying her face in her hands as we all erupted into even more laughter.

'What?' Jamie asked, genuinely confused. 'What did I say?'

'Aw,' Toni consoled, gently pinching his cheeks, 'it's a good thing you're pretty.'

Jamie gave her a wide, full-toothed smile before turning to me. 'A toast!' he announced, raising his bottle of beer to the middle of the table. 'To Ava, finally back to normal! Cheers!'

'Cheers!' we all cried, clinking glasses against bottles.

Normal? If only they knew...

***

'Welcome back, Ava.' Theo smiled once he'd unbolted the entrance door. 'You're late.'

I checked my watch. 'By literally two minutes.'

'Apology accepted,' he replied. 'Come through here.' He beckoned, waving me in.

He led me into what I called the Golden Room; it was the section that gave off the golden light. There was a rug, similar to the one we had laid on during our last meeting, flat

67

on the already carpeted floor, but Theo didn't motion towards it. Instead, he sat down on one of the plump indigo chairs beside the rug and gestured for me to sit on the one opposite him. As I did so, he leaned further back into his chair and smiled, his brown eyes never leaving mine. Once I was seated comfortably, I cocked my eyebrows in an impatient manner and bounced my right foot, but he remained silent and unmoving. If there was only silence, I couldn't maintain eye-contact for longer than four seconds at a time – with anyone. If I did, that meant they were looking at me for just as long, and I didn't like people looking at me for too long.

Theo continued to stare though, oblivious or simply unconcerned about my discomfort. He was handsome, in an obvious way, and there's nothing wrong with that. Brown messy hair that some would call "windswept", eyes that tended to sparkle, an untouched nose, an unintentional pout and a jaw line that couldn't really cut glass but looked like it could. Two years ago, being alone with him might have reduced me to a blushing, nonsensical mess, but I came to realise the hard way that the face doesn't always match the heart. If I did feel any attraction towards Theo, it was an attraction to his...*difference*.

After three more minutes of silence, Theo slapped his hands softly on his jean-clad thighs and said, 'Well, that's it for today!'

I jolted upright.

'Just joking!' he laughed and it was a masculine yet musical laugh that rang around the vast room. 'I was just wondering where to start, hence the long pause. You didn't make any plans with your friends or a boyfriend for later today did you?'

68

'No, my friends are all busy tonight,' I replied.

He waited.

So did I.

He waited longer.

'And I don't have a boyfriend.'

'Good,' he said, 'then I have you for the rest of the day.'

I looked away and scratched the back of my ear even though there was no itch.

'It really is difficult trying to figure out where to start,' he commented.

'What did you mean when you said I was gifted?' I asked

'*There's* a good place to start,' he acknowledged, leaning forward and resting his arms on his thighs. 'When a person is "gifted" it simply means they have a gift, a talent different to many. A supernatural gift.'

'I can read minds.'

'There's a difference between reading minds and hearing them.'

'There is? I thought they were the same thing,' I said.

'Essentially they are, but one is more advanced than the other. They're like training level steps; you start at basic and work your way up until you reach advanced. You start by hearing minds and then you read them,' he explained. 'Can you see pictures or images? Sense or feel people's emotions?'

'No.'

'That's reading minds, and you will.'

'How do you know this?' I asked, cautious by his knowledge on the subject.

'I know people like you, well, people *sort* of like you,' he answered. 'No gifted person is the exact same as another; no gift is a replica of another. I was talking to some people yesterday.'

'People like me?' There existed people *like* me? 'Can I meet them? Where do they live?'

His smile returned. 'They live...*elsewhere*.'

'I'm getting a little tired of that answer,' I said.

He laughed. 'I figured you would, it's understandable.' He stood up and went over to the rug. 'Come here,' he ordered politely as he sat down cross-legged on one end. 'Sit in front of me and do the same.'

'Are we going to meditate?' I asked, wary. I'd rather meet these people he'd mentioned than sit on a mat and stretch. Besides, I'd tried yoga once and pulled something I still didn't know the name of.

'Yes,' he said. 'A different kind of meditation though.'

'What kind of meditation?'

'I told you, a different kind.'

'What's it called?'

'Stop asking me questions.'

'Start providing answers.'

Theo rolled his eyes. 'How about this: if you do as I say, I'll *show* you.'

I opened my mouth to ask another question but he silenced me by raising his eyebrows.

'Alright,' I conceded.

'Good. Now, when I tell you to close your eyes you must do just that and not open them until I say.'

I nodded quickly, trying to ignore whatever it was bubbling inside my chest.

'Close your eyes,' he whispered, but with the room being so large, his voice echoed.

70

I closed my eyes and felt him reach into my lap, his indigo blue bracelet brushing against my thigh. He took my hands in his and held them tightly. My pulse raced, but I kept my eyes closed. I could feel the heat and energy pulsing through his hands, I could feel every nerve in my body awakening and standing to attention; it was nothing like I had felt before.

'Now, empty your mind,' he instructed.

I attempted to do that, but I couldn't get the buzzing sound out of my head. Something, his energy or my energy, his nerves or my nerves, I didn't know what, was commanding my attention.

'Ava? Empty your mind.'

I squeezed my eyes tighter in concentration but to no avail.

'Open your eyes,' Theo said. I saw in his eyes disappointment and sympathy. 'What do you dream of, Ava?'

'Nowadays? Not much,' I answered, my breathing slightly short.

'Hmmm,' he softly muttered as he thought for a moment. 'Well, that really *is* all for today.'

I hoped he might be joking again, but as he got up and headed for the door, my hopes were extinguished. Embarrassment and humiliation washed over me. I had failed and I hated failing, but what made it worse was that I didn't even know what it was I'd failed at.

'What was the aim of that?' I asked, getting up myself.

'Telling you that would only fill your mind, which wouldn't prove very beneficial when trying to empty it,' he said. 'Come back next Saturday, same time, but only if you feel confident enough to empty your mind. It helps to sit in a dark room.' With that nugget of advice, he gently ushered me out of the bookshop whilst he stood in the doorway, leaning on its frame.

'You're upset,' he stated.

I was going to retort with a sarcastic remark involving Sherlock Holmes, but it wasn't his fault I'd failed and so settled for silence instead.

'Try not to worry too much about it. It took me five weeks before I could do it,' he admitted.

'Five weeks? Really?'

'Yes,' he nodded, folding his arms. 'What I'm attempting to teach you isn't anything *ordinary*. It's extra-ordinary. Extra-ordinary things aren't easy to come by or achieve.' He smiled and leant forward, the side of his arm still resting on the doorframe. 'Because they're unique,' he finished and his eyes widened slightly at the word "unique" before resuming his previous position.

'Will you always speak in riddles?' I asked.

Theo laughed. 'Maybe.'

'You are quite unusual,' I stated. I hadn't meant to say that aloud. There must have already been too much going around in my head for my brain to process the difference between a thought and spoken words.

'Thank goodness for that,' he replied.

'What do you mean?'

'Well, what is unusual another word for? Different,' he said, answering his own question before I'd gotten the chance to. 'And what is the opposite of different?'

'Ordinary,' I answered.

His smile widened immensely so that his eyes narrowed and soft, young creases appeared and time momentarily stood still.

'Exactly, Ava,' he said. 'Ordinary. Let me ask you a question. Do I seem ordinary to you?'

I took a minute to think before answering. He appeared to look at the meaning of certain words from different angles, so if I shook my head, he might take it as me saying he was strange or weird and that's not something always taken in good jest. However, the way he seemed to revel in being called unusual made me think he'd take more offence if I nodded.

I shook my head and was rewarded with another smile.

'Why?' he questioned.

'I'm sorry?'

'Why don't I seem ordinary to you?' he clarified.

The glow. It was still there and it had been all night; even in the Golden Room Theo's glow had been discernible. If there existed a perfect moment to ask about his glow, this was it, but something stopped me from mentioning it. I realised that what stopped me and what had been stopping me all this time, was fear. Fear of the fact that I may be the only one who could see this glow. What if there was no glow and it was just my mind playing even more cruel tricks on me? It had grown fond of doing that lately.

'You look...different,' I finally answered, selecting my words as best as I could.

'Different?'

'Yes, different. You —' I hesitated.

'Glow?' he suggested innocently.

I stared at Theo and listened to the thrum of my pulse in my ears. In the few moments we stood outside, I had managed to convince myself that only I was able to see his glow.

'Yes,' I replied, stretching the word and narrowing my eyes in overt suspicion, to which Theo simply laughed.

'You're very cautious towards me, aren't you?'

'Why do you glow?' I asked, ignoring his question.

'Why do you glow?' he repeated.

'Yes, that's my question.'

'And it's mine too,' Theo said. 'Give me your answer and I'll give you mine.'

It took a while for me to understand what Theo was insinuating and once I had grasped the notion he'd been dangling in front of me, I took a sharp step back.

'I don't glow!'

'Yes, you do.'

I was about to childishly retaliate until I stopped to think. I thought back to the morning after the first night at *Hayven Books*, when I had stood in front of my bathroom mirror and spotted a faint hue surrounding me. I hadn't thought anything of it at the time. It seemed I'd been blaming my troubled mind for a lot of strange things.

Theo smiled knowingly.

I narrowed my eyes again and he copied, clearly amused.

'You are weird,' I said.

'Yeah? Well guess what? So are you now.'

'Now?' I asked.

'Yes, now,' he replied. 'So! Next Saturday?' Then he made to shut the door on me.

'Whoa! Wait a minute!' I cried in disbelief, using my right foot to block the closing door. 'Where are you going?'

'Elsewhere.'

I felt my throat vibrate.

Theo laughed and opened the door wider. 'Did you just growl at me?'

'Where are you going?' I asked again.

'That's a nosey question.'

'Then give me a useful answer!'

'Will you growl at me again if I don't?'

I pulled my foot back. 'Fine.' I turned around and made to leave.

'Ava, wait.'

'What?' I snapped and instantly regretted it. I never snapped.

'You're very impatient,' he said.

'Are you surprised?' I asked, my tone mildly softer.

'Not at all,' Theo confessed. 'I just said it because I thought you needed to hear it.' He smiled at me again before he continued. 'A friend once told me that patience is the key to a happy heart and in a woman's world, chocolate is too. Here,' and he produced a bar of chocolate from his pocket, unwrapped it, and then offered me a square.

'My mother told me I shouldn't take chocolate from strangers,' I said.

'Why not?'

'Because there's usually a windowless van parked around the corner,' I answered.

'I see. Did your mother not say anything against spending the evening with a stranger?'

I took the piece of chocolate and ate it.

'Better?' he asked.

'Not really.'

'Well that was a waste of my chocolate then,' and he pocketed the rest. 'Look, I know there's a lot for me to explain and my telling's so far have been rather cryptic, but I assure you, there's a good reason for that. What I'm trying to show you cannot merely be explained. If you practise hard enough, you might see it next Saturday.'

'But it took you five weeks. What if I can't wait that long?' I asked.

'Technically, you can wait that long and you're not me. I'm different, remember,' he said, pointing his thumbs in his direction. 'And so are you. There's no immediate rush. We'll see how long it takes you, and trust me on this: if it takes you a long time, it doesn't matter because it'll be worth it in the end. Ever heard of the saying, "good things come to those who wait"?'

'Ever heard of "patience is a virtue"?' I riposted. 'Well, it turns out, patience is a virtue I don't have.'

'Oh, I doubt that's true,' he said. 'But now isn't the time to get into your issues. You can wait. You'll survive.'

'But...five weeks...'

Theo sighed heavily and stepped forward so that we were now both standing outside. I felt myself catch my breath as he came closer.

'The words coming out of these...' and he pressed his forefinger to his lips, '...are going into here...' and he pointed to my right ear, '...and are leaking straight out of here,' he finished, pinching my left ear.

'Ouch!' I subtly ignored the sharp tang of electricity that stemmed from Theo's touch and the warm unfamiliar heat it ignited in the pit of my stomach.

Theo shrugged and turned to walk back into the bookshop. 'It takes patience and practise. A lot of practise.'

Then he shut the door firmly behind him.

CHAPTER SEVEN

I was not going to take five weeks to master whatever it was Theo wanted to teach me. So for the fifth night in a row, I locked my door, switched off the light, drew my curtains, sat cross-legged in the centre of my bed and tried to empty my head. I was surprised to find that as the nights went by, the assigned task became easier. I hadn't really known how to empty my head during the first two nights of practise until I settled on a black screen. With nobody around for me to intrude on their private thoughts, there was nothing but silence, and I could focus quite easily on the plain black image in my head. But whenever my focus wavered by a random sound from outside my door or window, a random image would pop into my head and it was usually an image of Theo.

Somehow, since our last encounter five days ago, Theo had really gotten under my skin, but in a way that didn't bother me too much. He fascinated me because I knew he wasn't your average Joe, I knew he was different. And the thought of being around someone who didn't quite fit the norm *excited* me. This was a dangerous position to put myself in.

On Saturday afternoon, I joined Theo on the rug and closed my eyes. He took my hands again and I paid minimum attention to the pulsating electricity coursing through them and focused on a black screen.

'Clear your mind, Ava,' Theo instructed.

I did and for a moment I was doing well, but my nerves got the better of me. It was easier to do it in my room alone because I hadn't been expecting any results then, but now I was and it was slowing me down.

'Try again,' Theo said softly.

I tried again and failed again.

'Maybe another week's practise is needed,' Theo said as he made to get up.

'No,' I said through gritted teeth and pulled him back down onto the rug. 'I can do this. I've been doing it for the past five days, so just wait.' I watched as he sat cross-legged opposite me before closing my eyes again, clasping his hands in mine and focusing until soon the dark image became natural. Spots of colour began to appear from the effort, but I concentrated only on their black canvas. I couldn't tell how long I'd been sitting in this state, but I sensed minutes passed until I felt Theo's hands loosen, melting and seeping through mine.

'Open your eyes, Ava.'

Theo's voice had shed its usual deep tone and had instead taken the form of a floating whisper, which seemed to dance across my shoulders and travel around my head, causing a shiver to run down my spine at the intimate proximity.

I opened my eyes and gasped soundlessly at the sight. Theo was *disintegrating*. From the tips of his Converses, upwards. Someone omniscient was rubbing Theo out with the end of their pencil and trickling out of their eraser were tiny, sparkling jewels that then floated freely in the air. Sparkling jewels of shimmering indigo blue that hung in the space around us, the pieces of him so minuscule they almost appeared invisible in the Golden Room. The sight was beautiful, frightening and mesmerising, all at the same time. The only thing that drew my eyes away from the sight was the tingling, almost numbing sensation that seemed to begin in my toes before slowly spreading upwards, taking over my entire body. My bones melted like heated butter and my mind swam in circles. It was a delicious feeling, a feeling of delirium, pleasure and ease.

I was disintegrating too.

I melted into pastel blue specks and became one with the air until I could see and hear no more, but only *feel* my specks begin to collide with Theo's. As soon as a speck of my being made contact with his, the pulse of electricity returned. It was only one pulse but it was stronger than before and the intensity of it caused our colours to attach and meld into one another. Next thing I knew, I had landed in an unknown city with Theo by my side. He was wearing the biggest smile I've ever seen anyone wear.

'Welcome to Hayven.'

CHAPTER EIGHT

I was bound to wake up soon from whatever weird dream I was having – because there was no way this was real – so I might as well enjoy the ride. I colourfully swore to mark the occasion.

We were standing somewhere…else, as a domino effect proceeded to take over my senses. The smell of fresh linen blended with the smell of warm summer evenings flew around the city. The heat from the sun serenaded my skin and warmed my entire body from the inside out. Overhead, birds flew in a V formation, the delicate sound of their wings mixing in with the sound of distant chatter and the gentle rustle of leaves. And the city was made of *gold*. Or rather, it gave that impression. The sun hid partly behind a sky that swirled in mesmerising colours of baby blue, pastel pink and dazzling white. Its rays breathed upon the snow-white clouds, melting their edges and causing the outer-linings of the clouds to glimmer and radiate a golden, almost copper-like hue, one that signified warmness and lazy days.

Apart from that, it was a regular city.

I hadn't been aware that we'd landed on a pavement beside a main road until I heard and then saw a car drive by, followed by another and then another. I was surrounded by big buildings, smaller houses, tall apartments, busy shops and exotic trees. This city could have been mistaken for just another charming town in England if it were not for the subtle golden hue resonating around the entire place, bouncing of the trees and hitting the sharp corners of buildings.

'I have some things to explain.'

I'd almost forgotten Theo was here with me. He was looking off into the distance with a small smile on his face and a soft sigh in his chest. He was home. Without warning, he started to walk forwards.

'Is this where you live?' I asked, trying to keep up. 'Is this "*elsewhere*"?'

Theo nodded and continued to walk in a pace caught between a casually strolling teenager and a man late for a now ruined dinner, which was not an easy feat to accomplish. I on the other hand, struggling to match Theo's Converse-clad feet, looked to be a cross between a lost toddler and a bewildered tourist.

'Are we going to your place?' I asked.

'Why? Eager to see my bedroom?' He kept his face straight except for the corners of his lips which rose slightly. He was teasing me.

Despite knowing this, I annoyingly started to blush. 'No. I…I didn't mean…I just…'

Theo laughed at my pathetic attempt to justify myself and marginally slowed his pace down.

'You're really easy to make fun of, Ava, which makes it so difficult not to,' he said. 'If you want, we'll see where I live another day.'

It was during times like this I really hated the relationship my brain shared with my mouth. I'd only assumed we were going to his house because I couldn't think of anywhere else he'd be taking me to talk. And that is *all* I wanted to do. *Talk.*

But I guess his house was a presumptuous place for me to think of.

'As for right now,' Theo continued, 'I thought we'd have lunch, so today I'm taking you to the home of amazing Italian food.' He slowed down as something occurred to him. 'Do you like pasta?' he asked.

'Of course I like pasta,' I confirmed with a nod and an incredulous look. 'Who doesn't?'

'You'd be surprised,' Theo said resuming his previous pace. 'We live in a crazy world these days. Some people don't like pancakes. Can you believe that? It's madness,' he mused aloud, genuinely befuddled.

I smiled affectionately towards him before I could stop myself, but luckily for me he had his eyes directed ahead.

'Well not me,' I clarified. 'I love pasta, it's my favourite meal of the day,' and as if to support my statement, my stomach audibly rumbled.

'A girl after my own heart,' Theo mumbled with a smile.

Theo would have made it a lot quicker to wherever he was taking me if he had been on his own and didn't have to deal with me constantly slowing down and stopping at almost every sight. To be fair to him, I was stopping to stare at normal everyday sights like clothes shops and old buildings, but it was like being in a foreign country. No, it was bigger than that. I was in an entirely different place that I hadn't known existed a few minutes ago. Everything looked ordinary whilst managing to be the exact opposite.

Once I had stopped for the eighth time, Theo sighed, clearly fed up. 'I should have just landed us in front of the

83

restaurant,' he said before grabbing my hand and pretty much dragging me across the street.

For a while, I merrily kept up, drinking in all the sights I possibly could, until we came by an area that required me to stop in my tracks. On the other side of the road were two large cherry blossom trees standing tall and opposite one another, the crowns of the trees so broad and wide, they touched, forming a lilac flowery canopy. In the middle of these two trees started a long, wide pathway that carried on so far down, I couldn't see where it ended. But what I could see was that on either side of the pathway were numerous multi-coloured blossom trees and the floor was beautifully littered with burnt orange, ruby red, dark and powder blue, soft lilac, emerald green and buttercup yellow petals. At the furthest end, a soft orange light emitted from the depths and it grew softer and softer the closer to the entrance it got. This phenomenon caused a light, apricot-orange air to surround the entire area behind the two cherry blossom trees. Mixed with the air's already golden tinge, it was the single most strikingly exquisite sight I had ever laid eyes on.

'Mysteria Park,' Theo introduced. 'You know, I've lived here for five years and I've seen that park almost every day and it never gets old,' he whispered, 'only more beautiful.'

I continued to look upon the park named Mysteria in wonder, finding it impossible to imagine growing bored of or even accustomed to the sight.

'I've never seen blue petals before,' I said. Then an image replaced the one in front of me. It was the dead of night and Mysteria Park was on fire. It was the fire that caused the orange hue behind the trees and its magnificent, liquid-like flames saturated the ground and consumed the trees.

Coloured leaves began to drop from branches, curling at the edges as mini goblets of fire blackened them, turning them into crisp, before they touched the ground, dead. I blinked and the image was gone.

'Ava? What's wrong?' Theo asked, addressing the stunned look on my face.

I stepped forward towards the park. Theo grabbed my arm and sharply pulled me back just as a car sped by, inches from where I stood.

'*Ava?* What is it?'

I looked at Theo and then back at the park. 'I don't know, the park was just...' but I trailed off. 'Nothing's wrong. I've just never seen anything like it,' I finished.

'Here you'll find a lot of things you've never seen before,' Theo said, his expressed concern fading. 'Another day,' he promised, gently tugging my arm and making me follow him once more. I looked back. The trees stood sturdy and proud, the leaves remained colourful and there was no fire or hint of smoke in sight. I looked away.

Soon enough, we stood in front of an old but handsome purple painted restaurant that had *Gordon's* written on the top in white italic writing.

'Here we are,' Theo announced proudly. He pushed open the door and a waft of enticingly, delicious smelling food escaped from the building. I stepped inside after him and inhaled the scents of roasted garlic, dried oregano and rich tomato sauce and felt faint from hunger.

The interior of the restaurant was what people described as *rustic* and was wonderfully decorated with brick walls, dark grey leather booths on one side, wooden tables and chairs on the other, polished wooden floors, large arc-shaped windows and hanging cage lights. At the furthest end of the room was a long counter where chefs could be seen talking to waiters and making orders and at the other end was an unlit brick fireplace. I'd been staring at the normalcy of those already seated and eating when a waitress with curled jet black hair that featured a black and white spotted bow, came up to us. She wore a nose ring, layers of black eyeliner and dark purple lipstick that suited her pale round face.

'Table for two please, Lola,' I heard Theo say.

'Right this way.' She smiled at us. *Who is she?*

I flinched at how loud she'd said that before realising that she hadn't said that bit aloud. I looked around the restaurant as something dawned on me. Why were her thoughts the only ones I could hear? I couldn't hear what anybody else in the restaurant was thinking, but Lola had now taken us to a table in a secluded corner, so maybe it was my proximity theory. But I hadn't heard a single thing in Theo's mind today either, or ever for that matter. Lola continued to subtly look questioningly at me, but I could tell she was merely curious. She had a friendly face and looked to be in her mid-twenties.

'Where's the gang?' she asked Theo as we took our seats opposite one another. We were sat right next to a window that gave us a view of a long patch of grassy land covered with countless oak trees.

'Scattered,' Theo replied with a warm smile. 'Bales is in London with Faye, Peyton's hiking with her parents in Wildehill Valley, Ollie is still travelling and who knows where Lucas is – and with whom.' He raised his eyebrows pointedly and Lola heartily laughed. I liked her laugh, it came straight from her stomach and if a laugh didn't come from your stomach, the joke wasn't funny.

'With a poor and unsuspecting girl most probably.' Lola laughed again. 'Your usual?'

'Times two please,' Theo said before turning to me. 'Do you mind if I order for you?'

I looked away from the window. 'Of course not,' I said. 'Whatever you recommend.'

'Coming right up,' Lola said before departing.

Once she'd left, Theo turned to look directly at me.

'Who are Bales, Faye, Ollie, Lucas and Peyton, was it?' I asked, playing with the napkin that held my knife and fork.

I hoped he didn't think I was being nosey. It's just that whenever Theo stared at me but never said anything, I grew hot and uncomfortable and felt a sudden urge to fill any silences we shared. This reaction never used to happen to me and quite frankly, it was starting to piss me off.

'My friends who live here in Hayven,' he replied. 'Well, everyone apart from Ollie, who lives in England. Lucas, Bales and I visit here often and most of the time, we come with my other friends: Oliver-Raine, Faye and Peyton-Jane. You'd like them. They're an…*eclectic* bunch. They go to the university here.'

Here. For a brief moment, I'd forgotten where I was. *Here*. Where was here?

'What is this place?' I asked in a whisper, leaning across the table.

'No need to whisper, people know where they are.' Theo chuckled. 'It's Hayven! It's a city only gifted people know about or have access to. Nobody knows for certain where it is on the map or if you can even find it on there. Of course people have their theories: some people believe we're right on top of London because it doesn't take as long to get here from there compared with other cities. Others say we must be somewhere in Europe because our currency is the euro; others believe we're on a faraway island in the middle of the Pacific Ocean.' Theo paused to take a breadstick from the basket on the table before continuing, 'I think it's more fun not knowing.' He smiled, snapping the breadstick between his teeth.

His enthusiasm was infectious.

'So, non-gifted people can't come here?' I asked, putting quote signs around "non-gifted" with my fingers.

Theo laughed – it came from his stomach. 'You don't need air quotes. That's what they are. It's like me putting quotation marks around "boys" and "girls".' He demonstrated to show how absurd it looked. 'But to answer your question, no, mortals can't get through the invisible barrier we have to pass in order to get to Hayven, or any other city,' he explained.

'Mortals?'

'Yes, that's what we call non-gifted people simply because it's easier when it comes to distinguishing between the two.'

'Are gifted people immortal?' I asked, disquieted.

'No! No.' Theo shook his head. 'We bleed and we die just like everyone else, we just live longer than the average human.'

'How much longer?' I asked.

'The average life span is seven thousand years,' he said.

'So, how old are you really?' I questioned.

This caused him to laugh again. 'Don't worry, I really am twenty. The ageing process only slows down considerably once you turn twenty-one.'

'Why twenty-one?'

'No idea.' He shrugged. 'The process could start at twenty, twenty-two or even twenty-three; no one really knows for certain, so I just say twenty-one.'

I took an olive breadstick from the basket and bit into it thoughtfully. If I was what Theo called "gifted" and this wasn't all a dream I'd wake up from in the morning, then that meant I was now likely to live for thousands of years. I couldn't do that. Yet, something tells me that being gifted doesn't come with a get-out clause. I hated the idea of immortality; watching all the people you love die before you and living seven thousand years was essentially that. But I guess that was only the case for me because if you lived here in Hayven, it was considered normal, like Theo said, it's the average life span. Children would still be expected to outlive their parents in this world. *But what about in my world?*

'If only gifted people are allowed here, Hayven must have a very small population,' I observed.

'Yes, it does. Just a little over two million people live here,' Theo said.

'Two *million*?'

'Yeah! Ava, did you think there were only thirty of us?'

'Yes, actually! Well, something close to that number.' Two million people with extra-ordinary gifts. Two million people who were not so different from me? Two million people the rest of the *entire* world doesn't know about? How was that even possible?

It was that thought that was interrupted by the arrival of our food. I looked down at Theo's regular: the largest bowl of tagliatelle bolognese I'd ever seen. *Challenge accepted.* It wouldn't be difficult to finish as the smell alone, of garlic,

89

onions, chilli, tomatoes and fresh pasta was intoxicating. I reached over to the middle of the table to where Lola had placed three bowls of cheese to find the middle one missing. Theo placed it back with half of its contents gone.

He shrugged. 'I like mozzarella.'

I didn't bother with the little spoon that came with the bowl and instead dumped the remaining contents into my bowl before winding as much pasta as I could fit onto my fork.

'So do I,' I said and shoved the entire forkful into my mouth. Flavour exploded in a way I'd never expect from such a humble dish. Chilli, basil, fresh tomatoes, pancetta, it was just one explosion after another. When the food tasted this good, etiquette was a thing of the past.

Theo smiled. 'Do you like it?'

I nodded. 'It's so good,' I said, reaching for the other bowl of cheese – parmesan. And it was by far the best pasta dish I'd ever tasted.

'If you like this, you should try my version,' Theo said.

I looked up, my loaded fork in mid-air. 'You cook?'

'Only spaghetti bolognese,' he said. 'I switch the spaghetti for linguine when I'm feeling adventurous.' He smiled again. 'My grandfather on my father's side is Italian and he taught me that dish. He believed it was important men knew how to cook.'

'Why?'

'Because good food is the best way into a good woman's heart.'

Once our desserts of apple pie with vanilla cream for me and a large slice of tiramisu for Theo arrived, he asked, 'Anything else you want to know?'

'Quite a lot, I'm afraid,' I replied, chewing on a spoonful of gooey apple filling. 'I just...this is so *strange*. Less than an hour ago, we were in Huxton and I had no idea there was another city...*somewhere*... It's like being in another world.'

'Well, I suppose it sort of is,' said Theo. 'Hayven is a city in a country called Naveya. It isn't just Hayven that mortals are restricted from but all of Naveya. Naveya Valley is the capital of this country, which is such an incredibly beautiful place. It's mainly hot springs, leafy trees and waterfalls there. It's also got the largest population of any city in Naveya, standing at around eighteen million last time I checked.'

If I had chosen to sip my lemonade at that very moment, Theo would have been very wet.

'Yes, Ava,' Theo smiled, sensing my shock, 'there are a lot of us. You're not alone. No one is ever really alone.'

I just couldn't wrap my head around it all. My head just wasn't that big and my inability to comprehend the situation reflected in my inability to form a coherent sentence.

'I just can't...I mean...what I can't...This is just—'

'— Insane?" Theo offered. "Ridiculous? Incomprehensible? Inconceivable? Yeah, it most certainly is, but isn't it also incredible? Exciting? Thrilling? You've gone through your entire life thinking you know all the countries that exist, or at least if someone said the name of one to you, you'd know it was real, even if you weren't sure where it was located. Then you come here and...and, it's exactly like you said, it's not like another country, it's another world.'

I smiled at Theo's obvious inability to contain his excitement. He'd said he'd been living here for five years. Imagine living somewhere for five years but every day was as exciting and new as the first day you arrived. *That's* the kind of place you settled in.

'It makes you wonder what else there is,' he said. 'There are probably a few more places hidden away somewhere that nobody knows about. The discovery of Hayven was an accident.'

'An accident?'

'Yep,' Theo said, depositing a forkful of coffee flavoured cake into his mouth. 'Thousands of years ago, a woman named Almone Errod discovered Hayven. It's believed that in order to try to come to terms with her newly discovered gift she practised meditation and one day she shut herself in a room, closed her eyes, lost herself in empty thoughts and when she opened her eyes again, she was here. The city was practically empty, nothing but golden-blue skies and luscious green land. Hayven was hidden until Almone found it, so who knows what else exists in the world, just waiting to be discovered? I'd love to find one,' Theo finished with a sigh.

That must be why Theo had left university. His mind wasn't one set for academic achievement; exploration and adventure were more suited to him rather than maths and science.

'So where did the name Hayven come from?' I asked.

'Her grandfather – Hayven Vent,' he replied. 'The only family member of Almone's who tried to help her once she realised she was gifted. Her grandfather was mortal, but he was the only one willing to understand. This must have meant a lot to Almone and since mortals can't come here, she named the city after him.'

'How many cities are in Naveya?' I asked.

'Thirty-two,' Theo answered. 'Almone discovered four: Willow City, Cayrio, Valton and Hayven. It was a friend of Almone, Aspen Guild, who discovered Naveya Valley and after insisting that Naveya Valley was the heart of the country, he named it Naveya. He was the first person Almone ever brought to Hayven.'

'She brought people here?'

'Well of course,' Theo said as he chuckled. 'She couldn't populate the country all by herself. After discovering her gift, Almone knew she couldn't be the only one in the world with extraordinary talents and went in search of others. Only gifted people can see when others are also gifted because we give off a sort of…aura.' He smiled intentionally, innocently turning his head a fraction to the left. 'Almone showed these people Hayven and many – after feeling like outcasts in their current home country – preferred it here and families began to settle and build their lives.'

I finally asked the question I had been absent-mindedly pondering ever since we'd arrived.

'If you live here, why do you work in Huxton?'

'Sidra was the one who found out that I was gifted when I walked into *Hayven Books* five years ago, looking for a summer job; she'd spotted it before my mum did. She showed me Hayven and told me everything I needed to know, but by then I had grown to love the bookshop too much to just leave it.'

I could understand why. After seeing Hayven, I now saw the true attraction of *Hayven Books* and especially the Golden Room. It was a piece of Hayven in Huxton.

'I keep telling myself I'll leave the bookstore and just get a job here,' he continued, 'but now that Sidra's gone...'

An immense sadness captured the brightness in Theo's eyes; the emotion so sudden, raw and almost impossible to look at. I felt my last piece of pie stick in my throat.

When I first met Theo I thought he might be Sidra's grandson, but now I saw that she was more to him than that. She was his mentor and his guidance to acceptance. She had shown him something nobody could ever take away from him – Hayven.

It was then that it occurred to me. 'Sidra gave me a gift, didn't she?' I asked. 'That's what happened when she held my arm and changed the colour of my veins. Did Sidra give you your gift too?'

'No, I was born with it,' Theo answered. 'There are only two ways to be gifted: either you're born with it and it's not always hereditary, or it's given to you. There are very few cases where a gift is given; not because it's impossible, in fact I think it's quite easy to do once you know how, but there are only a few cases because...well, why would you want to give your gift away?'

'Wait, Sidra didn't give me *a* gift, she gave me *her* gift?'

'Yes,' Theo nodded, 'her gift is now a part of yours.'

'A part?' I repeated.

'Yes. No two gifters can be the same because, well, I guess that's the whole point of being gifted; you and your gift are unique. So in giving you her gift, she made you gifted, meaning you now have your own gift. As the days go on your

94

gift will develop and you'll find you can do something in addition to Sidra's gift, making it distinctive and yours. There will be quite a buzz about you if people find out who made you gifted. Sidra was a very talented gifter – that's what we're called by the way – amongst a few of the best Naveya has ever known.'

I leant back in my chair. There was a lot more to this Sidra woman than Theo was letting on, I could just feel it.

'Who was Sidra Calix, Theo?' I asked, realising now that that should have been the first question I asked him today.

Theo let out a slow sigh. 'She was an old and very talented woman, Ava.'

'There's more to it than that, isn't there?' I asked, never taking my eyes off his.

'So much more,' he agreed, keeping his gaze locked just as firmly on mine. 'But today is not the day I tell you.'

When Theo went up to the front desk to pay, refusing my offer to pay after pointing out that I didn't have any euros, I couldn't help but wonder how much of an impact Sidra had on Theo's life and how much she now had on mine.

Stepping out of the restaurant, the first sight to greet me was a man jogging past us who then gradually disappeared, leaving a dusting of maroon coloured specks in his wake.

'What is that thing he just did?' I asked. 'That thing we did to get here?'

'We call it "travelling" because that's simply what it is,' Theo answered. 'There are other names for it but "travelling" is easiest for most.'

'People can travel standing up?'

'Yes, but it's less challenging for beginners to learn sitting down. Soon you'll be able to travel anywhere, anytime and in any position. Best not do it in front of mortals though.'

'What happens if they see?'

'Then good luck explaining yourself.' Theo laughed and his hand briefly held his stomach. It was nice to see him back to what I figured was his usual self after the unhappiness that had engulfed him when speaking of Sidra. 'I doubt anyone would believe them if they did say anything, people would just think they were mad.'

That made sense. Before today, I would have given anyone who claimed they saw someone melt into a coloured mist a wide berth.

'Does everyone have a different colour?' I asked as I watched the last few maroon dots leave Hayven.

'Yes,' Theo answered starting to walk back the way we had come, slower now that he was happily fed. 'Every person has a different colour or a variation in shade. People say the colour tells a lot about your personality and who you are.'

'Do you think that's true?' I asked, noting the soft scepticism in his tone.

'I don't know how you'd associate a person with a colour,' he answered my question without really answering it. He seemed fond of doing that.

'I'm blue,' I announced, sounding pleased. I couldn't imagine the colour pastel blue meaning anything bad.

Theo smiled at me as if indulging in my weirdness. 'How adorable,' he commented. 'I should take you back now,' he said after glancing at the watch on his wrist.

'What? I'm not going home! There's still so much I need to know.'

'There is a *lot* more you need to know, Ava.'

I kept quiet because I liked hearing him say my name. The pronunciation was correct and his accent English, but no matter the tone of the sentence he would always say my name softly and slowly.

'But I'm going to take baby steps when giving you information,' he continued. 'There is so much for me to tell you so try and be patient with me. I think the best way is to do something interesting whilst I load your unsuspecting mind with information. On your next visit we'll go to the university here – Fulton University.' He pointed in the direction of the huge white stone building I had spotted on arrival. 'You know, Sidra's great, great, great grandfather built and founded Fulton University.'

'Really?'

'Really.'

The more I found out about her, the more I was beginning to accept that Sidra Calix had indeed been someone special. In my mind she resembled a historic figure that'd changed the world somehow and was adored by all because of it. I was avid to find out more about her. Yet there was this feeling, this gentle prodding in the back of my mind, that suggested I wouldn't like all that I discovered.

As Theo walked, I followed, again taking in the sights around me. Everyone here looked so normal and nobody looked at me twice. They wore normal T-shirts, jeans, dresses, shoes and trainers; mothers pushed their strollers and held the hands of their small children; women and men carried shopping bags filled with food and brand new clothes; teenage girls chatted furiously and teenage boys on skateboards skated passed the girls, making them giggle. It was a very surreal moment; being in a completely different city that I never knew existed hours ago, that was secret to a very large percentage of the world's population and I was rather composed concerning it all. Shouldn't I be freaking out? Shouldn't I be wondering what this all means? Shouldn't I be worried that no matter how exciting this all was, my life would never be the same again?

Theo turned a corner into a road we hadn't walked down before and stopped near a small area of greenery. It was just a wide patch of grass and in the middle stood an apple tree.

'We can leave from here,' Theo said, grabbing a red apple from the tree before sitting down under its large head; its leaves branched so far out that when you sat under it, it formed a protective cave.

'Take my hands as before,' he said.

He popped the apple in his mouth, keeping it steady between his teeth, closed his eyes and offered me his hands. A snicker escaped my lips.

'What's funny?' he asked, as he opened one eye full of amusement.

'Nothing.' I laughed easily and placed my hands in his. 'Nothing at all.'

Back in the Golden Room, we sat opposite one another on the rug, smiling.

'Impressive, huh?' Theo asked, using one hand to hold his apple, which he had managed to take a bite out of somewhere along the line, and using his other to help me to my feet.

'Very,' I replied breathlessly; I was still waiting to be pinched awake at any moment. 'Why is it so dark outside?' I asked, looking out through the windows high on the walls. 'How long were we travelling for?'

'A few seconds,' Theo answered. 'Hayven time is behind England by four hours.'

Ah. That explained it. It had been nothing but bright sunshine and warm air in Hayven, but that was because it was afternoon there. I looked down at my watch; it was now 8.30 p.m. in Huxton.

'Would you like me to walk you home?' Theo asked.

'No, it's okay,' I replied.

'You sure?' he asked, leaning against the frame of the entrance door.

'Positive,' I said. 'If anyone tries to attack me, I'll hear them coming.' I tapped my temple with two fingers to reiterate my new gift.

I could still hear him chuckling softly as I emerged on the other side of the alleyway; the sound seemed to follow me as if unwilling to depart from my company. Or was it more that I didn't want to hear the carefree sound come to an end? It was more likely the latter. The sky was its usual dark blue and Huxton seemed a little dimmer than usual, but I felt truly elated. I couldn't help but look at the world differently now, with admiration. It had kept a hidden city, an entire country, away from me all this time and Theo had struck an interesting chord: who knows what else the Earth has concealed. It was nothing short of life changing.

That night, I lay in bed and dreamt golden dreams.

CHAPTER NINE

Getting to Hayven the second time around was a lot easier because all I had to do was picture in my head where I wanted to land. Theo told me only gifters who haven't seen the city before must think of nothing.

The university in Hayven – Fulton University – was nothing short of magnificent. It was surrounded by acres of vivid emerald grass where numerous students were either having their own mini picnic, enjoying the sun, studying, or simply relaxing with friends. In fact, the entire grounds seemed to be made up of grass and trees and concrete pathways. The university itself looked to be split into three, with the middle section resembling a tower, with a Roman numeral clock on its face. Attached on either side spread the rest of the building, spotted with golden arched glass windows and only reaching three quarters the height of the middle tower. The clay roof was a soft charcoal grey that glinted in the sun and suited the sleek white stone structure.

I assumed most classes were held in this building and others in the less impressive but still rather remarkable buildings dotted around the land.

'Am I allowed to just walk in?' I asked as Theo made his way up the stone entrance steps.

'Well, I don't know if you're *allowed* to, but I do.' Theo shrugged in that carefree way of his that I was growing accustomed to. 'No one knows you don't go here. I'm here all the time and I left last year.'

We stepped right into the middle of a long, wide corridor where lecture rooms were sprinkled across and lessons were taught behind large mahogany doors. The ceilings were high, providing the inside of the building with lots of natural light and the caramel marble floor positively gleamed, glinting as rays of light hit it. There were *hundreds* of students coming in and out of lifts, lecture halls and the building itself; walking up and down stairs, stopping to talk to their lecturers or fellow students and generally milling around. I'd imagine almost every student was thinking of *something*, but the sheer magnitude of people made it difficult to concentrate on the voices and I couldn't distinguish between the voices in my head and the voices outside of it. And for once, I didn't mind it. Each and every person here was like me; each of them had a gift.

Soon enough, the students began to clear out, heading home or to their next class and the corridor grew relatively quiet.

'Are we going to walk around?' I asked Theo and he nodded. I was glad because historic buildings were something of a secret obsession of mine, and Fulton was that extra bit special as it combined the historic with the modern in a very natural way. I adored the white stone statues mounted on matching pillars, the colourful tapestries hung on the walls, and the tall glass cabinets protecting artefacts and antiques. However, my favourite feature of the building had to be the plaques commemorating former students.

Gilmore Brandon
Year of 1739
Excelled in Physics. Gifted in Levitation.
Quote: Look at the world the way it really is, not how you wish it to be.

Another read:

Dylan Lexor
Year of 1943
Excelled in Psychology. Gifted in Agility.
Quote: Hopelessness is merely a state of mind.

Another read:

Jennifer Norton
Year of 1826
Excelled in English Literature. Gifted in Memory.
Quote: I read because life is too short to live just one.

The best plaque I found read:

Cara Braune
Year of 2004
Excelled in Architecture. Gifted in Telepathy.
Quote: I'd never wish to be normal because normal is boring, and nobody is good at it.

'I don't really have a tour plan,' Theo confessed. 'Fulton is just such a beautiful building, I thought you'd like to see it and get a feel of the place.'

'Why? It's not like I'm going to study here.'

Theo turned to me and smiled. 'You never know.'

I smiled back until I realised he was serious. I'd never thought about that. I'm sure I'd meet the criteria, so long as the criteria was good grades and being gifted, so that wasn't my concern. What did pose a problem was that attending Fulton University would mean leaving not only Huxton University but Huxton itself and coming to live in Hayven. And that was ridiculous. Hayven had its attractions and there were quite a few, but could I really see myself walking in and out of Fulton University doors daily, sitting and eating in *Gordon's* regularly, walking under golden-blue skies and taking frequent trips to Mysteria Park? Well...

'What did you study when you were here?' I asked, dragging my mind away from ridiculous topics.

Theo hesitated before answering. 'Law. I used to want to be a lawyer because my dad is one...it's a long story.'

'When you say it's a long story do you mean it really is too long to tell me now, or you're never actually going to tell me?'

Theo smiled. 'Why so interested in my life, Ava?'

'I don't know,' I answered. 'I just feel like there's a few things you're not telling me.'

'There are a lot of things I'm not telling you,' he said. 'We have only just met.'

'Well then, who better than a stranger to tell all your deepest, darkest secrets to.'

'Sometimes it's good to keep some things a secret.'

'And why's that?'

'For one, the present isn't always the best time to admit certain things. Two, it lessens the chances of you being judged.'

'You think I'll judge you?'

'Will you?' he asked.

'Depends.'

'On?'

'Did you kill your dad?'

Theo laughed. "No. Nothing like that.'

'Then I can't see why I would.'

'Nevertheless, somethings are best kept secret,' Theo said. 'But how about this. One day we'll have an hour of honesty. Sixty minutes to ask each other questions and all answers must be the truth, the whole truth and nothing but the truth, so help you God. How does that sound?'

'Sounds like you gave up on the law career too early,' I said. 'But other than that, it sounds good.'

He laughed again. 'Oh, Ava. You are special. Anyway, I used to study law and that's where I met my best friend…Bales.'

He was no longer speaking to me but addressing somebody else.

'Hey, Theo,' came a smooth, female voice.

'This is Ava,' Theo gestured towards me, 'the girl I was telling you about.'

It turned out Bales was a girl, quite a pretty girl actually. She had flawless brown skin and coffee brown hair that had been expertly cut into a shiny, sleek bob with one side tucked neatly behind her right ear to reveal her tragus piercing. Her brown eyes were currently regarding me in a cool manner underneath long eyelashes, and her full lips were pressed together. She was dressed casually, in skinny jeans, a fitted top, an oversized flannel and a satchel bag draped lazily across one shoulder. Her manicured hands were dressed in an array of rings, but her wrists were bare except for one purple leather bracelet and a cross symbol tattoo on her right lower wrist. She looked and smelt expensive. She looked me up and down once, gave me a non-committed smile and simply walked off.

Theo gave her a disapproving look as she sauntered past but I could tell he wasn't truly upset; he must be used to it.

'Must have been something I said,' I muttered.

'That's just Baleigh,' he defended lightly. 'Don't take it personally; she's always like that around new people. She's not the biggest fan of change and she has her reasons.'

'Does she think I'm going to steal you away from her or something?'

I meant it only as a harmless joke, but Theo's face suddenly stilled.

'She's not my girlfriend.'

'No…I was just…Theo, I was joking.'

But it seemed my attempt at an explanation was falling on deaf ears. Theo had a strange look on his face, he looked troubled and slightly guilty. Did he just *lie* to me? Secret number two. Was Baleigh his girlfriend? I doubted it. If she was, she didn't seem the type to take Theo hanging out with another girl all day lightly, so surely she would have made some sort of power move. Call him a pet name or kiss him goodbye. So maybe not his girlfriend. His ex? That would explain the rather chilled look she'd given me before leaving and the way Theo's face had stilled moments ago. Some way or another, Baleigh seemed to be a sore topic.

'So, you told your friend about me?'

'Oh, yeah,' he said and I watched his shoulders relax. 'Her mum can read minds too. Just like you,' he continued.

'I thought no two gifters were the same?' I recalled.

'They're not,' he replied. 'Like I said before, you have an additional gift. Like how you knew my name the first time you came to *Hayven Books*.'

I thought back to how I had simply brushed his hand and his name had popped into my head; I hadn't given that odd happening as much thought as perhaps I should have.

'I'm trying to arrange a day for you to meet and talk to Baleigh's mum,' Theo said as we headed outside. 'She can turn her gift on and off and I thought that might be something you'd like to learn from her. You'll like Mrs. Castel, she's really cool.'

'Theo, that would be —'

Suddenly Theo broke into something between a silent laugh and a smile. I looked up to see this hybrid of emotion directed at a guy who looked Theo's age.

'Lucas, we almost walked straight past you,' Theo said.

'No worries. You were obviously preoccupied,' the boy replied with a heady smile of his own before turning to me. 'Who's the pretty lady?'

I almost looked back to see who he was talking about, but remembered in time that there was nothing behind Theo and me but a white stone wall, so he must have been talking about me. I blushed shamelessly.

Lucas was very attractive; he was tall, with ash brown hair and pink lips; his eyes were hidden behind black Ray-Bans sunglasses, but I guessed they were either blue or green or a mix of both. Like Theo, he had a strong jawline and an infectious smile, and he was dressed similar to Baleigh had been, minus the skinny jeans. He wore multiple leather rope bracelets on his wrists, one of which – a fire red one – caught my eye, and he wore a plain silver thumb ring. He had a very effortless look about him.

'This is Ava, the girl I told you about,' Theo answered, gesturing to me for the second time today.

'Ah, it's nice to finally meet you, Avs!' Lucas leaned forward and practically swept me up into a bear hug. 'You smell good,' he casually commented before he released me. Theo rolled his eyes as I swallowed and looked away.

'Now, there will be plenty of time for us to get to know each other, but I need to find Bales. I think she's hiding from me,' Lucas said. He had a masculine but playful voice, like he was incapable of saying anything hurtful or offensive.

'Still chasing after her?' Theo asked with a mock-serious shake of his head. 'She'll chew you up and then happily spit you back out.'

That I could believe. But wait, that meant Baleigh couldn't be Theo's ex, not if his friend was happily going after her. Or maybe that was *why* Baleigh was such a sore topic for Theo. I snuck a quick glance at Theo to see if his true feelings would betray him. His face was relaxed, his brown eyes warm and his smile soft and easy. Either Baleigh was his ex and he was fine with the thought of Lucas and her together or he was a very good actor. My head began to ache dully.

'I wouldn't say chasing,' Lucas smiled, showing all his teeth. 'I would say I'm…suggestively following.'

I silently laughed whilst Theo laughed out loud and asked, 'What happened to Anna?'

'Well, you know how things go…' Lucas replied as he randomly scratched his right ear and avoided eye contact. 'She just wasn't for me.'

'That is a shame,' Theo said. 'I'm guessing that was the same for Lily, Kyra, Erin, Mia, Tanya, Stacey —?'

'Okay! Okay!' Lucas smiled, holding up his hands in surrender. 'Point taken! But seriously, where'd Bales go? Oh wait,' he turned to me, 'you're the psychic, so you tell me.'

I opened my mouth then closed it and repeated this pattern, caught in blindingly bright headlights as I tried fruitlessly to grapple for something to say.

Lucas's smile widened. 'You were right, Theo, she is easy.'

I blushed again. I had no other response for embarrassment. I'd blushed more times after meeting Theo than I have my entire life. People who know me know I'm not a blusher. I'm sure Lucas meant I was easy to play with as Theo had once told me the same, but I'm also pretty sure Lucas had winked at me from behind his sunglasses too.

He turned back to Theo. 'Direction?'

'That way.' Theo pointed his thumb behind him and Lucas smiled at us both before following the helpful gesture.

'How many people have you told about me?' I asked, trying to distract Theo and myself from the bright pink colour my face must have been.

'Just my friends,' he answered as we began to walk again.

'Lucas and Baleigh would make an…*interesting* couple,' I mused aloud.

Theo laughed as I'd hoped he would. 'If for some unknown reason you couldn't tell, Lucas is a bit of a ladies' man and Bales isn't one to take a lot of crap, so I'd say "interesting" is a very accurate word to describe them.'

'Do you think he's really interested in her?' I asked boldly.

'I do,' he replied, his expression fixed yet earnest. 'But who knows if I'm right; if only we knew someone who had access into his mind…'

I couldn't help but chortle.

Theo smiled at me and it reached his eyes. 'You'd have to be pretty brave to take a stroll through Lucas's mind,' he said. 'Then again, even if you were, you wouldn't be able to hear his thoughts anyway.'

'Why not?' I asked.

'Baleigh's mum taught Baleigh how to close her mind to readers and Baleigh taught us.'

Suddenly it all made sense. 'No wonder I can never hear your thoughts whenever I'm around you!'

'Have you been *trying* to hear my thoughts?' he asked, raising one eyebrow.

'No!' I shook my head adamantly. 'Believe it or not, I'm grateful for the silence.'

Mercifully, he took me seriously. 'Yeah, it must be quite a lot to handle, being practically forced to listen to unknown voices, especially if you don't know how to control it,' he said. 'Hopefully you won't have to suffer for much longer.'

A few hours later, Theo and I had covered the university's entire grounds and it had to be said, it was incredible enough for me to subconsciously consider attending Fulton in the future. But deep down I knew that wasn't possible. I lived in England and so did my family and my friends. That's where my life was and where it was to remain. Hayven would always be there to visit.

And Hayven is what I spent most of my days in Huxton thinking about. What the inhabitants of Hayven were doing at that moment, what colour the sky was then, and when my next visit would be. The city still didn't seem real to me, but that was what drew me in, the fact that there existed a city billions and billions of people didn't know about. Not even just a city; it wasn't just Hayven. There was Naveya Valley, Valton, Willow City, Cayrio and twenty-seven other cities. Maybe there was even another, an unlocked, twenty-eighth city…?

'Hey,' Toni whispered, nudging me with her pointy elbow.

'What?' I asked as she knocked me out of my reverie and my mind slowly and grudgingly focused back to the lecture class we were currently sat in.

'You're always daydreaming,' she said, nudging me again for good measure. 'You're away with the fairies so often, you must see them more times than you see me.' She chuckled quietly at her own joke.

'I've always been a bit of a daydreamer; you knew that within the first week of meeting me.'

'Yeah, but you've never been this bad! You've gone from beginner to professional in the last few weeks. If someone stops talking to you for longer than five seconds, whoosh, you're gone! What is it you even think about?'

Theo…Hayven…Theo…Fulton University…Theo…
Baleigh and Lucas…Theo…

'Just…random stuff.'

'Well, concentrate,' Toni admonished. For a second I
thought she meant concentrate on the lesson we were being
taught on the importance of marketing processes in an infant
industry, but one look at her face told me Toni had something
more important to share with me.

'There's this huge party tonight at Jungle and I really want
to go, so please come with me,' she said in one quick burble.

I sighed. I'd hoped Toni would never broach this subject
again. It looked like my hopes had been in vain. Of all the
clubs that I had ever been to – which to be fair, was not many
– Jungle, located at the furthest end of the town centre, was
by far the *worst*. The tables were always sticky, the air
always smoky, the bathrooms dirty, the bartenders sleazy, the
music practically one sound, and the club itself was so dark
you could never catch the stranger who had just groped you.

The lecture ended and whilst everyone around me stood
up, I stayed in my seat, faced Toni and placed my hand on
her left shoulder. 'Toni, you know I love you so try not to
take it the wrong way when I say, I would rather swim
through shark infested waters with an open cut on my foot
than spend an hour in Jungle.'

Toni smiled with an exasperated look. 'Really? You don't
think that's a bit much?'

'You're right,' I said, packing away my books. 'Ask me
again.'

'Will you come to Jungle with me tonight?'

'No, thank you.'

111

'Oh, come on. Please!' Toni begged, following me out. 'I can't go on my own!'

This was an interesting statement since whenever we did go to a club together, I'd end up taking a taxi home on my own. Toni always wanted to stay later than 2 a.m., because according to her, 'The party's only just started!'

'Well, I'm afraid you're just going to have to,' I said, remembering the vow I had made to myself to never set a clean foot in Jungle ever again after the last time. 'Just don't jump into any strange cars or accept drugs that look like sweets and you'll be fine.'

'Ava! Don't be so boring all the time! You need to loosen up,' Toni insisted. 'All you do is go to lectures and sit alone in your room all day!'

That's all you think I do.

I hadn't – and couldn't – tell Toni about my frequent trips to Hayven, so she obviously thought that was all I did. However pathetic and sad it made me seem, I was happily okay with allowing her to maintain her view.

'What are you even doing tonight?' Toni questioned as we left the building.

'I'm going back to my room to —'

'Relax?' Toni finished. 'Yes, you do a lot of that. Relax from your busy day of doing nothing. Please, just come with me. Blake Shayne is meant to be coming tonight!'

'Who? The orange guy from the reality show you like?'

'He is not orange,' Toni defended in laughter, 'he's tanned!'

'If you say so,' I said. 'Why don't you ask Susie or Lauren?'

'Lauren is going with her girlfriends,' Toni explained. 'She said I could tag along but I don't know her friends that well. And you know Susie hates Jungle.'

I wonder why…

'Come on, Ava, please,' Toni continued, gearing up to make me an offer. 'If you come tonight, not only are the drinks on me, *but* I won't pester you about coming out with me for another…four months. Deal?'

Despite how resolute I had been mere seconds ago, much to Toni's delight I couldn't help but waver. Toni had played it smart and gotten my attention with her offer, which sounded very appealing. Not the free drinks part because any drink consumed in Jungle had a forty per cent chance of already being spiked before the bartender even handed it to you. No, the appealing part was Toni promising not to bother me about going to any more clubs for an entire four months.

There's a club on campus called The Green Sea and Toni's there at least once every fortnight, and even that wasn't enough for her. She constantly complained that Huxton was too quiet and boring and attempted to make up for it by hitting any clubs she heard were in the vicinity. Distance was never an issue, even if it was miles away; she'd drive there, get too drunk to drive back, take a taxi home, then collect her car the next morning. And *every* time she went to any club, she harassed me into going with her. This deal was more advantageous on my part because tonight I could just leave Jungle early, like I normally did, and then be free for four months.

'Deal,' I said, shaking her hand.

'Yes!' she squealed. 'Dress code is black and white.'

'Of course,' I replied. Jungle was famous for its originality.

I thought I'd done pretty well with my outfit choice when I met Toni downstairs at ten that night, but based on her outfit *and* the disapproving look she was currently giving my choice of wardrobe, I obviously hadn't done too well.

'I suppose it will have to do,' she sighed at my black skinny jeans, white loose top and suede high-heeled boots. At least I had worn heels, despite them not being nearly as high as some of the stilettos the other girls at Jungle often went for. Toni had opted for a tight black and white bandage dress, black high heels, a full face of make-up that accentuated her green eyes, and wore her hair in loose curls that bounced on her shoulders. I had gone for a more natural look, as in, no make-up at all and my hair in its usual ponytail.

We were only there an hour before I was ready to go home. Jungle had outdone itself tonight; my shoes stuck to the floor with every step, which explained the huddle of people around the bar – they weren't interested in buying more drinks, they just simply couldn't move. The toilets were unsanitary and my bum had been grabbed a grand total of five times. The choice of music for tonight was slow songs, allowing everyone the opportunity to mesh onto each other on the dance floor, and that mass of pheromones happened to include Toni and a guy I had never seen before. He had his hands all over her and I couldn't tell whether it was appreciated or not, but I stayed exactly where I stood having learnt my lesson from the first time I'd come to Jungle with Toni.

That night, she had done the exact same thing with a guy she had just met; the next thing I knew he had his tongue down her throat and his hand up her dress. I'd thought that was an unwanted advancement, so I had gathered my courage, walked over to the dark corner of the room they'd inhabited and attempted to pull her away. I had gotten a mouthful of abuse from the guy and another mouthful from Toni, warning me to mind my own business and to stop 'killing her vibe'. Funnily enough, when I had done just that, the guy's girlfriend suddenly showed up, having emerged from a shadowed area of the crowd and started having a full-blown shouting match with Toni. Almost everyone had stopped what they were doing to tune in and even the DJ had turned *down* the music so that he could hear.

The guy's girlfriend had not looked like someone to be reckoned with, as her six-inch heels combined with her naturally tall stature made her tower over pretty much everybody at the club, including some of the security men. Her red lipstick had been heavily applied at least three times in the past hour and matched the colour of her blood-red painted nails, which I could only liken to talons. Her raven black hair had been messily piled high on top of her head, and the gold earrings swinging from her earlobes had been the size of my breakfast bowls at home. I had expected Toni to take one look at this woman and wisely back down, but Toni was as stubborn as they come and seconds later a real cat fight had broken out, which resulted in Toni being dragged away from the girl by a burly security guard.

The entire journey home I'd had the irrepressible joy of Toni questioning what kind of friend I was for not defending her. I had then asked her if she had known the guy had a girlfriend before they started kissing and she had said, 'He might have mentioned it.' I'd kept my mouth shut after that and she'd refused to speak to me for three days.

With several similar experiences at various other nightclubs under my belt, I now knew that my job really was to drop her off, hang around for sixty minutes, and after that I was licensed to leave. By that time, Toni had not only made some new friends she would never see again, but was also steadily drunk and no longer interested or aware of my whereabouts.

'Whoops, sorry love!'

Just when I'd turned around to leave, someone "accidentally" spilt their sticky beer all over my top, effectively turning it transparent.

'Looks pretty soaked,' the guy said. 'You might want to take your top off.'

It was so dark in the club I couldn't identify the culprit and fortunately they couldn't see me turn bright red. I swatted the air violently anyway, hoping to find a rough cheek, but was unsuccessful. Instead of heading to the bathroom to try and clean myself up, I left to go home. Luckily, I was accustomed to such behaviour in Toni's outing choices and had stuffed a spare jumper into my shoulder bag. I changed swiftly near a bush outside and then paid for a taxi ride home where I made another silent vow never to return to Jungle.

CHAPTER TEN

'You know, you still haven't told me what your gift is.'

I was back in Hayven with Theo and we were currently enjoying the ice creams Theo had finally allowed me to pay for.

'That's because you never asked,' Theo answered, swallowing the last bit of his ice cream cone. 'I'm a shifter.'

'A shifter?' I repeated. 'What does that mean?'

'It means, dearest Ava, that I —'

And he disappeared, literally vanished into thin Hayven air. Less than a second later, he appeared again behind me.

'— can do —'

And again, in a blink of an eye, he disappeared before materialising in front of my very eyes.

'— that,' he finished.

He could *teleport*? I was about to comment on how unreal that was and ask if he could show me again, when it struck me how close to my face *his* face currently was. For once, it seemed impossible to break eye contact with him and my mind momentarily shut down.

His stare subtly focused on my lips and I heard myself begin to breathe deeply. He turned his stare back to me and I couldn't read him. I'd never seen his eyes so *gentle* and warm, but with kindness were two other emotions hidden within its brown depths: confusion and sadness. He slowly lifted his palm to my cheek. I flinched, unsure of his purpose and he hesitated. I stilled again and let his palm rest on my

117

cheek. He sighed as soon as he'd made contact. It was a very strange moment and it was one I wasn't sure how to perceive. If I was watching this happen between two other people, I'd assume they were about to kiss. But why would I kiss Theo? We weren't dating and there hadn't been any inclination that we would. Did I want to kiss Theo? It's not something I ever thought about when I thought about him – and I thought about him often. His eyes provided my reflection and the confirmation that my facial expression mirrored his: confusion. Neither of us knew what was going on or why. His face came dangerously close until his lips were an inch from mine and he closed his eyes. I took one last look and closed my eyes too.

'Not interrupting, am I?'

Theo's hand slipped from my cheek and he sprang to my side.

Lucas stood in front of us with his regulation Ray-Bans on, but despite the sunglasses, I could see the disapproving look he was giving Theo and once Theo saw it too, he shifted guiltily on the spot.

Lucas pushed his sunglasses up to rest in his hair and revealed his blue-green eyes. 'Summer's back,' he said stoically.

I heard Theo gulp before he turned to look at me, his eyes large and apologetic. He bit his lip and fumbled nervously with the bottom of his T-shirt before he said, 'Ava, I should tell you —'

'Theo!'

At first, I thought it was Baleigh screaming Theo's name, but the voice was too high and shrill for the cool mien Baleigh seemed to prefer. I turned my uncomprehending gaze from Theo and watched a blonde girl in a floral dress bound up to us and stand right beside Theo.

'Hey, Lucas!' the girl shrieked again, as if he wasn't centimetres away.

'Hey, Summer,' he replied in a more ear-friendly decibel. 'How was Russia?'

'Cold!' she giggled before turning to Theo. 'I missed you,' she said and she kissed him. On the lips. Theo attempted to pull away, but she was adamant, and anyway, it was too late.

I felt as if the earth had lurched beneath my feet for a split second before abruptly halting to a standstill. Then the world began to move again, to carry on as before.

'Who is this?' the blonde girl asked once she'd detached herself from Theo. I noticed how she hadn't asked in the same shrieking tone she had used when speaking to Lucas.

Theo could hardly look at me, but I gave him his due when he managed to say, 'This…this is my friend, Ava. Ava, this is Summer. My girlfriend.'

CHAPTER ELEVEN

I should have just walked away.

'Nice to meet you,' I said instead. I took a three-second look at Summer and found my stomach could take no more. Her looks reminded me of Susie, long, blonde hair and blue eyes, but Susie's features were softer. Susie weighed hardly anything but she had a round face and round-shaped eyes, whilst Summer was more angular; her face shape resembled a diamond and her eyes were blue almonds.

'It's nice to meet you too,' she said politely before turning back to Theo to stroke his cheek with affection, like he had mine a few seconds ago. And just like that, something hit me. Confusion washed away to leave *sadness* in its place. Summer bothered me. The fact that Theo hadn't told me he had a girlfriend bothered me. He'd been about to *kiss* me.

'Are you a friend of Theo's?' Summer suddenly asked. 'Because he hasn't mentioned you, and the last time we spoke was last night, wasn't it, Theo?'

He didn't answer her, just continued to look at me, as if I had the answer. I had known Theo for almost three months now and I hadn't heard a single thing about Summer, so I wasn't surprised she'd heard just as much about me. Why hadn't he mentioned her? I looked at Theo, as if to ask him why I'd never heard of his girlfriend, but I stopped myself. And just looked at him. The air thickened further with every second Theo refused to take his eyes off me, and Summer was beginning to notice that something wasn't right.

Something's going on between Theo and this girl. I don't like the look of her. Where'd she come from anyway?

I guessed Summer's thoughts weren't unreasonable. I'd been thinking the exact same about her a few seconds ago.

'Well,' Lucas said, 'Avs and I will leave you two to it. We were just on our way to get ice cream.'

Summer looked down at the steadily dripping ice cream cone in my hand.

Lucas took it from me and threw it into a near-by bin. '*Another* ice cream,' he corrected. 'Come on,' he finished, draping his long arm around my shoulders and steering me off. Not once did I look back.

'Well, that wasn't awkward at all,' Lucas said, releasing his arm once we reached a good enough distance from Theo and Summer.

'You okay?' he asked me softly.

'Of course,' I answered, feeling slightly dazed. 'I'm fine.'

'I don't believe you.'

'Why not?'

'Because you're a girl and when a girl says she's fine, she's lying.'

He had me there.

'It's nothing, really. I just didn't know he had a girlfriend,' I admitted.

'Yeah, I figured you didn't. He did want to tell you, Avs, but it was difficult for him. He's in a sticky situation,' Lucas explained. 'I think he's falling for you.'

I looked at Lucas and remained mute. No. Guys like Theo didn't fall for girls like me; they fell for girls like Summer.

'Lying's always the worst thing to do, so sometimes it's just easier to say nothing rather than tell the truth,' Lucas said.

'You look sad,' I blurted out. I hadn't meant to be so pointed, but the expression on Lucas's face hung oddly on him. It was as if the emotion didn't belong. His sudden sadness tugged at my heart.

'Do I?'

'Yes,' I answered. I would have left it there but there was something haunting behind his dark blue-green eyes that made me want to know more. 'Why are you sad?' I asked.

Lucas turned to look at me, contemplating something. Then he shrugged as if to blow caution to the already fierce wind. He pulled down his sunglasses before speaking.

'Have you met Baleigh properly yet?' he asked.

'Yes,' I replied thinking back to when I had first met her and the joyous conversation we'd both shared.

During my visits to Hayven I usually just hung out with Theo and Lucas, or just Theo. Whenever we did see Baleigh, she would never say more than two words to me but talk to Theo or Lucas only. She didn't seem to like me very much and I didn't know why. Maybe she was close friends with Summer and thought I knew about Theo and her being together and chose to be around him anyway. She probably thought I was some kind of homewrecker.

'Two years ago, she was my girlfriend.'

I had not seen that coming.

'You two dated?' I asked.

'Yes. Our relationship didn't end very well and it was entirely my fault. It's an incredibly long story and it's not one I particularly want to share, not today anyway.' Lucas sighed.

'Baleigh is a strong girl, Avs, and I don't know if you've noticed but she hates to show any sign of weakness; the day we broke up, she cried.' Lucas flinched slightly as he retold the story. At first I had put that involuntary action down to him thinking of the consequence that followed if Baleigh ever found out he'd told me, but the more I studied his face, the more I came to realise that the flinch stemmed from the memory of Baleigh crying, and the recollection seemed to cause him *pain*.

Baleigh was another person I believed had a face that sadness would not suit. While I could imagine her *feeling* sad, I couldn't imagine her actually showing it, especially with tears. But that's the thing about people who don't show certain emotions, when they finally do, it isn't something you were likely to forget and that's what seemed to be silently haunting Lucas.

'The sight of her crying…isn't an image I've been able to get out of my head,' Lucas confessed, unknowingly confirming my theory.

'Even after two years?'

'Even after two years.'

I hated to see Lucas like this, he looked so *sad*. There was just no other word to describe it; his face and entire demeanour seemed to *crumble*. And for someone who is usually full of laughter and energy, it's not a sight you hope to see again.

'But you both seem fine now. Theo told me you guys all hang out together,' I said.

'Yeah, we do,' he said. 'She forgave me about six months ago, but she hasn't forgotten; she never will and as much as I want her to, I can't expect her to.'

123

Bales isn't one to take a lot of crap. Theo's words jumped to attention at the forefront of my mind. Maybe Lucas's jokey remarks about chasing Baleigh may not have been jokes after all.

'Do you want her back?' I asked and deep down, I knew the answer.

'I never stopped wanting her, but she just wants to be friends, so I've been making do with that.'

'I don't understand,' I said. 'If it's Baleigh you really want, why do you date so many other girls?'

Whenever I was in Hayven with Theo we would take an hour out of our planned schedule to just walk and talk mindlessly about this, that and the other, and because Fulton University grounds was the perfect place to do this, that's where we often went. I had yet failed to see Lucas in the distance, without his arm around a girl's shoulder or his lips pressed against hers, and I never saw Lucas with the same girl more than twice. And if Theo and I always saw this and didn't even attend Fulton, then who knew how much Baleigh saw.

'I don't really know,' he said and shrugged. 'My motto is "life is better when you're laughing", so I just always try to have a good time. When you're having fun, you don't overthink. I don't know,' he repeated. 'Theo thinks it's a coping mechanism, I just think I'm selfish.'

'I don't think you're selfish,' I said instantly.

'That's sweet of you to say, Avs, but you hardly know me...if you knew...' Lucas took a deep breath before straightening up and shaking himself off. 'Look at us! We make such a miserable pair.'

Lucas was right. I hardly knew him. I didn't know his full name, I didn't know what subject he studied; I didn't know his travelling colour, I didn't know whereabouts in Naveya he lived, I didn't even know how old he was. But with all I didn't know, I was good at judging people, I always have been, and Lucas was a good person.

I stood on the tips of my toes to give Lucas a hug. It was a very out of character thing for me to do, but I doubted anyone had seen this vulnerable side to Lucas, except perhaps Baleigh. But for whatever reason, he had shown me, and call me easily-pleased, but that somehow made me feel rather special.

After a few seconds of deliberation and hesitation on his part, he hugged me back. At that moment, I knew I had made a friend for life in Lucas, and for once, since the day I met him, he dropped his mental barrier and I heard him think the exact same about me.

Lucas Ayden was a seriously cool guy. He sort of reminded me of Jamie: good-looking, cocky in a harmless way, and a real softy at heart. I spent two hours discovering all kinds of basic things about him. I learnt that he studied Microbiology at Fulton, lived with his parents in Hayven but has plans to move out before his twenty-first birthday. He's part-Greek thanks to his dad and he has one of the coolest gifts ever – he's a firider, meaning he has the ability to produce fire with his hands.

He showed me his gift by simply holding out his hands, palms facing upwards, and I watched in deep captivation as his hands begun to glow a soft, sunset pink before turning into a crimson red, then a canary yellow, finally turning a molten orange, before his entire hand spontaneously ignited and went aflame. 'It doesn't hurt,' he assured me once he'd caught sight of my panicked expression.

He also introduced me to Peyton-Jane Levi. A pretty, hippy-like girl who wore a long skirt that tickled the ground and hid her feet, a cropped plain tee showing off her defined stomach, and a cardigan almost as long as her skirt. To complete her bohemian look, she wore a thin white and pink flower band tangled in her brown-blonde curly hair and multiple bracelets on each wrist, one of which looked strikingly familiar. Unfortunately, I didn't get to look at it more closely or even speak to her because she had been running late for class. Lucas had laughed and said, 'She's always late for class,' and so all she could do was throw me a slow-drawled 'Hello', kiss me on each cheek and rush off towards Fulton's main doors.

I was disappointed that I hadn't been able to hang out with her; she seemed a lot friendlier than Baleigh and she had this sort of really chilled and loveable ditzy vibe surrounding her. There was also something about her emerald eyes that made me feel calm and *safe*. I'd thought it had something to do with her gift until Lucas told me her actual gift was earth manipulation, meaning she could pretty much control things connected to the earth – trees, rocks, rivers, etc.

I dreaded the moment I'd have to say goodbye to Lucas and the moment came too soon. He travelled with me to *Hayven Books* and even walked me under the arched alleyway before he stopped and let out a long, slow whistle.

'So this is Huxton?'

'Haven't you been here before?' I asked.

'Nope.' He shook his head before looking around. 'Not past this arch anyway. Sometimes I'll come to bug Theo at work, but that's as far as I've gone. My family and I took loads of holidays together, but who goes to Huxton?' He smiled and added, 'No offence.'

'Offence taken,' I said, despite being unable to hide a smile myself.

Yes, Hayven may be lighter, brighter and all round magical. The streets were usually busy, the skies swam in multi colours as the clouds melted into one another, the weather was always balmy even when the sun wasn't out and yes, Huxton did seem to be the complete opposite. It was January now and whilst Hayven was warm all year round, Huxton on the other hand was absolutely freezing and despite it being only five in the afternoon, Lucas and I stood alone on the street.

So, whilst admittedly Hayven was more *alive* than Huxton, I had lived here for over a year and in doing so, had developed a rather quaint and unexplained fondness for the town's usually quiet streets and elderly residents.

Lucas continued to look around the empty streets. 'Yeah, well, it's a good thing that when people say "no offence", it really means, "prepare to be offended".'

I punched him on the arm as a payment for his cheek. After doing so, he turned to me with big, innocent eyes that were currently in a state of concern.

'What is it?' I asked, worried.

He looked down to where I had punched him. 'I think a fly just bumped into me, but I can't be sure.'

It took me a second to realise that Lucas was ribbing me, unsubtly implying that my punch had been weak. So I punched him again.

'If I hadn't seen you do that I would have been convinced a fly was after me.' He smiled. 'You hit like a girl.'

'That's sexist,' I stated.

'Thank you.'

'*Sexist*. Not sexy.'

'I heard "sexy",' Lucas replied, 'so that's what I'm going to go with. Alright, I'm leaving now, this town is slightly depressing.'

I looked around the dull town and noticed something.

'Your glow is making Huxton shine,' I smiled softly, reminiscent.

'Yes, well, my presence does often have that effect.'

I rolled my eyes. 'It's your gifted aura. You're glowing.'

'Oh yeah?' He smiled again. 'So are you. See ya!' And then he was gone in a cloud of cherry red dots.

I instantly missed him.

He had been a healthy and friendly distraction. I had guessed that as soon as I was on my own with only my thoughts for company I would think of Theo and Summer, and annoyingly I'd been right. The worst part was I couldn't understand why my brain was so obsessed with the two of them. Even with Lucas, every now and again my mind would wander back to those two. Common sense would dictate that I was jealous of Summer, maybe in love with Theo. Perhaps the first part was true; maybe secretly I wanted to be the only female Theo gave his attention to, which really wasn't like me. The latter part of that assumption was more than false. I wasn't in love with Theo. I didn't fall in love easily and the last time I had, I'd crashed and burned.

CHAPTER TWELVE

Four weeks had passed since I'd last been to Hayven and I was suffering from what I could only liken to withdrawal symptoms. I'd been tempted more than once to go on my own, but still wasn't confident enough to do it by myself with no supervision, especially since I didn't know what happened if you did something wrong whilst travelling. Not to mention I'd have no one to roam about with. Lucas had given me his number, but he had his own life and his own friends and I didn't want to seem a bother. I could go and finally take a walk in Mysteria Park, but what if I couldn't get back to Huxton somehow, or worse, I saw Theo and Summer in there, holding hands and…being a couple?

So I did what I knew I could do – sulked. I stayed in my room with nothing but my school work, numerous DVDs and mountains of food for company, which I suppose isn't so terrible. I went out whenever Toni or the others suggested we did and whilst I pretended their plans always sounded good to me, deep down I always agreed reluctantly. I couldn't deny that hanging out with Toni, Susie, Alfie and Jamie often disconnected my mind from my head, taking my dark thoughts with it, but I also felt I *had* to agree. It was like the Sidra Calix incident all over again; I just didn't want any of them to figure out that something was up with me because that led to questions, and because I couldn't give them truthful answers it led to lies, and lies led to a very complicated life. Sadly, it was just easier to pretend.

'Something's not right with you, Ava.'

It took a while for me to realise that Toni was talking to me, despite her having used my name. We were on our way home from a lecture and once again, my mind had packed its bags and taken off without permission.

'Why do you say that?' I asked.

'You're different,' Toni explained. 'It's like you're not happy or something. You hide it well from the others, but you can't hide it from me.'

When I failed to provide an answer, she asked, 'So, why aren't you happy?'

Could I tell Toni? Not about Hayven of course, but maybe try to explain the Theo situation without revealing too much. She knows much more about boys than I do, so maybe she could tell me why I felt so woeful all of the time, especially over someone I wasn't in love with. But how could I possibly explain it when I didn't understand it? She'd want to know too much and if I wasn't careful I'd let something slip.

'I just feel very lonely at times,' I replied, disclosing only half of the truth.

'But why?' she asked, her dark green eyes big and sincere. 'You've got us and we're always here for you.'

'I know…' I started, eventually trailing off. I felt even worse now. Toni, Susie, Alfie and Jamie had been nothing but great friends to me, and yet I chose to sulk around my room thinking about a place I couldn't even share with them.

I had friends in Huxton I could depend on, family I loved in London and who loved me too, and a university I enjoyed and was sure I'd enjoy even more once I'd found the right course to study. But no matter how much I tried to convince myself that I was better off here, Hayven would never leave me alone. I couldn't seem to give the place up and that was what frustrated me more than anything. I hadn't noticed my shoulders were tense until I felt them droop as Toni took my hands into hers.

'You're not depressed, are you?' she asked gently. 'Like, clinically depressed.'

'No,' I answered. 'No, I'm not.'

'Oh good,' she said relieved, 'because that is way out of my zone of expertise.'

A random image suddenly came to mind, of Toni years older, sitting behind the desk of a therapist's office. She wore glasses that weren't prescribed perched haughtily on the tip of her nose whilst she rolled her eyes and tutted impatiently as her clients told her of their problems. I chuckled softly.

'You hardly do that anymore,' she said with a smile.

'I'll try to,' I promised.

'Good. I like hearing you laugh. It makes me laugh, and I love to laugh.'

To prove her point, Toni attempted to laugh but because it was forced, it sounded strangled, like she was having a coughing fit. Then she actually *did* have a coughing fit, which made me laugh and that in turn made her laugh. It felt good to laugh and truly mean it. Toni was right; I hadn't done that in a while.

'Come here,' she said and she wrapped me in a big hug. Toni was tiny but her hugs managed to make you feel as if you were in the arms of someone a lot bigger. I leant my cheek on her shoulder and inhaled her usual, expensive, flowery perfume she often doused on her neck, and a breeze of nostalgia hit me in the chest and the back of my throat. The smell made me feel at home and made me want to cry.

'Are you sure you don't want to come to dinner with us?' she asked after releasing me, unaware of the effect her hug had had on me.

'No,' I replied. 'I desperately need to catch up on some work. I'm so behind.'

'Want me to stay back and help?'

'No, no, go to dinner. Have fun,' I ordered. 'Tell the guys I said hi.'

'Okay, will do,' she promised. 'See you tomorrow?'

'Yes, see you tomorrow.'

I let myself into my room, took off my jacket and sat at my desk. I opened my textbooks and notebook and managed to get through an hour of study before throwing my pen down and falling back in my seat.

Theo. Theo. Theo.

Why did I not know how to feel about him? Why didn't he tell me he had a girlfriend? Why hadn't he called me? Why was he taking up so much brain space?

I needed to talk to someone, someone who wouldn't ask too many questions. I picked up my phone and dialled her number.

'Hello, Ava, darling! It's so nice to hear from you! How are you? Is everything alright?'

In the background I could hear bubbling, sizzling, and the gentle clatter of pots and pans. Mum must be experimenting in the kitchen. I smiled before it fell.

Ever since I left for university my parents would call me once a week, just to check in. Ever since the very first incident at *Hayven Books*, their calls have gone up to three times a week and I'd always tell them I was too busy to talk now, or we'd have a very brief conversation. Sometimes, I'd accidentally miss their call and forget to ring them back. I should have made more of an effort.

'Hey, mum,' I said into the receiver, 'everything's fine. Just wanted to call and check in. How are you and Dad?'

'We're well! Your father's at work at the moment. I'm just busy in the kitchen!'

Homesickness replaced sadness. I loved being in the kitchen whenever Mum was experimenting. I'd sit on the dining table whilst she hovered over one pan and stirred another. Asking me to try this, that and the other. Her blowing on the spoon in case it was too hot, just like she always did when I was younger. An unexpected tear rolled down my cheek.

'What are you making?' I asked, brushing my cheek with the back of my hand. 'A new recipe?'

'Yes!' she answered. 'Recently, I've grown rather tired of cooking the old regulars, you know, lasagne, chicken pie, etc. So, today I've decided to give something new a try. Now, it's a little unconventional, I must admit, a bit exotic, but darling, hear me out. Chocolate pasta.'

I laughed and Mum did too.

'I knew you'd chuckle,' she said. 'Your father did too when I first told him of it. Yet, it's always you and your

135

father who enjoy my unconventional twists the most! Remember my blue cheese and pumpkin mashed potato?'

'I do. That was pretty good actually.'

'You see! Your mother knows what she's doing in the kitchen!' she trilled.

I smiled and hugged the phone closer to my ear. 'So, how do you go about making this chocolate pasta?' I asked, knowing that if there was anything my mum enjoyed most about experimenting with food, it was talking about it.

'Well!' she started. 'Last Saturday, I was at the farmer's market with your father, simply browsing around, when we came across a stall run by a couple selling flavoured dried pasta. Such a clever couple. They had all sorts on their stall – chilli pasta, squid ink pasta, saffron pasta, beetroot pasta and cocoa pasta! I bought three bags of their cocoa fusilli and have been experimenting ever since!' I heard a lid being placed on a pan. 'I tried to make it into a savoury dish at first,' she continued, 'with tomato sauce, cheese and all of my usual pasta ingredients. It wasn't *too* bad, but I've been having better luck transforming it into a dessert. I've added pecan nuts and a caramel sauce and it's rather delicious! I might serve it as a dessert for my next dinner party. Alongside something more conventional, perhaps a lemon drizzle cake, you know, for the less adventurous.'

I sighed. 'I love you, Mum.'

'Oh, darling. I love you too.'

I heard a chair scrape across the laminate floor and assumed she'd sat down at the kitchen table.

'Is everything alright, Ava?' she asked. 'You sound a little despondent.'

'I've met someone. A guy.'

'I see,' she said. 'Is it not a bit soon after...Alex?'

'We're not dating, it isn't like that,' I replied. 'To be honest, I don't know what it's like. I'm very confused.'

'Why don't you tell me everything, darling, so that I can understand a little better.'

I told Mum everything minus Hayven and elaborated only a little on the details.

Theo was a guy I'd met at a bookshop. We got on really well. Before I found out he had a girlfriend, I saw him as only a friend. Or maybe I was forcing myself to see him as only a friend, to keep him at a relatively safe distance. We don't talk anymore and he hasn't tried to get in touch with me. But I miss him. I just don't know in what context.

'Hmmm,' Mum said quietly. 'Well, Ava, you know all I want to do is protect you and so my head is telling me to advise you to stay away from Theo. Yet my heart urges me to advise you to follow yours. I know it's a very cliché answer to provide, but when it comes to how one feels, no organ can instruct you better than the heart. I wouldn't say you're in love, but usually, it is the men we think about the most, the men who make us question how we feel, that end up being the men we eventually fall for. Whether you want to be with Theo forever or just for now is perhaps not something you need to decide right away. What needs to be decided is how important this man is to you *now* and whether that level of importance is likely to change any time soon. There is no pressure to be with him, sweetheart,' Mum pointed out. 'You can have him as a friend, but never be afraid of admitting how you feel to yourself. Acceptance is your key to understanding, Ava. You cannot live your life pretending you don't feel certain things when you do because in the end, you have fooled no-one, not even yourself. Try to decipher your feelings for Theo and see if you can answer this: Are you upset he didn't tell you he has a girlfriend, or are you upset that he has one? Your answer is where the truth lies.'

***

I was in a concrete maze. Trapped in a building consisting of only locked grey doors, plain walls and flights of stairs. I held onto the bannister and pulled myself up the next set of stairs. My T-shirt clung to my back and sweat dripped down my face, salty droplets hitting the floor. I reached the door at the top of the stairs and grabbed hold of the handle. I pulled down. Locked. Next flight of stairs. Door handle. Locked. Stairs. Door. Locked. Stairs. Door. *Unlocked.*

I opened the door only marginally at first, the metal of the handle cool in my palm, before pushing the door open completely. I put a step over the threshold and a tall lamp to my right flickered on. Another step forward turned on a lamp to my left side. The door shut on its own accord behind me. There was nothing in the dim room but a small square desk. Someone sat at it with their back to me. I walked up to the person and placed my hand on their shoulder. Their hood fell down, causing an explosion of orange hair to be released. Pale, elegant fingers that could only have belonged to a woman pulled the hood back into place. She slowly stood up. Her plain robe swept the floor. She stepped to the side and revealed, sitting on the table, a crystal ball. It didn't move. It didn't roll. Despite its curved, edgeless body, it remained perfectly still in the middle of the table. The only thing moving being the dancing wisps of clear smoke captured inside it.

Suddenly, the woman turned around, her head bowed low, her hood covering every facial feature, her hair unnaturally contained. She presented a dagger from her side and walked towards me. Every step she put forward, I took one step back until she was left with no choice but to run. She caught up to me, placed her palm on my chest and pushed until my back found a wall. She raised the dagger higher before bringing it down to my chest. The sharp tip pierced my skin.

I screamed and woke up.

Someone was knocking on my door. A yellow post-it note was stuck to my forehead. I'd fallen asleep at my desk. My hand flew to my chest, but there was no blood or stab wound. It had been just a dream.

'Who is it?' I asked, my voice dry.

'It's me. Alfie.'

'Oh. One second, Alfie.' I took of my sweat-soaked T-shirt, replaced it with a dry one and peeled off the post-it note before answering the door. 'Hey, Alfie. Come in. What's up?'

'Hey, Ava,' he said, stepping inside. 'I just…are you okay?'

'Yeah,' I replied, closing the door. I sat on my bed and Alfie took the desk chair. 'Why?'

'It's just, you look very…wild-eyed,' he answered. 'Are you sure you're okay?'

'Yeah, yeah, I'm fine,' I said dismissively. I looked at my watch; it was 8 p.m. 'How was dinner?'

'It was good,' Alfie replied. 'Missed you, though. We went to the Indian restaurant next to the town centre.'

'I've been meaning to try there. Any good?' *What a weird dream that had been.*

'Yeah, really good,' Alfie said. 'I'm glad you're interested in trying it because there is something I've been meaning to ask you.'

'Oh, really? What is it?' I asked. *Who had been that cloaked figure who had tried to kill me?*

'Well, I was just wondering…'

What was that weird ball on the table?

'If, I don't know…'

Why was there smoke inside it?

'If maybe, you know. If you weren't busy or anything…'

What building had I been in?

'If you wanted to have dinner with me tomorrow night. Just you and me.'

I'd only been half-listening to Alfie's stammering's, but unfortunately, I had caught the last bit of what he'd said.

'I'm sorry?'

'What?' he asked.

I stared at him like I hadn't understood the question he'd thrown at me, but I did understand it and I really didn't want him to repeat it. I continued to stare dumbstruck at his hopeful yet puzzled face and I came to the horrid conclusion that I would have to say something regarding his question.

How was it that he was still interested in me? It's been almost half a year since I'd first heard him think about asking me out and pretty much since then, I'd gone AWOL. Okay, I needed to provide an answer. Alfie was still staring at me, waiting for me to say something.

Just say no. Just say no.

'Yes.'

CHAPTER THIRTEEN

At least once in a person's life there is a moment of panic felt
when a certain question needs to be answered. But because
that person either doesn't know what to say, or doesn't want
to say what they should, they instead say the first thing that
pops into their head. I *hated* those moments and unluckily for
me, the latest one occurred at the worst time possible.

What had I been thinking when I'd said yes to Alfie last
night? I still didn't feel that way about him and I didn't know
if I ever would, but it was too late to think about that now. I
couldn't cancel our date because we were both already here,
sitting at our table in the Indian restaurant Alfie and the gang
had visited the previous night. I did like Indian food and that
was mainly because of the smell, but today the smell of
roasting chicken and skewered lamb wafting in from the
kitchen, combined with all the exotic spices and scattered
pieces of incense and potpourri filling the air in the dining
area, was beginning to make me feel nauseous. I pulled down
the menu I had strategically placed to cover my burning face,
to peer over the top at Alfie. I was greeted by the sight of a
pair of hands, slowly turning pink, tightly gripping the edges
of his menu. I'd been unaware that he'd been mirroring me,
pretending to study his meal choices with furious intensity,
and I couldn't help but wonder what we must look like to
fellow diners.

We were both studiously ignoring each other and unfortunately, this meant I had to listen to his thoughts as the only other option was removing the menu from my scorched face and attempting a plausible conversation.

Maybe this was a huge mistake…she won't even look at me. Alright, just say something; start a conversation about… about the work she was catching up on last night.

Despite everything, I couldn't resist. I lowered my menu just as he did, masked my face with a look of pure innocence and said, 'You'll never guess what happened to me last night when attempting to catch up with my uni work.'

'Oh…urm, what happened?' he asked. 'How strange. I was just going to ask you how last night went.'

'Oh, really? That is strange…Well, I'd been working solidly for an hour before I had a phone call with my mum. I remember saying goodbye and pressing the end call button, but I can't seem to remember anything after that. I just fell asleep. I don't even remembering closing my eyes!'

Alfie laughed and I noticed his shoulders drop to a more relaxed state and I felt mine do the same. Alright, *this* was normal; just think of it like having dinner with everyone, minus Toni, Susie and Jamie. Just remind him how easy it is being *just* friends. *What could I talk about to reinforce that idea?*

'I was just in the toilet before you came.'

'Oh…really? Great! Everything…go okay?' he asked.

Tread lightly, Ava. 'Yes, everything went fine. I just had a bit of a…runny stomach, that's all.'

Kill me now.

Alfie pressed his lips firmly together and stared down at his menu.

'I'm ready to order,' I announced. I had actually no idea what I wanted to order, but I did know I wanted to move away from the topic of me on the toilet. 'Are you?'

'Just one second.' Alfie pulled the menu back up to his face as if to study his choices again, but I could hear suspicious noises coming from his end of the table.

'Are you...' I paused to make sure. 'Are you laughing?'

'No! Of course not! Why would I? There is nothing funny about what you just said.' He tried his best to maintain a straight face, but the strained effort was making me smile which in turn made him smile.

After that, we were able to slip into ordinary everyday chatter, which I was grateful for because the more he talked, the less he thought, and it had only cost me my dignity. Unfortunately, the same didn't apply to me. As my mouth moved, my mind wandered. I just couldn't shake last night's dream off. It had been so *vivid*. I had felt a strong pinch when that dagger had touched my skin.

Our food arrived and we managed to maintain conversation throughout our three courses. We discussed university, the increasing difficulty of my course, how his course was going, life in Huxton, how much I missed my family in London, how much he missed his family in Kent and anything else we could think of. Regrettably, the inevitable end to our conversation now made it impossible to ignore what Alfie was thinking.

This is going really well. I'm so glad I asked her out to dinner...she's so easy to talk to...she's perfect.

Alfie's opinion of me was a blow to the chest. I wish I could tell him how far from perfect I actually was because I should never have said agreed to this date in the first place. I

143

couldn't keep trying to convince myself that this was just a dinner date with a friend when I knew that it was more than that to Alfie; I was leading him on. He'd made such an effort tonight. For me. He'd brushed his hair back from its usual tousled state, he'd shaved his stumble, he'd worn smart clothes, and was wearing aftershave that must be new because I'd never smelt it on him before. He didn't deserve this.

I considered just being his girlfriend; it wouldn't be so hard. Guys weren't exactly throwing themselves at my feet, and after my last relationship – if you could call it that – it would be *nice* to be with someone like Alfie. Someone kind, caring and considerate, someone who actually liked the way I looked and was in no rush to change me…but I didn't feel that way about him and the longer I kept him believing I did, the worse it would be. I'd been there.

The entire journey home consisted of Alfie talking to make up for my sudden silence. I didn't have anything else to say now because I needed to think about what I was going to say next. I knew the looming conversation I needed to have with him wasn't going to be easy and it wasn't a speech I'd ever given, only heard.

The wind had picked up considerably since entering the restaurant and the darkness of the sky had caused the air to adopt a blustery and icy persona. I reluctantly hunched deeper into Alfie's dinner jacket. I hadn't wanted to accept it, but the involuntary shiver that had taken over me once we had taken one step outside hadn't escaped Alfie's notice, and he'd graciously taken off his jacket and kindly forced me to put it on.

We'd arrived at my building when a gaggle of squealing girls, clearly drunk, staggered past us in a rush to get out of the door Alfie was currently holding open. One of the girls stumbled on her thin stick of a heel and accidentally bumped into me, causing me to lose my footing and lean onto Alfie for support. It had been either that or land sideways on the concrete floor. Perhaps I should have taken the floor.

Entering the building came as a warm relief, but soon I felt myself grow too warm; a heat that had nothing to do with the buildings radiators but all to do with what I had to say to Alfie. Now that we were both outside my bedroom door, I couldn't put it off any longer.

'Alfie, listen, I —'

'Ava,' he interrupted, 'just wait.'

And then, he kissed me. It was a soft and gentle kiss, as light and as delicate as springtime air, but I couldn't kiss him back, I couldn't even attempt to.

I felt a sharp and slow stinging sensation build at the back of my eyes and I had to blink rapidly to avoid what threatened to spill out. But the rapid blinking only seemed to encourage the tears and a few wet drops managed to escape.

Afterwards, Alfie stepped back to look at me, but instead of looking him in the eye, I looked down at the floor.

'You're not interested in me, are you?' He'd asked in a whisper but the silent hall seemed to amplify each word.

'Not in that way,' I confessed.

'Right.'

And that was all he said.

'I'm so sorry, Alfie, I —'

145

'Then why did you say yes to this date, Ava?'

I'd expected him to be angry about the fact that I'd led him on and then let him down, and I'd rather that than how I knew he really felt – disappointed. I'd rather he was angry because anger was easier to cure than disappointment. Disappointment sticks with you.

'I thought maybe I could change my mind.'

'And why can't you? Is there someone else?' he asked softly.

'Yes. No. I don't know,' I whispered. 'It's very complicated.' And it was. Theo had nothing to do with how I felt for Alfie. I felt the same way about him now as I did before I met Theo; nothing had changed. Yet, I couldn't help but bring Theo into it. I had taken my mum's advice and had tried to decipher how I felt about him. I still couldn't pinpoint it exactly, but I knew that whatever I felt for Theo may not be unbearably strong, but it was stronger than what I felt for Alfie, and that wasn't something I could put into words. How did you even begin to explain that you had met a guy who was different; that you had met a guy who made you feel *something*, something you've never felt and therefore can't articulate? You don't know what that *something* is or what it could lead to, but you know it's there. And then go on to explain why you chose him over someone you'd known longer, someone you were friends with, someone who'd never let you down or hurt you, and someone who probably never would. You couldn't.

I slipped off Alfie's dinner jacket and held it out to him, knowing that there was nothing left for me to say.

'I'm so sorry,' I said.

'Yeah, me too, Ava.'

He took hold of the jacket in the middle and for a moment, I hesitated, refusing to let it go. That is how we stood for that short moment, him holding onto the middle of his jacket and me still clasping the top. A part of me couldn't and didn't seem to want to let go because I knew that if I did, that was it. I'd lose Alfie as a friend. But I couldn't change the way I felt. I released the jacket and watched Alfie walk away.

I let myself into my room, exhausted and ready to collapse into bed, but someone was currently occupying it. I nearly jumped out of my skin at the unexpected sight of her.

'Baleigh!'

'Well, that was awkward to listen to,' she said.

I patted my chest softly with a shaky hand, in a vain attempt to calm my heart. I thought I might be hallucinating but after subtly pinching myself several times, I came to accept that Baleigh Castel was in fact, sitting cross-legged on my bed. In my bedroom. In my flat. On my university campus. In Huxton.

She sat, all dressed in black – black skinny jeans, a black turtle neck jumper and black combat boots. She had her hair in her signature style, loose with a strand tucked behind her ear, and her hands were again, decorated in multiple rings. I didn't know whether it was because my room was dimly lit, or because she was wearing all black, but surely even non-gifted people could see her glow, it was so bright.

'What are you doing here? How did you get in?'

'I'm here to take you to Hayven, and I came in through the *door*,' she replied, getting up and looking at me as if I was the crazy one out of us both. 'Relax, I didn't climb in through the window.'

'How did you know where I lived?'

'I don't know. I'm smart?' she ventured, adding a casual shrug for emphasis. 'Come on, I haven't got all day…' She trailed off, looking me up and down.

I looked down to examine my outfit. For my disastrous date, I had chosen a purple velvet dress that I hated, but was the only dress I owned, black tights and plain black ballet pumps.

'That dress is a sin. Change your clothes, please,' she said once her inspection was over. 'I wouldn't want people to think *we've* been on a date.'

I'm embarrassed to admit that Baleigh did scare me a little, so I did as I was told. I changed into a more acceptable jeans, jumper and Converse combo in my bathroom. Once I emerged, she stood in front of me in the middle of the room.

'Ready to go?'

'Well…yes…I think so.'

Baleigh raised a perfectly plucked eyebrow. 'You *think* so?'

'I've never gone on my own,' I explained.

She heaved a laborious sigh at this. 'Well try,' she insisted. 'If you can't, I suppose you can hold my hand,' and she paused to think about what she had just said. 'But I'd rather you tried first.'

I closed my eyes in an attempt to focus, knowing all the while Baleigh was watching me, but I pushed my nerves to the side and pictured Hayven instead. It was all too easy to do since Hayven is all I've been thinking about for the past few months. I embraced the tingling sensation that started at my feet and spread through me, as I allowed my bones to melt. When I opened my eyes, I was standing in front of Fulton University. I smiled, pleased with myself.

Seven seconds later, violet coloured specks formed Baleigh beside me.

'I'm impressed,' she said, entering the university. 'I didn't think you'd be able to do it so I didn't even ask you where you'd go. I checked *Gordon's* before I came here.'

'Why are we going in here?' I asked, pointing to Fulton's front doors. 'It's almost eight at night.'

'My mum works here,' she answered.

'The one who can read minds?' I asked.

'I only have one mum.'

I was about to tell her that I knew that and was only excited to finally meet her mother, but she cut me off before I could start.

'Theo told me everything that happened with you, him and Summer. He feels really bad so he's been bugging me to get you to meet my mum so she can teach you how to control your gift; as if that'll get you to forgive him or something.'

She turned a corner to walk up the grand staircase with golden railings that reminded me of the staircase in *Hayven Books*.

'So, he told you everything?' I asked.

'That's what I said,' she answered.

Baleigh was a strange girl. She had a way of bluntly answering a question without sounding sarcastic or offensive; she simply answered questions without any true emotion behind her reply. She turned round from leading the way to look at me and decided to take pity.

'Look, if it makes you feel any better, I prefer you over Summer, which I suppose speaks volumes seeing as I don't even know you. Summer just bothers me.' After that short

149

yet blasé statement, she turned around to walk across the second level of the university.

I couldn't suppress how smug I felt. Coming from Baleigh, that was a compliment…sort of. To be fair, it really just meant she could stand my presence more than Summer's, but I knew when to be grateful.

'I don't think Theo would be too pleased to hear you say that,' I told her.

'Why? He's heard me say it before,' she said.

I wasn't surprised. Baleigh mincing her words to protect somebody's feelings, even those she loved, seemed as likely as me sprouting wings at this very moment and taking flight. Perhaps even *more* unlikely than that, given where we were.

'And to be honest, I think deep down, he agrees with me.'

What, that Theo agrees that Summer is annoying, or that he also prefers me to Summer? I thought about asking Baleigh to clarify before swiftly deciding against it. No, I didn't want to seem like a complete loser in front of her. Knowing that she'd heard what happened between Alfie and me ten minutes ago, I liked to think I'd ran out of embarrassment cards for the day.

Baleigh had stopped in front of dark mahogany double doors and proceeded to push them open to reveal a vast classroom decorated in deep purple, with rows of tables and chairs, and a desk at the very front where a woman sat.

'Hey, Mum. Avery's here,' Baleigh announced.

It was weird being called Avery; even all my teachers at university called me Ava.

'You can call me Ava,' I said.

150

'I know,' she replied and then looked down at her watch that glinted gold with its own personality; it looked suspiciously like a Rolex.

'Okay, I'm going to go now; I'm meeting Faye and Peyton. I'll see you some other time, Avery.' She blew her mum a kiss with a softness I hadn't thought she could manage, and made to leave but then paused and turned to face me again. She twirled her keys around her index finger and regarded me questioningly.

'Are you hungry?'

I wasn't expecting that question but having not eaten much in the last six hours, I was *famished*. I hadn't particularly liked what I had ordered at the Indian restaurant, so most of it went uneaten. The constant talking, the dream from last night, and the nightmare of having to tell Alfie the truth hadn't done much to aid my appetite either.

'Very,' I answered.

'Okay, Faye, Peyton and I are going out to dinner later. Do you want to join?'

Was this a trap? Did she want me to say yes just so she could say, 'Well, you can't!'? No, it couldn't be; she wouldn't be that mean to me with her mum in the room, would she? There was only one way to find out.

'Yes, please,' I answered, holding my breath.

'Alright, I'll see you in an hour then.' She continued to look at me with an expression I couldn't place before giving me a smile and walking out. The smile was a little less forced than the one she'd given me when I'd first met her, but her lips had still remained firmly closed. Nonetheless, she seemed to be making an effort when she really had no reason to, and I appreciated that.

As she closed the door behind her, my eyes were drawn to a painting of a bowl of fruit that hung on the wall beside the door. The painting was so striking I couldn't help but take a few steps towards it.

It really was nothing more than a painting of a bowl of fruit, but the bowl was an ornate glass that sparkled as if constructed out of polished diamonds, and the individual pieces of fruit were drawn with such precision and detail, you couldn't miss one and you couldn't ignore another.

A green vine of shockingly red cranberries sat at the very edge of the fruit bowl so that it overlapped the bowl's rim and hung languidly over. Dark orange peaches sat on top of each other beside the cranberries, and a yellow pineapple was placed next to them, towering over the entire contents of the bowl. Next to the pineapple were small kiwi fruits, the hairs on their brown skin drawn so intricately that they were clearly visible, despite the fact that the painter had drawn the kiwi in halves to reveal their emerald centres. A bundle of tiny blueberries took up a small space against the vivid green kiwis. The further the blueberries got from the kiwis the darker they appeared in colour, so that right before the edge of the bowl, where rich violet coloured plums were drawn, were indigo blueberries, so dark, they were almost black, a complete contrast to the pale blue ones drawn at the start of the blueberry cluster.

'Incredible, isn't it?'

I started at the voice that reminded me I was not alone and turned to face Baleigh's mother, unaware of when she had moved from behind her desk to stand behind me.

'The painting,' she said, her voice gentle, soft yet perfectly audible.

'It really is,' I said, turning back to the painting for another look.

'It was painted by an extraordinary artist named Leonardo Santano,' Baleigh's mother explained.

'I've not heard of him,' I said.

'I'm not surprised. Unfortunately, not a lot of people have. He's very talented, so naturally he's under-appreciated,' she sighed. 'His paintings are so simple yet different. See? The colours of the fruits in the bowl form a rainbow, and instead of using the conventional fruits that are usually associated with such colours, for example, orange for oranges and yellow for bananas, he went for something different.'

'They look so real,' I commented, enthralled by the skill and ability of Leonardo Santano. The fruits were alive; the cranberries so small yet so large in detail, water droplets clung onto the surfaces of the ripening blueberries, and the spikes on the head of the pineapple looked sharp and well-defined.

Baleigh's mother sighed in agreement and walked back to her desk. I reluctantly turned away from the painting and followed her.

Closer up, it was easier to spot the resemblances that existed between Baleigh and her mother. They both had the same flawless skin tone, brown eyes and face shape, but the mother's hair was longer and her expressions softer than Baleigh's.

On my arrival to the front of her desk, she pushed aside the papers she had been previously writing on before smiling warmly.

'Hello. Please allow me to introduce myself properly,' she said. 'I'm Iris Castel, Baleigh's mother. And you are Ava, was it? Or do you prefer Avery?'

'Ava,' I answered. 'It's nice to meet you, Mrs Castel,' I said, clocking the wedding ring in time.

'Call me Iris, all my students do. Please sit,' she patted her desk to gesture for me to sit in the chair placed under it. I pulled the padded seat out and sat down so that there was nothing between us but her large oak desk.

'So, you think Baleigh takes after me?'

Oh! I'd forgotten she could read minds too; that *is* why I was here. I silently hoped I hadn't offended her.

Mrs Castel laughed a dulcet chime. 'It's alright,' she soothed, 'you haven't offended me in the slightest and you wouldn't be the first to say something like that. Baleigh does take after me considerably, but she tends to keep a straight face around people she's just met. She has a lovely smile, but doesn't seem that eager to show it. Stick around and you'll see it eventually.

'The first thing I should probably tell you, Ava, is that, as you've probably already guessed, we are not the only ones in the world who can read people's thoughts, and that is extremely important to remember. Not all gifters are the same, but we can be similar. I can only read people's minds, meaning I can hear their thoughts, see the pictures or scenes they play in their heads, and sense their true emotions, but my abilities stop there.'

'I can't see pictures, scenes, or sense emotions,' I said.

'Oh, but I think you will,' Mrs Castel replied. 'It's not something I need teach you, it will come to you in due time. It takes a while for a gift to fully develop; I suspect there

154

have been times when you wouldn't hear anybody's thoughts for a while, and then they would randomly return?'

I answered with a nod.

'I thought so,' Mrs Castel said. 'I hope it didn't alarm you at the time, a gift being weak at first is to be expected, it's normal. Well, as normal as it can be under the circumstances. Now, Theo tells me you can see people's names if you both come into contact. Is that true?'

'Yes,' I replied. 'Well, I think so. It's only happened once. And I think it only happens if I don't know the person's name already.'

'Alright,' she said as she rolled up the right sleeve of her dark purple blouse. 'Touch my arm and tell me my middle name.'

I hesitated at first, afraid to disappoint, but then did as she asked. The name Freya came to mind.

'Freya?'

'Very good,' she congratulated. 'Yes, my mother was rather eccentric when it came to naming her children. My brother's name is Cabe Dewey Caraway,' she said, pulling a face.

I smiled; Theo had been right when he'd said that I'd like Mrs Castel. She seemed the perfect balance between a teacher and a friend.

'However, Ava, I feel there is more you can do, but I cannot tell you what they are because I do not know; we'll just have to wait and see. The first thing I wish to teach you is how to close your mind so I – and others – cannot read or hear it. This will in turn make it easier for you to then block out other people's thoughts as well.'

155

I nodded eagerly; Mrs Castel had no idea how much I wanted to learn how to do this.

'I have some idea,' Mrs Castel smiled. 'I used to be in your shoes.'

I need to stop thinking aloud.

'I heard that too,' she said. 'Now essentially, what it all comes down to is the obvious – *not* thinking aloud. Whether you believe it or not, it *is* possible to do such a thing because they are *your* thoughts. You must learn to control your brain and not the other way around, because once you let your brain control you, insanity creeps in.'

I thought back to the first few weeks when I started hearing people's voices in my head. I'd assumed I was going insane, and now I saw that was purely because I was letting other people's thoughts take over my own. If I had been weaker and not returned to *Hayven Books*, I'd probably be mad.

'All you need is self-control,' Mrs Castel continued. 'It is all about having an empty mind but a full brain. It is said to prove an easier task if you say your thoughts aloud instead of keeping them to yourself – Baleigh's chosen method – but that is not always…recommended. Let's give it a try, shall we?'

'Oh. Now?' I asked.

'Yes, you needn't worry,' she comforted. 'Just try. I won't scold you or give you a bad mark for failing. I've always said "you can't fail at practise".'

So I closed my eyes and tried, and for a while I thought of nothing, but I soon realised that was because I *couldn't* think of anything. As soon as I thought *that*, a magnitude of random thoughts began popping into my head. Thoughts of

London, my parents, Huxton, my essays, the painting of the fruit bowl, Theo and Alfie.

'Oh-oh, boy trouble,' Mrs Castel observed, picking up on the two thoughts I had dwelt on longest.

I felt my neck and cheeks burn. *How embarrassing.*

'It's not embarrassing,' Mrs Castel placated. 'You think the male kind are troublesome now, wait until you marry one.' She smiled before gently urging me to try again.

We did this for the rest of our allotted time; I focused on keeping my thoughts clear and my mind empty. I had been at it for eight minutes straight when the door to the room opened. I turned round to see Baleigh, Peyton and another girl who must have been Faye, standing at the entrance.

'That's all for today,' Mrs Castel said. 'Meet me here next week and we'll see how far you've gotten. Nothing but practise, Ava. You have seven days to impress me.'

Despite feeling as if seven days was quite a short period of time, I felt surprisingly optimistic. I had made progress today and that was something. I made a mental note to practise for at least two hours each day. I really did want to impress Mrs Castel.

She smiled, obviously having heard my thoughts again. 'Off you go then,' she dismissed kindly.

'Thank you. Goodbye, Mrs Cast – I mean, Iris. See you next Friday.'

***

'How was your first lesson?' Baleigh asked as we headed out of the building.

'Good actually, really helpful.'

I was glad it was Mrs Castel and not Baleigh who could read minds, as I still wasn't sure what to think of her. She hadn't been particularly welcoming during our first meeting and that moment was one I found hard to forget, but perhaps for some reason I couldn't yet figure out, she was warming to me.

'Good. Peyton says you've already met, so this is Faye Parks.' She gestured towards the other girl. 'Faye, this is Avery or Ava. She doesn't mind which.'

I took one look at Faye and liked her instantly. She had long, spiralled, light auburn hair, her blue eyes were protected behind square-rimmed glasses, her cheeks and nose featured a liberal splash of freckles, and she wore baggy blue dungarees over a woollen jumper. She was adorable.

'Hello,' she said shyly.

'Hello,' I replied, just as bashful. I imagined we'd get on great.

I was grateful to learn that we would not be going to *Gordon's* for dinner as I had only Theo-filled memories in there. We went to Vanilla Shake, an American retro diner that served things like turkey burgers and bacon with pancakes, and had red vinyl booths for seats. I sat with Peyton beside me, Faye across from me, and Baleigh diagonally opposite. I took a furtive interest in seeing what the girls ordered because it helped me sense the kind of person they were without me having to ask a lot of typically boring questions.

Baleigh ordered a stack of pancakes with butterscotch sauce and a tall vanilla milkshake, which gave away her sweet tooth. Faye ordered chips, a chicken burger and a glass of lemonade, which hinted at her age (I later found out she was the baby of the group at a newly turned nineteen). Peyton ordered a vegetable burger with a side of salad and a glass of sparkling water because she was a vegetarian. I purchased a steaming mound of macaroni and cheese made with three different cheeses, and a chocolate milkshake.

'So, Ava,' Peyton started in her calming drawl, 'are you planning on attending Fulton next year?'

'Oh, well, I hadn't really thought about it.'

That wasn't technically true, as it was more of a downright lie. Every now and again, Fulton University took centre stage in the midst of my mind. Whilst those thoughts lasted for no more than a minute at a time, they were still thoughts I couldn't get rid of.

'Are you happy at wherever it is you go now?' Peyton asked.

'Huxton University,' I answered, 'and not particularly. My International Business course isn't as exciting as I thought it would be,' I confessed.

'Really?' Faye asked wide-eyed behind her glasses. 'I study International Business at Fulton and it's great! In our fourth year, we get the choice of studying abroad.'

'Oh. We don't get that option,' I said, suddenly feeling very disenchanted with Huxton University.

'Fulton does things differently,' Baleigh stated. 'I used to go to Phillips Grace University in London, but I left to come to Fulton. It's much better here.'

'What do you study?' I asked.

'Law,' she answered simply.

Oh yeah, Theo had mentioned that that's how they'd met.

159

I wondered how the law system differed here compared to England. I hadn't seen any police cars or police stations as of yet, but surely they existed. I needed to keep in mind that Hayven was basically another city rather than another world, even though that is what it often seemed like.

'What about you?" I asked Peyton.

'Veterinary Science. I absolutely love animals,' she gushed.

'Yes, it's just a shame you don't *love* being on time to your classes,' Baleigh said.

Faye giggled softly.

'It isn't always my fault,' Peyton said, smiling. 'I tend to oversleep, or end up daydreaming for too long.'

Now that was easy to imagine. Peyton, sitting on a bench somewhere with a faraway look in her eye, as her lecturer began teaching the class she was supposed to be in.

'If you did come to Fulton, would you keep the same course?' Faye asked me.

I had thought of this too. 'I'd probably choose another one,' I answered.

'Well, Fulton has a wide range of courses. You can discuss it with my mum the next time you see her,' Baleigh suggested.

This is what I meant. I was beginning to feel more confused over Baleigh than I was about *life*. A couple of months ago, I'd gotten the impression that I wasn't allowed to be a part of her world, yet here she sat practically inviting me to study at Fulton, meaning I'd most likely relocate to Hayven. I hated to admit it, but I secretly desired to be accepted by Baleigh. Mainly because, at the present moment, she was my only connection to Hayven – if it were not for her, I probably wouldn't have visited again. My mind plugged back into the conversation.

'What does your mum teach?' I asked intrigued.

'Architecture,' Baleigh answered. 'She designed some areas of Fulton and my dad's company's building.'

So her mother designs buildings and her father has his own company. Maybe that *was* a Rolex watch I had seen earlier.

Peyton's mobile phone began to beep to indicate she had a message.

'Oh shoot,' she said calmly, reading the text. 'I'm late to meet my mum.'

Baleigh shook her head whilst Faye giggled again. It seemed being late was a typical trait of Peyton's behaviour. I smiled fondly at the girl I'd only met twice.

'Okay, I'll see you guys later,' Peyton said, popping the last bite of her burger into her mouth and waving a bracelet-laden hand at us before dissolving into a bundle of emerald green specks.

I looked around the diner to see if anyone had noticed. They had, but it was as normal to them as someone walking out of the door; nobody batted an eye. I sighed contently and sank deeper into my seat.

Once back in my room, I decided to do something I hadn't done for a while. I decided to draw. It was now three in the morning in Huxton, but I wasn't tired. I brought out a large white canvas from my makeshift art supplies closet near my wardrobe and propped it up horizontally on my wooden easel. I tipped out my different coloured pens and pencils from my pencil case, and sat on my drawing stool beside my desk. I slowly drew Baleigh, Faye, Peyton and me with tiny, shimmering coloured dots floating above each of our heads to symbolise our travelling colours. Luckily, Faye had left before I had so I was able to witness her dissolve into bright sunshine-yellow dots.

Soon, I fell into a state only drawing could put me into. I loved the speed at which my hand moved as I shaded, as if entirely independent from my mind and body, the way my wrist bent languidly as I drew around corners, and the way my fingers clutched my pens and pencils lightly yet firmly. I couldn't remember when I'd finally crawled into bed.

CHAPTER FOURTEEN

'Hello,' I croaked into my phone.

'Ava! What were you thinking?' came Toni's shrill voice from the other end. I sat up straight, suddenly alert.

What had happened? What had I done?

'What are you talking about?' I asked.

'You going on a *date* with Alfie, not even bothering to tell me, and then telling Alfie you're not interested!'

Suddenly, it all came flooding back. Oh-no...please, no. I didn't want to remember the disaster of last night. I had gone to bed happy and peaceful, knowing that my only concern for the day ahead was handing in my essay on time, and now Toni's reminder made that *thing* happen. When you remembered something bad that's happened, something you managed to forget for a while, and that triggers the remembrance of everything else. So when I thought of Alfie, I asked myself why the date had ended so badly and that brought back thoughts of Theo and Summer. I rubbed my forehead in a futile attempt to erase unwanted images.

'Ava? Are you still there?' Toni shrieked.

'Yes, yes, I'm still here.' Unfortunately. I sank back into bed.

'Well?' Toni questioned exasperated.

'I don't know what to tell you, Toni.'

'No way,' she said. 'You're not getting away with it that easily. Alfie told me you told him that there was someone else, but I know you were lying to spare his feelings because there is no other guy. I still want to know *everything*, so meet me in the quad for coffee in an hour. I'll bring breakfast.'

'No, wait, Toni, I —'

But I was wasting my breath; she'd already hung up on me.

My happiness from last night evaporated, leaving me dry and tired. I sighed and rubbed my eyes. I imagined I'd gone to bed at around five in the morning and it was only 10 a.m. now. I looked down at the drawing I had done last night, leaning against the legs of my desk and somehow felt slightly better. I liked looking at my art work with fresh eyes; I appreciated it more then. It wasn't complete, but it was getting there.

With drooping eyes I sat on a bench waiting for Toni; my hot shower had done very little to dispel the tiredness currently weighing me down. Thankfully, the quad – a large patch of grass on campus with benches – was empty apart from the odd person occasionally walking past. The sun hid behind a few clouds but still managed to spread enough warmth for me to shed my heavy jacket.

'Tell me everything!' Toni squealed, planting a cup of coffee, a cup of hot chocolate, and two blueberry muffins in front of me. I had sensed Toni coming up behind me without having to turn my head; I could feel her buzzing with excitement and this sudden charge of energy managed to stifle the air.

'Didn't Alfie tell you everything already?' I sighed, peeling the case off my muffin.

'Yes,' Toni admitted, doing the same to her muffin, 'but I want to hear it from you.' Her eyes were practically twinkling which was no surprise. Toni loved gossip and the more embarrassing the better.

So to placate her, I told her everything, but rather than tell her I walked into my room to find Baleigh on my bed, who then took me to Hayven where I met her mother and her friends, with whom I'd then had dinner, I told her that I got into bed, cried and fallen asleep. Which I'm sure I would have done if Baleigh had not been there.

'How mortifying!' she commented. 'For both of you! How are you going to be around each other? It'll be so awkward. I would hate to be you right now.'

'Yes, Toni, I get your point, thank you.' She wasn't helping by mentioning everything I was too scared to admit to myself, but I took the opportunity she had unknowingly provided me and used it to my advantage.

'*Friends* should not date,' I said, hinting heavily at her and Jamie.

Unless they're really hot...

'No matter how *cute* or funny they may be,' I continued, addressing her thoughts. 'I've learnt my lesson and won't be making that mistake again.'

Toni seemed undeterred as she took another bite out of her muffin and spoke on. 'So, what are you going to do? You can't avoid Alfie forever.'

'It only happened last night!' I pointed out. 'I'm allowed to avoid him for a bit.'

'I'd say it'll be awkward when we sit and have lunch together, but you never come out to eat with us anymore anyway,' she said.

165

'I come out with you guys,' I defended.

'Hardly,' Toni counter-argued. 'You go through weird cycles. Some weeks you're with us every day, other weeks you completely disappear. Then you repeat.'

I changed the subject swiftly before she could analyse my disappearance patterns any closer.

'What do you think I should do?' I asked.

'Face him,' she answered plainly. 'Get the inevitable awkwardness out of the way.'

The thought made me shudder, but it was better than all of my ideas put together.

I found Alfie in the library the next day when I went to return a book. He was sitting amongst his friends from his English Literature class who I identified as Omar, Anton and Layla. He caught me staring and turned around. I smiled at him as genuinely as I could and waved before he could pretend he hadn't seen me, and he smiled back. But his smile didn't reflect his thoughts.

It's too soon to be back to normal again, Ava.

It was as if he knew I could hear what he was thinking, but he turned his head away soon after to persuade me otherwise. I thought of maybe forcing myself on him; maybe ask if I could sit with him and his friends as I knew he was too kind to say no. I was close to doing just that when I remembered that Alfie and I hadn't just gone to dinner, we had also kissed. Well, he had kissed me and I got the feeling I hadn't reacted as positively as Alfie would have liked me to. If I attempted to repair our friendship so soon afterwards, it would look as if I was all set to move on; it would look as if I was acting like it had never happened. It'd look like I was brushing the kiss to the side as if his feelings meant nothing to me, which just wasn't the case.

Thoughts of my date with Alfie were tormenting enough, and when something as awful as that happens, despite you wanting to do otherwise, you just can't stop thinking about it. Unfortunately, thoughts of Alfie always led to thoughts of Theo, and apparently, in my head, there was no Theo without Summer.

And as if I couldn't feel any worse, as the day went on I started recalling the dream I'd had this morning. It had been another vivid dream; I'd answered a knock on my bedroom door to Theo. He'd been explaining how he had gotten my address off Baleigh when the ringing of my phone had woken me up, disallowing him to divulge any further.

It was late into the afternoon when I got back to my room and a few stray leaves had managed to cling to me, following me home. I stopped in front of the mirror hung on my bedroom wall to pick out a stray corner of a leaf that had gotten tangled in my hair. I never looked into mirrors for very long. Don't ask me why, I just hardly ever did. I didn't need a mirror to put my hair into a ponytail, and I didn't wear any make-up so there wasn't any point in me doing so; I knew what my face looked like. I only ever really looked into the mirror before leaving my room for the day, just to make sure my face was still relatively normal. But now that I'd been stood in front of it for more than a few minutes, I couldn't help but pause for longer.

I didn't look awful, well, I didn't think I did anyway, but I'm by no means absolutely gorgeous. I'm just...*okay*. I could be worse.

So what was it exactly that Summer had that I didn't? We have different coloured eyes, but there's nothing wrong with brown eyes, in fact, they're my favourite eye colour. People say brown eyes are boring; I think they're deep and warm in a way no other eye colour can be; common but special. But that was my preference; I didn't know what Theo's was. Was it the hair? I pulled out my hairband and let my hair fall in layers down to my back. Is it because she's blonde and I'm not? I twirled innocent strands of chestnut-coloured hair around my finger. What's wrong with brown hair? He has brown hair, but maybe he *prefers* girls with blonde hair? No, it can't be that; Theo isn't shallow. I tied my hair back up. Maybe it's her personality. I wouldn't say I'm particularly funny; people usually tend to laugh at me rather than with me. Theo always laughed at me, in a friendly way though, just whenever I said something random, weird, or sarcastic, but he'd smile at me afterwards, as if to suggest that what he's just laughed at has made him really happy. Maybe Summer was *naturally* funny... She didn't look the comedic type; she looked as if she'd actually be quite bland, but I wasn't her boyfriend so what did I know? Okay, what else could it be? Lips? Smile? Or the one thing I didn't want to admit – body shape.

If you looked at only my face, you wouldn't know I wasn't skinny. I was one of those girls whose face shape didn't reflect their waist shape. Even if you went a little lower, stopping after my boobs, you still probably wouldn't guess. My boobs weren't huge, but they weren't very small. The problem was what came after my boobs: my stomach, hips and thighs. I was a size fourteen some days, a size twelve on others. My size never used to bother me because I was quite tall, so I kind of balanced out. It only started getting to me last year, when I was dating Alex who thought it was okay to...

I sighed before turning away from the mirror. I clearly needed something to distract myself from stupid thoughts and the best way to do that was to be productive, but my uni work did the exact opposite of keeping me focused. So instead, I pulled up the picture of Baleigh, Faye, Peyton and me and decided to add a bit more. I always did that with anything I drew because I always felt like I could never just finish a drawing. There was always something more I could add, whether it was an extra blade of grass or a deeper inner shading of a cloud.

Time passed by as I sat absorbed in putting the "final" touches on my artwork when there was a knock on my door. That was strange. You needed to press the buzzer to gain entrance to the building if you didn't have a key and I hadn't answered one. Perhaps I just hadn't heard it. Or maybe it was Izzy next door, asking if she could borrow some milk again. But I'd told her she could help herself to anything on my shelf if she needed it. The number and tempo of the three knocks did however strike me as familiar, but I couldn't figure out why. Putting down my pencil, I crossed my room and answered the door to...*Theo*. I felt my hand slip a little off the door handle.

The first thing I noticed was his faintly altered appearance. His hair was a little on the scruffy side, his brown eyes had dulled, there was a hint of dark bags under his eyes, his cheeks seemed to have sunk in slightly, and his usual tanned skin seemed paler. Was it even possible to be pale in Hayven?

'Ava! Oh! Hi…'

He seemed shocked to see me here. Was he at the wrong address?

'Theo? What are you doing here?' I asked, just to make sure it *was* me he had planned to visit.

'I just…well…I owe you an explanation, don't I?'

I hardened. 'This "explanation" of yours was due over a month ago,' I said. 'It's no longer needed, but thanks for stopping by.'

'Wait, please. I know. I know, Ava. I'm sorry it's taken me so long,' he said, ruffling his hair and causing me to inwardly wince at the sight of such a familiar gesture. 'It's been difficult trying to put into words what I want to say. Please, just… hear me out. Can I come in?'

At that question it hit me, the unmistakable feeling of déjà vu. I knew what I was going to ask next, and I knew his reply.

'How did you know where I lived?'

'Baleigh told me.'

There it was again.

'Alright, come in,' I said, stumbling slightly on my words, as this part of the conversation didn't feel so natural. As Theo nervously shuffled past me, his standard scent of Hayven, fresh coffee and books filled my nose. The sun took this moment as an opportunity to stream through my window, illuminating my room. I wasn't very pleased to note that the sun seemed to have put in an appearance for Theo's sake, especially when it was only the rain that enjoyed my company. Its butter-yellow rays made his gifted aura more conspicuous; it brought life to his cheeks and more prominence to his handsome features. I gazed involuntarily.

170

'Did you draw that?'

I turned to see what had suddenly trapped Theo's attention. It was the drawing I'd been working on before he'd arrived.

'Yes,' I answered.

'That's incredible,' he breathed and he sounded genuinely awe-struck. 'It's so...*realistic*; you've perfectly captured everyone's features.'

I felt pleased by Theo's compliment, as the girls' features had taken me a very long time to master. There had been a lot of erasing going on and continuous changes being made, but I was pretty happy with the drawing at this stage.

Baleigh stood with a confident yet relaxed expression on her face and I had given Faye a shy, easy smile. Peyton stood wearing a peaceful and dream-like expression on her face whilst I had drawn myself as I felt I looked when I'd been with them, content and smiling, as if I belonged.

'I can't help but wish you'd drawn me,' Theo whispered to himself.

'Maybe I will.' I shrugged. 'I'll draw you...and Summer of course. We can't forget about her, can we?'

I turned to face Theo and he looked at me as if I had slapped him. His expression was a combination of startled shock and horrendous, heart-felt hurt. It made me feel sick that I was the cause of that. I folded my arms and looked away.

'What do you want, Theo?'

He cleared his throat. 'I want to apologise, Ava. I should have told you about Summer. I *know* I should have, but the longer I put it off...the harder it became.'

'Fine, whatever. Apology accepted.'

'What? Just like that?'

'Yes, just like that,' I repeated. 'At the end of the day, you don't really owe me an explanation. Who you date isn't my business. Why would it be?'

He bit his lip. 'You don't think it's your business?'

I could tell he wanted me to disagree and say it was my business, but *why* would he want me to do that? Nothing positive could come from me saying that, and if I did say it, it would be a lie. It isn't my business because Theo isn't my business.

'No,' I replied. 'It isn't. Like I said, why would it be?'

He shuffled on the spot for a moment. I think he was staring at me, but because I was looking out of the window behind him, I couldn't tell. 'Okay,' he said finally, defeated. 'It isn't your business.'

'Exactly.'

But if I truly believed that, why had I been feeling the exact opposite ever since I found out about Summer? Why had I been secretly waiting for Theo to explain? Why had I felt like he'd led me on and then dumped me as soon as someone better had come along? Because it had happened before? *Resentment*. Is that what I'd been feeling lately? Is that the emotion connected to Theo that I couldn't pinpoint? What I'd thought was jealousy and even considered might be love, was resentment. Resentment because Theo and Summer was just another reminder that guys like him didn't go for girls like me. I'd been told that once before, and it seemed I hadn't forgotten it.

I breathed out. I could finally answer the question my mum had given me. I wasn't upset Theo didn't tell me about

Summer. I wasn't upset that he had a girlfriend. I was upset that his girlfriend looked like Summer.

'What am I to you, Ava?'

'I'm sorry?'

'What am I to you?'

I'd heard what he'd said. I just needed more time to answer a question I didn't want to answer. Theo wanted me to say he's more than a friend, but I couldn't admit something like that if I couldn't find a justifiable reason to do so. I wouldn't put myself out there to be hurt again. I'd admitted the truth to myself and that was enough; nobody else needed to know.

'You're my friend,' I answered. 'I hope.'

He bit his lip again before nodding slowly. 'Your friend? Okay. I should take what I can get.' He breathed deeply. 'A hug?' he asked brightly, his arms outstretched.

'Don't push it.'

'Yeah, you're right,' he backed away, 'too soon. Okay, well, looking at you is slightly more painful than I bargained for, so I'm going to go now. I'll see you around?'

'Sure.'

He smiled a small, grateful smile and then he was gone, leaving me with only a few glittering indigo blue flecks before they disappeared too.

I didn't have it in me to resume my drawing. Instead, I curled up tight and found solace on my bed. Theo had done the right thing by apologising, no matter how late it was, and he still wanted to be my friend…which was what I wanted. If I was to be completely honest, I had felt better before he'd visited because now I had to deal with the truth. I'd been carrying on for the past year as if I was okay, mended. Alex was old news, and I'd cried about him at the time, but now I was over it. He didn't like me for me, but that was okay. *I* liked me for me, and that's all that truly matters. To think that for more than twelve months and to then meet someone who unknowingly forced you to realise that you'd been lying to yourself all along. I was still hurt. I was still broken.

And it was that realisation that finally released my tears.

I cried and cried and cried until there was nothing left. It felt good to let it out, to let loose everything I'd been keeping caged up inside me. I cried about Alex and the things he'd said, I cried about Theo and Summer, I cried about Alfie, I cried about Lucas and Baleigh, I cried about Sidra Calix, I cried about Hayven, and I cried about missing my family at home. I cried about everything so that nothing would be left bottled inside. I cried until my throat grew drier, dry, then dried, and I was left with only a few hiccups and a sore throat. I was exhausted. I kept my cheek on my tear-drenched pillow and was just about to succumb to the heaviness weighing down my wet eyes before a violet coloured cloud of sparkling dust began to drift in under my opened window and settle in the middle of the room. Violet? That was…

'Baleigh!' I exclaimed, fiercely brushing my damp eyes with the back of my hands, but I knew it wouldn't make any difference; my eyes and the tip of my nose must have been red, my bottom lip undeniably shaky and my cheeks flushed.

She took one look at me and rolled her eyes. Good thing I hadn't been expecting a hug because I would have been sorely disappointed.

'Good grief. I knew you'd be like this,' Baleigh said. 'Once I saw the state of Theo back in Hayven I just knew you'd be similar or worse. Look, you two aren't Romeo and

Juliet, okay? You're just two regular – by Hayven standards, of course – young adults, one of which just happens to have a girlfriend. Or maybe both of you do; I'm currently unaware of your sexual preference and also, uninterested.

Nonetheless, consider me your stylish fairy godmother, with all the sparkles but no crown or wand. I'm here to deliver a very important message that Theo has already graciously heard. Are you ready for it?'

I sat up straighter to hear.

'Pull yourself together.'

I shouldn't have expected anything less.

'You look an absolute mess,' she continued. 'Your cheeks are streaked, your eyes are red, your hair is a birds nest – is that a leaf?' She rolled her eyes once more. 'Listen, hanging out with Theo is starting to feel like work because he's just miserable all the time and he's managed to consume my months' worth of ice cream in *four* days. I don't want you to turn out the same in my company. I'm still unsure of our pending friendship status so don't ruin it. Right, I'm off.'

I was about to ask Baleigh to stay because, despite her no-nonsense, straight-talking attitude, she had the same effect Theo *used* to have on me, she made me feel better.

She had turned to float back out of the window when she caught sight of my drawing. It was procuring a lot of attention today.

'*Oh,*' she breathed, as her brown eyes widened. 'Did you draw that?'

'Yes,' I answered, flipping my pillow over dry-side up before she could notice the damp stain.

'It's really good!' Her smile widened to show off her perfect white teeth. Baleigh's mum had been right. Baleigh had a lovely smile that made her face prettier and softer because her eyes slimmed slightly and you saw the faint imprint of dimples on both cheeks.

'It's me, Faye, Peyton and you…and our colours!'

She must have then realised how excited she sounded and hastened to compose herself. 'That's really cool.' She shrugged, turning back to face me. 'I didn't know you could draw so well; I didn't know you could draw at all.'

I shrugged back. I was glad she liked it. Maybe I'd get a chance to show Faye and Peyton one day too.

Baleigh took one last look at the picture and sighed. 'Alright, well, I really do have to go now or else I'll be late for class.' She paused to consider my face. I had cheered up marginally since her arrival, but she could tell I was still despondent. The gleam in my eye couldn't hide the previous tears, the proud flush I'd gained failed to mask my tear-stained cheeks, and my smile could only last for so long.

She stepped forward as if to give me a hug but then hesitated. She looked as if she had silently decided that it wasn't her style and instead patted me softly on the head. 'Cheer up, Ava, the world is never as bad as it seems.' It wasn't until the last smattering of violet dots had disappeared that I realised she had called me Ava.

CHAPTER FIFTEEN

I decided to heed Baleigh's words and cheer up, and to do that successfully, I threw myself into my artwork, so much so, that my bedroom was beginning to resemble an amateur art gallery. After I finished the drawing of me and the three girls to a state I was pleased with, it allowed me to move on. I drew Huxton Park, Huxton University and then Fulton University. I drew Toni, Susie, Alfie and Jamie; I drew Theo and Lucas and their colours, deep indigo blue and fire red. I drew Baleigh and her mum, but left space for her dad to complete if ever I met him, and I drew the enthralling and exotic entrance of Mysteria Park.

These accumulations of artwork took weeks of undivided attention and I hardly noticed winter give way to spring. Drawing for me was therapeutic, and I preferred to do it more than anything else. Whenever Toni tried to convince me to come out with her and the others, I rejected her invitation by telling her the truth – I'd rather draw. I knew that soon I would no longer be considered as part of that group and the five would turn into four. It was mainly because of the Alfie situation. I'd heard Jamie's thoughts enough times to know that after breaking Alfie's heart, he wasn't particularly fond of me anymore. Also, having tuned into Toni's thoughts during the lectures I did bother to attend, I found she'd ignored my advice about not dating friends.

It turned out that during a party on campus that our four-month deal meant I didn't have to go to, Toni and Jamie had each gotten really drunk, although I'm guessing more so in Jamie's case than Toni's, and they had slept together. Only thing was, whilst Toni was interested in pursuing a relationship, Jamie was pursing the exact opposite. It wouldn't be long before things blew up between them, and I think I owed it to myself to not be around when it did. The less they saw of me, the more I hoped they'd forget about me.

I went to very few lecture classes, caught up online instead, and purchased a new bicycle. Whenever I wasn't in class or drawing, I was most likely riding my pastel blue bike around Huxton Park, practising mind exercises.

I'd attended my weekly classes with Baleigh's mother enthusiastically, and was making remarkable progress according to Mrs Castel. I had so far mastered how to empty my mind to the point of it becoming a natural state, and soon enough Mrs Castel found it impossible to hear my thoughts. It was a strange feeling – thinking of nothing whilst still thinking; it consisted of me keeping my mind blank and empty whilst still being able to *feel* my thoughts in the back of my mind. My gift had advanced like Theo and Mrs Castel had said it would, and I could now see the pictures and scenes people played in their heads. On Wednesday, I was excited to show Mrs Castel how far I'd managed to get with our next step, which was to block out unwanted voices. I was to meet her at 5 p.m., but chose to make my way to Hayven an hour earlier instead. After Theo and Baleigh's visits almost two months ago, I hadn't just decided to stop feeling sorry for myself, I had also decided to move on.

Today, before meeting Mrs Castel, I was going to take a walk through Mysteria Park. I'd practically forgotten the first time I'd come across it and had seen…whatever it was that had made me think the park was on fire, but time alone managed to bring back things that were probably best remembered. I had been given a gift by a woman who meant for me to have it; I could no longer ignore that fact. What Sidra Calix wanted me to do with this gift, I was unsure. Why she'd given it to me of all people? Well, that baffled me more than anything. One thing I did know was that I had to do *something* in order to gather answers and for some reason, Mysteria Park was the first thing that came to mind.

I focused on the road the prepossessing park was located on as I had a clearer image of that than the park's entrance location. Most of my Mysteria Park drawing was assumption and guesswork, and probably inaccurate, but I would find out today; I would only need to walk up a short distance. I watched my feet instantly dissolve into minuscule pale blue dots and smiled. No matter the colour, travelling was truly a remarkable sight.

Once in Hayven, I felt my mood immediately lift. The golden air was comforting, and the soft breeze relaxed my bones and soul. I felt at home.

I walked up the road, feeling lighter, shyly smiling at people I'd never met before. One gentleman even tipped his hat to me whilst riding on his bike. It's funny how a stranger can make your day. I reared up to the park's entrance and saw Faye leaving with an empty bread bag.

'Faye! Hi!' I called out to her.

'Ava!' she called back, spotting me and walking up to give me a hug; she was quite small and the top of her head reached my nose. Her hair smelt of strawberries. 'It's good to see you! What are you doing here?'

179

'Well, I was just on my way to —'

'Oh yes! You're meeting with Mrs Castel. Well, I'm on my way to class, we can walk together!'

I didn't have the heart to tell her I was actually on my way to Mysteria Park. Besides, Mysteria Park would always be there. Also, there was quite a bit of a walk to the university and it would be nice to get to know Faye a little bit more.

'What were you doing in the park?' I asked, even though I had a pretty good idea in my head by the scrunched up bread bag she had just deposited into a bin.

'I went to feed the ducks,' she answered. 'I do it so often I think they recognise me now. Whenever I go there they swim up to me expectantly,' she said.

I couldn't help but smile. Faye was truly a child at heart and it was a warming sight. Even I enjoyed feeding the ducks every now and again when I visited Huxton Park. I hadn't known there was a pond in Mysteria Park. It must look beautiful.

'Maybe I could come with you the next time you go?' I asked.

'Yes, please! It would be nice to have some company. I went with the girls once but that didn't go so well…'

'What happened?' I asked, preparing myself for the funny anecdote that awaited me, judging by the guilty look on Faye's face.

'Well, first I took Peyton because she loves animals,' Faye began to explain, 'but she refused to leave until every duck in the pond had gotten a handful of oats. It is such a big pond and some of the ducks were really far away and refused to come near us. She had to use her gift to cause ripples in the water so the current forced the ducks closer, but it still took a while. By the time they'd all been fed, it was dark and I'd missed my opticians' appointment. So…I've, urm…*forgotten* to invite her back.'

I spotted the faint, pink tinge on Faye's cheeks and bit my lip.

'Fair enough, what about Baleigh?'

'Baleigh was the exact opposite of Peyton,' Faye answered, adjusting her glasses. 'She kept giving bread to only one duck because she said it "looked nicer". Understandably, the other ducks didn't take this too well and, you see, there's a gate that separates us from the edge of the pond. Someone had left it open and one of the ducks escaped and started chasing her, pecking and squawking at her with every step! Baleigh's not been back since.'

Faye turned to look at me with innocent blue eyes and I pressed my lips firmly together to inhibit any laughter from escaping, but Faye had now begun to do the same and so naturally, we both ended up laughing.

'I brought Lucas once, but he got bored very quickly and bribed me with ice cream in order to get us to leave. Ollie's come with me a few times, he likes the ducks and they like him too, but he's normally quite busy, so usually I go with Theo.'

The mention of Theo's name caused me to miss a step, but luckily Faye hadn't noticed.

'But most of the time I just go on my own,' she continued. 'Mainly on my way to Fulton when I've been able to smuggle some fresh slices of bread out of the kitchen without Mum noticing. I usually feed them oats and seeds because bread isn't the best for ducks, but I think a little treat is alright every now and again.' She smiled, brushing her

181

unruly, auburn hair back from her face. In doing this, I saw a piece of metal glint from her wrist. Faye was wearing a bracelet identical to Theo's midnight blue one, but her bracelet was yellow.

'Faye, where did you get that bracelet from?' I asked.

'This one?' Faye asked shaking her wrist. 'Peyton made them for us almost a year ago, faux leather, of course. Baleigh, Peyton, Ollie, Theo, Lucas and I each have one in our colours.'

Now it made sense; the purple bracelet on Baleigh's wrist was not purple but violet, and Theo's indigo blue. I had wondered why Peyton and Lucas's bracelets looked so familiar; they were replicas, but in different colours.

'That's talent.'

Faye nodded by way of reply. 'Peyton loves to make her own things because she always says that things have more sentimental value if they're unique.'

'I couldn't agree more,' I said before we lapsed into a comfortable silence.

'So, how have your mind training lessons been going?' Faye asked.

'Really good actually,' I replied. 'I finished learning how to close my mind to readers two weeks ago, and now I'm learning how to block out people's thoughts.'

'Already?' Faye questioned astounded. 'It took me almost four weeks to learn how to close my mind. It must be interesting hearing people's thoughts though.'

'I suppose so,' I said, thinking the exact opposite. 'What's your gift, Faye?'

'I'm a shield.' She smiled proudly.

'A shield?' I repeated.

'Yes.' She nodded before continuing, 'I project this invisible force field around me so no one can get in unless I project it around them too. Do you want to see it?'

'Definitely!'

For a few seconds, Faye did nothing but watch me expectantly.

'Try to touch me,' she finally said.

I brought my finger towards her arm, but about four centimetres before I could reach her jumper, my finger met an invisible barrier instead. It gave my finger such a sharp shock it vibrated through my entire body, almost knocking me off my feet.

'That's incredible!' I said once I'd shaken the shock off and the vibrations stilled to a soft thrumming. 'And painful,' I added playfully.

Faye giggled. 'Sorry! But that's the lowest intensity level I can put it on.'

'*Seriously*?' I asked, amused. 'I'd hate to feel your maximum.'

'Me too!' She laughed.

'Were you born with your gift?' I asked as we resumed our walk to the university. I could still feel the tingle of electricity, softly pulsing through my veins. It was quite a nice feeling, once it settled down.

She nodded in response. 'My dad isn't gifted, but my mum is; they divorced when I was five years old. I found out about my gift when I was thirteen. I was at school!' She turned to me with large eyes. 'I was heavily bullied for my ginger hair and my glasses, *and* I had braces back then too,' Faye said, shaking her head at the unfairness of it all.

'I had used my shield by accident when I knew Tina Mint was coming to pick on me again, like she always did whenever she saw me. Somehow, I had projected my shield without even knowing it and before I knew it, Tina was knocked off her feet and flat on her back! I had no idea what had happened, but luckily Peyton – who went to the same school as me at that time – saw everything. She knew I was gifted and spoke to my mum about what had happened, who then explained everything to me. You don't get your aura until you've used your gift for the first time, so Mum didn't even know I *was* gifted until then. To this day, I still don't think Tina knows *exactly* what happened to her, but for the rest of my time at that school she never came near me again.'

'Wow,' was all I managed to say. I was baffled by how anyone would want to bully sweet and innocent little Faye, but some people just get a disgusting kick out of picking on someone so soft. It made sense for her gift to be a shield; I was glad it was.

'So you've known Baleigh and Peyton for a long time then?' I asked.

'I've known Baleigh for just over a year now, but I feel as if I've known her longer because when I started at Fulton, Peyton had told her my story and she's been looking out for me ever since. Once, a boy accidentally pushed passed me, and I dropped my books all over the floor. I knew it was only an accident but Baleigh saw and made the boy apologise and pick my books up for me! She's always trying to feed me too; she thinks I'm too skinny.' Faye waved her thin right arm at me as if to make Baleigh's point.

Faye *was* quite skinny, but not due to lack of eating; in fact, Faye had the appetite of a trucker, it was just her metabolism. You wouldn't think she was skinny on first glance because she has plump, rosy cheeks, and hides her thinness under baggy jumpers and over-sized dungarees.

'I've known Peyton for five years now,' she continued. 'Her mum and my mum really helped me come to terms with my gift. It was incredibly difficult at first because I didn't know how to control it, and people weren't allowed to touch me or come too close, so I grew very lonely. Once a teacher at my secondary school went to pat me on the back to congratulate me for a history piece I'd handed in and she fainted from the shock my shield gave her! Luckily, she was alright afterwards. Then I came to Fulton and fortunately Mrs Castel knew a professor who taught me how to turn my gift on and off, and manage the intensity levels.

'How did you get your gift?' Faye paused before answering her own question. 'Theo told me Sidra gave it to you. That's so lucky to have gotten your gift from *the* Sidra Calix. She was an incredible gifter. I didn't even know she'd still been alive.'

I had been meaning to ask Theo the question I was about to ask Faye, but I had never gotten the chance and who knew if I ever would.

'Faye? Why is Sidra Calix so...*famous*?'

Faye turned to face me with wide blue eyes once more as we entered the university building. 'Don't you know?' she questioned, surprised. 'She restored peace and light back to Hayven. Sidra Calix *saved* Naveya.'

I froze. I'd always thought Sidra just had an incredible gift, or was some sort of humanitarian at most, but to *save* Naveya? Save it from what?

'Faye, what do you mean —?'

185

'Ah! Ava, you're early, good,' Mrs Castel interrupted as she descended the staircase. She wore her hair in a long, sleek ponytail today, which accentuated the facial features she shared with Baleigh.

'Hello, Mrs Castel,' Faye said cheerily.

'Faye, I've told you. Please, call me Iris.' Mrs Castel smiled cordially. 'Oh, here,' Mrs Castel said, delving into her pocket and producing a chocolate bar. 'Baleigh said, and these are her words not mine, "If you see Faye, give her some chocolate. She's too skinny." Make any sense?'

Faye blushed, gave me a quick side glance, took the chocolate bar from Mrs Castel's proffered hand, and nodded. 'I'd better get to class,' she said, waving as she left.

Mrs Castel turned to me. 'It's good you're early, Ava, because I must get home to see to my builders.'

'Builders?' I asked.

Mrs Castel laughed. 'Yes, gifters are normal people who need things done for us at times, Ava.'

'Oh, right,' I said with a nod and a smile. 'Should I come back tomorrow?'

'No need, we'll just have the lesson at my house. My car is right outside.'

She began to head to the university car park before she stopped to study me.

'Are you doing that on purpose?' she asked me.

'Doing what?' I asked.

'Hiding your thoughts.'

'*Oh*. No. I hadn't even realised I was doing it.'

'Goodness, Ava. I'm very impressed. It's natural to you after such a short time. Good for you.'

CHAPTER SIXTEEN

The Castel residence was…big to say the least. The house formed a U-shape, and the front of the house was smooth concrete where Mrs Castel parked her Audi beside a two-toned Range Rover. The house's exterior was wonderfully designed; all glass windows and shiny polished wooden doors, with exotic pot plants dotted here and there. The house's interior was not much different, as in it was perfectly decorated and furnished.

After pouring two drinks, Mrs Castel led me into her study room as the builders were going to be busy in the kitchen. The room was decorated in soft autumn colours and in the middle were two brown leather sofas opposite one another with a glass table in between them. The floor was carpeted and metres in front of the large glass window sat a desk similar to the one in the classroom where we'd had our first lesson. There was a picture of Mr and Mrs Castel and Baleigh hanging up on the wall, and a baby picture of a chubby, smiling Baleigh in a silver frame perched on Mrs Castel's desk among stationery, papers, two separate piles of books, and a lamp.

'Is apple juice okay?' she asked.

'Perfect,' I replied. She handed me a glass and set her own down on a coaster near her chair before taking a seat.

We spent over an hour, with my eyes closed, trying to get me to ignore Mrs Castel's ardent thoughts whilst simultaneously focusing on her not being able to hear mine.

It wasn't easy doing both things at the same time, but Mrs Castel assured me that because I had mastered blocking my own thoughts so quickly, I'd be able to block hers and everybody else's soon. Whilst the activity of strenuously focusing on my own thoughts rather than hearing someone else's was nowhere near as easy as quietening my own mind, it was not dissimilar to tuning out someone's voice. I had to focus on what she was thinking for a while in order to blur it out.

'Alright, let's give your brain a rest for today, but as you now know, practise is key and soon it'll become so natural you'll only be able to see and hear what you want to. We'll see where you are next week.'

'Thank you again, Mrs Castel. I really appreciate you helping me with this,' I said, but I made no motion to leave. I wanted to ask her something I had a feeling she'd know the answer to.

'You kids are never going to stop calling me Mrs Castel, are you?'

Before I could answer, voices floated in through the gap underneath the study door, and then Baleigh and Mr Castel walked in. Baleigh's dad looked exactly as I thought he would, even before I had seen the portrait on the wall. He was tall and handsome, with only a few of Baleigh's features, and he wore a crisp midnight blue suit that looked like it was made from silk, and a silver watch that glinted on his wrist.

'Hey, Mum. Hey, Ava,' Baleigh said, lazily popping purple grapes into her mouth.

'Ah, so *you're* Ava, the famous mind reader,' Mr Castel said after giving his wife a kiss. His voice was deep and his smile reminded me of the smile Baleigh wore when she'd seen the picture I had drawn in my room, minus the dimples. 'Hope my wife isn't working you too hard,' he said.

'Of course not. When do I ever push my students too hard?' Mrs Castel rhetorically asked.

I heard Baleigh suspiciously choke on a grape behind me. It was true, Mrs Castel was demanding during our lessons, and I was given no breaks, but if it weren't for that regime I probably wouldn't be learning so quickly.

'Hmm,' Mr Castel murmured disbelievingly. He'd obviously been given classes too as I could not hear a single one of his thoughts, in fact, the entire room was silent; it was nice.

'Right, I'd better see to the builders,' he said making for the door. Before he left, Mr Castel reached out his hand towards Baleigh and the bowl of grapes she'd been eating from flew out of her hand and into his. Baleigh tutted as her father popped a stolen grape into his mouth and departed with a cheeky smile. I could feel my mouth gaping.

As if *she* had the ability to read people's minds, Baleigh answered my silent question. 'That's his gift. His hands are like magnets to everything. Anyway, since you're here, the girls and I are going to the cinema for a late night movie. Want to come?'

'Yes, please,' I answered, wondering what a Hayven cinema would be like. 'What are we watching?' I asked as I got up and shrugged into my cardigan.

'Well, it's Faye's turn to choose, so most likely something sad and depressing,' she answered.

'Well, you girls have fun,' Mrs Castel dismissed warmly.

Baleigh went over to kiss her mother goodbye as I stood behind the chair I had just vacated.

'Before I forget,' I said, recalling why I hadn't left earlier. 'I know this may sound a bit *strange*, but I just wanted to ask, what do you know about Sidra Calix?'

'That's not a strange question at all,' Mrs Castel said. 'Sidra Elise Calix was an extraordinary gifter. She made such a positive impact on life in Hayven that she is the only ever person to be buried in Mysteria Park. Do you know of Mysteria Park?'

I nodded, ignoring the goose bumps that had begun to creep along my arms and across the nape of my neck. I knew whatever was going to be said of Sidra Calix was going to affect me some way or another.

'What you probably didn't know was that Sidra was seven thousand, five hundred and twenty-six years old.'

'Really?'

Mrs Castel was right; I hadn't known that, but I remembered what Theo had said about the ageing process slowing down at around the age of twenty, and Sidra had looked to be nearing ninety.

'Anyway,' Baleigh said, forever wanting to reach the point, 'Sidra Calix is the sole reason Hayven is the way it is now.'

I looked confusingly at them both. Mrs Castel then began to explain. 'About one thousand years ago, the city's halcyon days came to an end and Hayven went through a dark time, a very dark time indeed, figuratively and literally.'

'Literally?' I repeated.

'Yes,' Mrs Castel answered, her voice sombre as she spoke. 'There was nothing *but* darkness.'

My nerves came alive and prickled at the word 'darkness'.

'…you must win…or…*terrible* darkness.' Sidra's hoarse voice rang faintly in my ears.

'Hayven had no king or queen, but people lived harmoniously. Of course we have laws and regulations, and the government, police and criminal justice courts deal with any law-breakers, but there were hardly any reports of crimes. Everyone treated the city with love and respect, until one woman decided it wasn't right, that it wasn't natural somehow.'

Mrs Castel paused for a moment, thinking. But I didn't need to read her mind because I could read her face. She was deliberating over something and one side seemed to be winning. What she was going to tell me was something she wasn't sure she should, but it seemed she saw in the end that it would cause no harm.

'She believed that people were gifted for a reason and that reason was so they could be ruled.'

I stared questioningly at Baleigh's mother. I couldn't understand how being gifted meant you had to be controlled or led by another, but the answer to that question wasn't the one I cared for.

'What was her name?' I asked, attempting to keep my voice steady. I feared I already knew the answer.

'Madrina,' Baleigh answered.

Fireworks exploded inside my chest and I felt that unsettling feeling of nausea build in my stomach.

'Madrina believed her gift to be the most powerful and unique of them all,' Mrs Castel continued. 'Madrina had the ability to absorb other gifts from any gifter she laid hands on, and use them as her own for a limited period of time; it made her almost all-powerful. Over time, Madrina quietly but

191

successfully gathered followers, those that chose not to join her, were killed.'

'What were her followers called?' I asked.

Please...don't be...

'Cliders,' Mrs Castel answered and Baleigh involuntarily flinched at the word.

Seeing Baleigh shudder wasn't a comforting sight. I hadn't known Baleigh for long, but sometimes all you need to do is meet someone for a minute, you don't even have to get their name, but you know...you know something about them that everybody who has met them knows too. When it came to Baleigh, with her effortlessly straight posture and unshakable confidence, I'd believed she feared nothing.

'Cliders,' I repeated, hating the way it tasted on my tongue; it tasted of poison.

'The Cliders have returned...growing each day in strength and numbers...' Sidra's voice rang out in my ears again, more prominent than before.

'Cliders are corrupt and vicious hooded gifters who were closest to Madrina,' Baleigh explained, mistaking my repetition of the word for confusion. 'It was said that the people who saw their faces died shortly after, which made the Cliders impossible to identify and near impossible to stop.'

'Where does the darkness come into it?' I asked.

'...or...*terrible* darkness.' Sidra's voice rang even louder, its echoes bouncing off the walls of my mind. 'How did they cause darkness?'

'She took the stars,' Mrs Castel answered plainly. 'Madrina plucked the stars from the dark sky, one by one, and with no stars, there is no sun, and with no sun, there is only darkness.'

'The *actual* stars in the sky?' I reiterated. I couldn't believe it; it sounded ludicrous. 'What did she do with them?'

'Word has it, she fashioned a silver orb from the silver stars and apparently this orb gave Madrina knowledge and power never seen or witnessed before,' Baleigh explained. 'It's written that the only way for Madrina to have lost all her power was for the silver orb to be destroyed, allowing the stars to re-join the sky. But some stars are still missing.'

'Missing?'

'Missing.' Baleigh nodded. 'Rumour has it the silver orb is still out there somewhere, but smaller and less powerful, having been created with only a few stars, yet its brightness is said to be still near blinding.'

'I don't understand,' I said shaking my head. 'Why do you keep saying things like "word has it" and "it was written", as if there's doubt to the legend? Did nobody ask Sidra Calix what happened, seeing as she's the one who destroyed Madrina?'

Mrs Castel exchanged looks with her daughter before answering me.

'The thing is, Ava, whilst Madrina was gone, the majority of the stars back in their rightful place and Hayven brighter than ever, Sidra Calix never remained the same,' she said sadly. 'She had lost her entire family during Madrina's rule. Her first husband and her four sons were killed. Whenever questioned about the events by anyone, she would claim that she could not remember most of it, so we assume that Madrina had taken Sidra's sanity along with her beloved family.'

Mrs Castel was wrong. Sidra had lied. Sidra Elise Calix had remembered everything that had happened, every last detail concerning the events of Hayven under Madrina's rule.

'*The Cliders have returned...growing each day in strength and numbers...Madrina...Hayven...you must lead as I once did...you must fight...you must win...or...terrible darkness.*' Her faint speech rang resolute, unyielding.

I made sure to keep my thoughts hidden from Mrs Castel.

'She pretty much kept to herself. No one ever really saw her, only the people she truly trusted, which I'm guessing was only her husband.'

I didn't believe that either. I had no doubt in my mind that that's what Baleigh, Mrs Castel, and probably almost every gifter in Hayven believed, but if Gaige Calix was not Sidra's first husband it's unlikely that he was her true love as well, so I doubted there was much Sidra told him. But, there was one person who I could bet anything on, she'd trusted. A young fifteen-year-old boy who had come to her looking for a job, but she had ended up giving him so much more.

'Is that all you know?' I asked.

'That's all anyone knows,' Mrs Castel answered.

'Are you okay?' Baleigh asked, looking down at my hands tightly clutching the top of the chair.

'Ava, darling, you look rather pale,' Mrs Castel remarked. 'I didn't mean to frighten you. This happened over a thousand years ago. Madrina is gone.'

'*The Cliders have returned...growing each day in strength and numbers...Madrina...Hayven...you must lead, as I once did...you must fight...you must win...or...terrible darkness.*'

'Do you need to lie down?' Mrs Castel asked, concerned.

'No, no, I'm okay…but, I can't come to the cinema,' I said to Baleigh. 'I just remembered…I have an important night lecture class to attend.'

I wasn't fooling Baleigh one tiny bit with my lie, but thankfully she didn't push the subject.

'Perhaps you should skip this lecture nonetheless and get an early night's sleep,' Mrs Castel suggested.

I nodded in agreement and before they could say any more, I was gone in a haze of shiny blue dust.

CHAPTER SEVENTEEN

I didn't intend to go to sleep that night, but as soon as I had reached my room, I blacked out. When I awoke, the top half of my body was slumped on my bed and the bottom half was on the floor. My clock told me it was 7 a.m. My body was stiff and my head was aching, but I needed to draw.

I moved the canvas I had been previously working on off the easel, cast it aside and searched for a fresh white canvas, but I'd run out. That didn't stop me or even slow me down. I had to draw what I could remember from my dream before I forgot. With my pulse in a state of panicked frenzy, I began to draw on the white wall. I had no sketch, plan, or idea of what I wanted to draw, but my hands did, so I allowed them to work. When I started to run out of space, I pushed my easel and desk to the other side of the wall, pulled down my notice board, and drew on the plain white space that I'd uncovered. I sketched, drew, and coloured until my back, neck, arms, hands and wrists begun to ache. I carried on regardless.

I drew a tall, thin woman, draped in a black satin cloak that covered her feet, shimmered quixotically, and had a blood red fastening in the middle. She had orange, curly hair splayed around her face in a way that reminded me of Medusa's snakes. Her eyes were a piercing blue, her smile indifferent, and her skin milky white. By her hair alone, I identified her as the woman who had tried to kill me in my dream.

I then drew eleven other figures that followed behind her with plainer black cloaks and dark purple fastenings; these eleven had their large hoods hiding their faces, but I could remember certain features. One had golden eyes, another had long, jet black hair that camouflaged against her cloak and was only visible when it flowed over her purple belt. One was particularly muscular so the robe seemed tight and strained around his broad chest, and one was several inches shorter than the rest. I was surprised to find I could remember such tiny details, but I was even more surprised to find that I could effortlessly remember each and every one of their colours.

Silver, dull grey, harsh pink, cyan, dark purple, moss green, crimson red, pitch black, burnt orange, pale yellow, coffee brown, and an off-white colour that looked close to being cream but didn't quite reach it.

Once I had finished, the drawing covered the entire side of the wall. It would have been a true work of art if it had not been for what it represented.

After waking up for the second time that day, late in the afternoon, I finally came to terms with what I had drawn. Madrina and her Cliders. I continued to sit on top of my bed, my knees pulled to my chest and my nails digging into my duvet.

'What does this mean?' I whispered.

I needed fresh air. I showered and fetched my bike. The wind slapped my face as soon as I opened the building door, wiping away any residue of lingering tiredness. I walked my bike to Huxton Park and then rode around in endless circles.

Sidra had said that the Cliders had returned, but Mrs Castel and Baleigh were certain the woman was mad. I was more inclined to believe Baleigh and her mother, but was that because I trusted them more, or because I'd rather their take on the matter be true? Maybe Sidra Calix *was* senile, but then…how did she die? Everyone was convinced she died naturally from old age, but as much as I wanted to, I couldn't believe that. The blood may have vanished into thin air, but it had been there; it had been no trick of the light or a hallucination brought on by shock. Sidra Calix had been murdered. And Theo knew it too.

I pedalled furiously. I remembered the look on Theo's face on the night we'd spent on the roof of *Hayven Books*. How he'd looked when he'd told me that Sidra hadn't died naturally. He hadn't been there when she had died; he hadn't been there to see the blood, but he knew. How had he known? Did he know who had killed her? I doubt he knew *exactly*, but I was certain he had his suspicions.

Only Sidra Calix knew what truly happened on the night Madrina was destroyed, but the more I thought about it the more I doubted the truth died with her.

Was Madrina still alive? If she was, where was she? Why was she back? Where had she been for a thousand years and how had she returned?

Apart from me there was only a stray walker and his dog, so I pedalled like a crazed woman, like my life depended on it, riding half on the cycling lane and half on the grass, crushing weeds and daises underneath my tires. My legs worked endlessly, spinning the bicycle's wheels in blurred circles. My thighs ached and cried, my hands chaffed red from the tight grip on the handlebars, and I dripped sweat.

Seven laps around the park later I dropped my bike and staggered over to a bench nearby. I sat with my head between my legs, breathing deeply until the burning in my chest subsided and the spots of colour behind my eyes disappeared.

I sat back. Alright, say Madrina was alive, where could she possibly be and why had she come back *now*?

Because Sidra was dead? Because her biggest threat in this war had been removed?

Who would stop her now when the only person who knew how to destroy her was permanently out of the picture? Perfect timing.

I stretched my neck to the left to get rid of a stiff ache and noticed something move in the corner of my eye. I turned to look at the far edge of the park where I knew it was only trees and further back, a black gate. There was nothing out of the ordinary. *Must be hallucinating.* I no longer attempted to explain anything weird that happened to me. I was gifted; I would never be "normal" again.

Then it happened a second time, a flash of movement, but I caught something this time. The tail of a long, black coat. Or it could have been a skirt, only seen by a small patch of light on the ground. Like what I'd seen months ago. When I'd thought someone had been following me.

I slowly rose and reached for my bike, never taking my eyes off the shadow now clearly lurking amongst the dark trees. People at university called that area of the park, 'the forest' because the trees were so many and so close together that inside was nothing but darkness, even in the daytime. I grabbed onto the handlebar of my bike, but it slipped through my moist palm. When the bike crashed to the ground, the shadow moved deeper into the forest. I stepped backwards and it moved forwards. Even without a face, I could see that whoever it was, or whatever it was, was cautious…towards *me*. I stepped forward again to retrieve my bike and the shadow stepped backwards. I took another step forward to reach for my helmet that I'd thrown to the ground, and the shadow retreated, but this time it didn't take just one step back. It kept retreating until it disappeared and a few seconds later, flecks of colour emerged, floating amidst the darkness. Miniscule dots that could have easily been missed by an untrained eye – somebody's travelling colour. I gasped, dropped my helmet, and ran. I ran to the edge of the forest and hurtled inside before reaching the black gate. Two coloured dots swam in front of me but it was so dark I missed the exact colour before it disappeared. If I had to guess, I'd say grey. I looked around for more specks, but my foot found something hard instead. Semi-covered by a pile of rotting leaves, was a shard of glass, illuminating the darkness.

Thanks to the absence of light, I could see clearly something moving within the shard. I picked it up and focused on what seemed to be wisps of smoke confined within the thick glass.

Where have I seen this before?

I returned home to find someone occupying the middle of my room, staring at the drawing on my wall. He must have heard me open the door, but he either knew it had to be me or simply didn't care.

'Theo?'

He didn't turn to face me, but merely continued to stare at the wall. I went to stand beside him and we stared together.

'That's Madrina and eleven of her closest followers,' he finally said.

'I know.'

He turned to face me with a stern and daunting expression that managed to throw a little fear into my chest.

'But *how* do you know?' he asked.

'I dreamt it,' I answered truthfully.

'You dreamt it,' he repeated quietly to himself before turning back to face the wall. 'It's impossible to dream so accurately of real people you've never seen before,' he paused, taking a final step back from my drawing before looking me in the eye. 'Which means you didn't dream it, you *saw* it.'

I paused for a moment to take in the true meaning behind what he was saying.

'Is that the future?' I asked, gesturing to the wall.

'That's my guess.' He nodded. 'Can you see into the future?'

I was about to shake my head until I thought back to the day Theo had turned up at my door to apologise. How I'd had a dream of him doing exactly that, but had thought it was nothing more than déjà vu, whilst also knowing at the same time that it had felt *realer* than that too.

'I think so,' I whispered.

His jaw tensed. 'Then it's the future.'

My hand went to my pocket. 'Theo, I was in the park just now and found —'

'Come with me,' he said, taking my hand and cutting my sentence short. I ignored the pulse of electricity. I could travel on my own, but now didn't seem the time to remind him, so I let him take me to the entrance of Mysteria Park.

Theo looked at me before he walked in with his hands behind his back.

Inside the park was a wide and soft orange mist-obscured concrete pathway that stretched onwards before eventually branching off into two different directions. Just like I had seen before, different coloured cherry blossom trees – violet, orange, blue, emerald, yellow and red – surrounded the pathways and their petals littered the ground. The orange glow I'd also noticed before hid behind the trees but streamed in through the open gaps the trees provided. I gasped at the sight of it all.

'Magical, isn't it?' Theo said and he turned to smile at me. I could only give a weak smile in return.

'Why were you in my room?' I asked, as we chose the left pathway to follow.

'Baleigh came to see me yesterday, saying something was up with you after her mum told you about Sidra and Madrina.'

I knew she hadn't bought my pathetic lecture story and I'm glad she hadn't. I needed answers.

'And you came knowing...'

'Knowing what?' he asked.

'That I know.'

'Know what?'

'That the story people believe about what happened between Sidra and Madrina is the story Sidra *wanted* people to know,' I said, my thoughts finding their own voice, tumbling out of my mouth quicker than I could control. 'She didn't lie, she just left out crucial parts and those parts didn't die with her; she was much too clever for that. The truth isn't with her husband Gaige either; whose surname she only took because she knew people would be interested in her story. If anyone *were* to question what happened on the night Madrina was destroyed, they'd ask Gaige, assuming that he would be the only person Sidra had told the entire truth to. Whatever story he retold would be taken as the truth, and it is exactly that, but like I said, there are parts *missing*.'

I turned to look at him as we continued to walk. Theo kept his face still and his eyes forward, but the slight acceleration in his pulse, evident by the increased movement of his chest, gave him away.

'I'm guessing,' I continued, 'that there is only *one* person alive who knows what truly happened.' I caught him flinch. 'And it just so happens, he's standing right next to me.'

He stopped dead in the middle of the pathway and turned to look upon me intently.

'You're more than you seem, Ava, and *I'm* guessing that is why Sidra gave you her gift,' he said. 'The story Mrs Castel told you has been around for over a thousand years and no one has so much as battered an eye at its validity, but you worked it out in, what? Twenty-four hours?'

'Tell me the full story, Theo.'

'I will,' he replied and he continued to walk, 'and I knew I would have to eventually. I had no intention of keeping it from you. If anything, I had planned to tell you during a walk in Mysteria Park, but that was before things got…complicated.'

'Oh yes,' I said, remembering *why* things had gotten so complicated. 'How *is* Summer by the way?'

'Don't be a bitch, Ava. It doesn't suit you.'

My head jerked at the word he had just called me and suddenly I felt small and petty.

'Just tell me,' I pleaded, defeated.

Theo sensed my softening and his facial features reflected this, but his shoulders remained tense.

'Madrina is Sidra's daughter.'

CHAPTER EIGHTEEN

'I don't believe you.'

'I have no reason to lie,' Theo replied.

'How could Sidra kill her own daughter?'

'Kill?' Theo repeated. 'No. Not even gifted people can come back from the dead, Ava.'

'So, what *really* happened to Madrina?'

'Sidra knew Madrina was a threat to Hayven, but she couldn't kill her own child.' Theo heaved an arduous sigh and looked flustered for a moment. 'I should start from the beginning.

'People are greedy, Ava, never forget that,' he said turning to look at me, his brown eyes set. 'No matter who you are or where you're from, greediness is something that is in everybody's nature. It is the *level* of greediness we indulge in that determines who we truly are and in turn, what we will do for the things we want.

'Sidra had five children with her first husband, Sadler Osborne; four boys and one girl. Madrina was the youngest and by far the greediest. It's said that you can tell a lot about a gifter from their gift. *This* I believe to an extent. People say I can shift because I love to travel, which is true; I hate to stay in one place for too long. People say the ability to shape shift means you're uncomfortable in your own body and would rather take the form of others. The ability to project a shield means you need protecting and the ability to produce fire means you're afraid of the cold. People may say that your ability to see the future is because you were born to *change* the future,' he said, throwing me a meaningful look before continuing.

'Madrina's gift was to absorb other gifts. Sidra told me she was always caught taking her brothers' gifts and when it wore off, she would take them again. As Madrina grew older, Sidra noticed that Madrina only really spoke to her rather than the rest of her family, and that she didn't have any friends. Sidra described her as a "queer child", always preferring her own company, and that's not completely normal for someone so young. When you're a child and you don't know the realities of the world, it's sort of like you live in your own world, a world full of sticky candyfloss and bright balloons; the postman can become your best friend in two seconds and the milkman next when those two seconds are up. Sidra once asked Madrina why she didn't have any friends and she'd replied the reason for her selected solitude was because nobody understood her. Then in Madrina's teen years, she finally found a friend, Sia Valour.'

Theo didn't have to describe Sia to me because somehow I knew who she was by the drawing on my wall. She was the Clider with long ink-black hair that I had subconsciously drawn closest to Madrina.

'Sidra couldn't remember much about her as a child because she liked to keep the hood of her jacket up, even in the boiling heat, but from what she could remember, Sia had long, jet black hair that fell to her waist, and pale white skin; her gift was flight.

'Soon after Madrina had met Sia, they moved in together, far away from Hayven. Madrina left the family home only giving her mother her new address, but when Sidra hadn't

206

heard from Madrina for a few months, she decided to pay her a visit. However, she found the address to be just an empty warehouse on a quiet lane. Sidra then went to the university her daughter had claimed to attend, but the school had no records of Madrina Osborne or Sia Valour. It was around this time that Sidra noticed the days grow shorter and the nights much longer. Rumours began to float around Hayven like deathly whispers, taking the lives of those who dared to utter them aloud. Madrina was taking over, trying to rule Hayven. Not only were stars disappearing mysteriously from the sky, but people were too. People who were known for their extraordinary gifts were seen one moment, gone missing the next. But through all this, Sidra turned a blind eye and a deaf ear, refusing to believe that her youngest child had anything to do with the dark times consuming Hayven. Perhaps her biggest mistake.

'One day, when Sidra had visited the abandoned warehouse in another vain attempt to find her daughter's true whereabouts, she found Madrina waiting for her. Sidra hadn't told me everything regarding what had passed between the two of them, but she had told me Madrina's ultimatum: her family were to either join her cause, or die. After Sidra passed on the message, her sons and husband were determined to fight against her. They went about collecting their own followers and in doing so, started a rebellion against Madrina, in which they died fighting. Days after that, Hayven began to burn.'

'Burn?' I asked, enraptured in his tale.

'With wildfire,' Theo clarified. 'Do you know what wildfire is, Ava?'

'Is it the kind of fire Lucas produces?' I ventured.

Theo shook his head. 'Fortunately not. Lucas can only produce fire that you would get if you burned wood, struck a match, or poured gas on an already roaring fire. What one of Madrina's Cliders could do was produce wildfire. A substance that does exactly what it says on the tin. It is fire that is wild and what is wild cannot be controlled. Once wildfire takes over, nothing can extinguish it. Ice cold water and other things with similar properties can keep it at bay but never put it out. It must go out on its own, which doesn't happen until the thing that was set on fire has been completely consumed by its bright orange, red, and green flames.'

'*Green* flames?' I questioned.

'Green flames,' Theo answered. 'Of course, I wasn't born at the time so I can only imagine…' he said, and I felt him shiver beside me. 'When Sidra told me the story she'd often choke on her words, and sometimes if I looked closely enough, I *swear* I could see the flames of wildfire lick wildly in her blue eyes. Sidra mentioned that Hayven grew darker and darker until there was no day, only night, and the only source of light came from the few remaining stars and the fires emanating from burning houses and streets.

'Adults and children ran around helplessly in fear as their houses and property burned; shouts and screams filled the streets, and manic laughter from Cliders rang mercilessly around Hayven. You almost couldn't blame people for joining Madrina; it was either that or their lives and their children's lives. Of course, Madrina wouldn't take everyone because not everyone could be trusted. Many had to prove their loyalty in ways Sidra dared not share, but one way she did tell me about was that new members had to prove themselves faithful and loyal by killing non-members; people fighting against their "true" cause, and that often included members of their own family. She seemed unstoppable.'

Hayven was warm this time of year and it was even warmer inside Mysteria Park, but I had never felt so cold.

'How was she stopped?' I asked.

'Sidra betrayed her,' Theo answered. 'Sidra had always tried to help Madrina and it was obvious Madrina, perhaps not loved but, *cared* for her mother. So there was no question of her loyalty and no test to pass as all of Sidra's family had died by that point. However, Madrina was not so stupid as to believe that Sidra was now one hundred per cent on her side, seeing as she had been the cause of their family's deaths. So Madrina kept Sidra at a safe distance and trusted her with very little. But Sidra managed to gain the trust of somebody else. She never told me the name of the person, only that they weren't a Clider but a hostage because of their gift, and it was from that person Sidra learnt Madrina's secret.'

'The silver orb,' I whispered.

Theo nodded. 'The silver orb was made from the stars and it is said that nothing is more powerful and knowing than the stars in the sky, and so the orb gave Madrina power and knowledge that made her invincible. But is someone truly invincible if they rely on something else for their strength? That was the question Sidra asked herself when she learnt of the silver orb. She knew that to destroy Madrina she would need to destroy the orb that gave her so much power.'

'How?' I asked immediately.

'She smashed it,' he answered, looking and sounding unconvinced.

'What? On the ground?' I questioned, knowing it would take more than that.

'I don't know,' Theo replied, defeated.

'What do you mean you don't know?'

'Sidra didn't tell me and I didn't ask. And before you say it – I know! I know I should have asked, but I thought she'd tell me eventually or maybe I'd have years to question her and find out more. Besides, I feel she would have lied to me anyway or why not just tell me straight away?'

'People say the silver orb is still out there,' I blurted. 'Rumour has it.'

'Sadly, some rumours are just unproven truths.'

'You think it's true,' I said. 'You think the orb is still out there?'

'I think the reason Sidra didn't tell me how she destroyed it is because she didn't,' he replied, answering a question I hadn't yet asked.

'Why couldn't she?'

'Listen to what I'm saying, Ava.' He turned to face me. 'I don't think she *couldn't* destroy it, I think she *didn't*.'

'Why wouldn't she want to —?'

At that moment, all the pieces of what Theo was trying to get me to understand finally slid into place. 'When you said Sidra couldn't kill her own child…'

'Yes.'

'Is that…*your* assumption?' I asked.

'No.'

'Sidra told you that?'

'Yes,' he answered. 'If the silver orb was smashed completely, then Madrina would have no chance of returning, she'd die. Madrina paid a heavy price for the stars and gave her soul to that orb, and one cannot live without their soul. But if the orb was made...let's say, less powerful...smaller perhaps?'

'Sidra let Madrina live,' I said, cutting Theo off and allowing the haunting truth to settle in.

Theo hung his head. 'As a mortal, yes.'

I found myself holding my breath and my head swam from the lack of air. I blew out slowly. My heart still raced ahead. So I'd been right. Madrina is out there, and she's been out there for over a thousand years.

'But, if she's mortal, she must be long dead,' I suggested, clutching at whatever short straw I could find.

Theo sensed my hopefulness and crushed it with a single shake of his head. 'She was born gifted and so mortal or not, gifted blood runs through her veins. Therefore, she can live as long as we do, only without her gift. She is simply a mortal who ages slowly and lives longer.'

We all get these moments when we feel something but can't actually name it, and then it hits you. You remember what it is that brought on that random emotion and you're able to pinpoint what it is. I was angry.

'Sidra Calix was *nothing* special,' I spat. 'She didn't save Naveya and she didn't bring peace to Hayven. She didn't end a war like everyone believes. She just postponed it so others would have to deal with it when she was dead!'

Theo, however, remained as calm and still as untroubled waters.

'Would you have been able to kill your daughter, Ava?' Theo asked.

He turned to me again at this question, and I could see in his eyes that his query didn't conceal disbelief or judgement, only curiosity.

I thought it would be easy to say 'yes' since it was Madrina we were talking about, but the point of Theo's question was for me not to think of it as if it were someone else's child, but my own. So I thought on it and the more I did, the more I questioned whether my prepared answer was true. *Could* I do something like that? It took me hours and a lot of built up courage to kill the tiny spiders that lurked in the corners of my room, but my own flesh and blood? To kill the little girl I had given life to and watched grow up. The little girl I had bathed, clothed and kissed goodnight. A girl whose first sight would have been me, a girl I would have told 'I love you' countless times, and would have heard 'I love you, too' from just as often.

'Sometimes I find myself judging Sidra too,' Theo said, interrupting my silence. 'Because you're right, Ava, she didn't end the war. She only suspended it and people love and praise her for essentially giving them false hope and a promise that they'll never have to go through something like that again. Madrina killed innocent people, stole gifts, set houses on fire, ruled by force, destroyed lives and destroyed Hayven. So she deserves to be destroyed too, right? But who are we to say that? Who gets to decide? Who says we can elect the rules regarding vengeance and redemption? If Sidra had killed Madrina, aren't they then both the same? Are they both not murderers? Are they both not murderers of their own blood? Often I find myself thinking about it; thinking deeply, and I try not to judge, but I'll admit, sometimes it can be difficult.'

Theo's eyes grew anxious and he stared at me for a while before deciding on something.

'Well, I may as well tell you since I've told you everything else. Sidra was an incredible gifter, not just for what she did for Hayven but for another reason. She possessed two gifts.'

'Yeah, so do I,' I pointed out. 'Telepathy and the weird seeing-into-the-future thing.'

'Pre-cognition,' Theo corrected with a smile. 'And yes, but your gift was given to you, and in order for it to be yours, another gift had to be added. For born gifters, no one in recorded history has possessed two gifts – except for Sidra.'

'So, if you're born gifted, it's not possible to have two gifts?'

Theo smiled his genuine smile. 'Is anything *im*possible?' he questioned. 'We're essentially talking about a crazed woman with a crystal ball that gives her special powers. How can anything be impossible after that? People say flying is impossible, but look at Sia Valour. People say reading minds, seeing the future, and teleportation is impossible, but look at you and me. Ava, people *are* the impossible, but most of us don't see it, and that's what limits us: the frequent use of the word "impossible". That word is only an excuse used by very lazy people. Just think, if the word "impossible" had never been introduced into the English language…well, I think it's fair to say humans would have achieved a lot more than we have today. I believe that we all – gifted or mortal – have *something* that once we unlock, the word "impossible" becomes only a word with no definition.'

'You really believe that?'

He turned to look at me and gave me smile that softened his face. 'I really do, Ava. Do you want to know what I believe most of all? That, when it comes to gifters, sometimes, that *something* we have to unlock, isn't always our gift.'

I sighed. I wanted nothing more than to just walk, softly kicking stray flower petals up and back into the mist that swirled around our feet, whilst dwelling on the truth of what Theo had just said, but I knew it wouldn't be best, even if the opportunity to do so presented itself. If Sidra's story had taught me anything, it was that time was not guaranteed, even to gifters.

'Are they coming back, Theo?'

Theo took a deep breath. 'They killed Sidra,' he said. 'They are already here. Sidra knew it and now you've seen it.'

We had now walked up to the end of the pathway, which led to the entrance of the park; I wasn't even surprised.

'What do we do?' I asked, turning back to look at the entrance and the path we had started and now ended on.

'We destroy them,' Theo answered. 'We destroy them before they destroy Hayven.'

CHAPTER NINETEEN

It wasn't long after I'd landed in the middle of my room that I heard a frantic knocking on my door.

'Ava! Ava!'

I opened the door to Toni. Her eyes were so welled up with tears they looked as if they'd never stop running; the whites of her eyes were a soft pink, a temporary effect of endless crying, and her cheeks were stained with black streaks thanks to her non-waterproof mascara. I had seen Toni cry before, and it was always a similar picture, but somehow she looked different. It had been a while since I had last seen Toni and one look at her face made me realise something: I hadn't missed her.

'You were in here the whole time?' she accused. 'I've been knocking for two straight minutes!'

'I just got in,' I said absent-mindedly.

'What? How? I've been standing outside your door!'

'I meant...I just woke up. I was asleep,' I corrected falsely.

She looked down and furrowed her eyebrows. 'In your Converses?'

I looked down at my traitorous black and white footwear. Good thing Hayven was warm and I hadn't worn a jacket. 'It's...been a long day. What's wrong? Come in.'

'You'll never guess what I just found out,' Toni said, forgetting the oddity of my shoes and freshly made bed. 'It turns out Jamie is – Ava! What have you done to your wall? And…what are *these*?'

She gestured to all the canvases I had placed one on top of the other beside my desk; I'd drawn so much lately, they created a towering pile. Inviting Toni in had been what I was beginning to realise, a big mistake. I should have told her my room was inhabitable and suggested we go out for coffee.

'Oh…well…I did tell you I was always drawing.' And thank goodness for that otherwise this would have been a lot harder to explain. 'I ran out of fresh canvases for the…' I gestured weakly to the picture on the wall.

'So you went for the wall?' she asked incredulously.

'It's not *that* strange,' I defended, believing the exact opposite.

'It very much is!' Toni argued, believing just as much. 'Not to mention it's creepy! I mean, it's a good drawing and everything, but goodness, Ava, they look…*evil*.'

You have no idea.

'Well, not all pictures can be of rainbows and daisies,' I said. 'So, what happened with —?'

'Who are they?' she asked.

I was about to say I didn't know, that I had made the faces up, but I turned to see that she was no longer looking at the wall. She was looking at the stack of used canvases and was in the process of lifting one up, the picture of Baleigh, Faye, Peyton and me.

'Oh,' I fumbled as my heart rate elevated. 'Just…some people I know.' I began to sweat as I fearfully pondered how low down in the pile the picture of Theo and Lucas was.

'People you know?' she repeated disbelievingly.

I couldn't say I blamed her. Any people I knew, she knew, and because I spent so much time alone and Toni did the exact opposite, she knew more people than I did.

'Yeah…I drew you too! It's somewhere in the pile,' I said in an attempt to distract her. 'I drew you, Susie, Alfie and Jamie.'

'Where did you meet these people?' she questioned, refusing to be dissuaded.

'At…a coffee shop…in town. I took my bike there when…I wanted something to drink.' I was really sweating now – profusely. Sweat droplets that would be clearly visible if Toni came any closer. How much more could I explain without letting something vital slip?

I took the picture firmly from her hands and laid it face down on the pile of canvases.

'So, what happened? Why were you crying?' I asked in a vain attempt to change the subject yet again. Thankfully, this time it worked.

The drawings forgotten, Toni went over to fling herself lifelessly on my bed.

'Jamie is what has happened! He is such a pig when it comes to girls!'

'Yes, but we're his *friends*,' I said, emphasising the final word. 'Well, more you than me at the moment but still, we know this about him.'

Toni shone a guilty shade of red, obviously catching my hidden meaning, and looked at me coyly.

'Ava…there's something I haven't told you.' She really did look embarrassed and uncomfortable, and I would have felt sorry for her if, firstly, I hadn't warned her about crushing on Jamie. Secondly, if she hadn't witnessed the outcome of Alfie and me dating. And thirdly, if she hadn't been getting wet mascara stains all over my brand new white pillow. *How was I going to wash that out?*

'For a few weeks now, I've been really…into Jamie…' she continued, fiddling with the corners of my now ruined pillow and avoiding eye contact. '…and last week…well, we slept together.'

I felt so emotionally drained from my meeting with Theo and with, well, the fact that Hayven may soon be set alight again, that it took all I had to feign surprise.

'You are joking!'

'No!' Toni said, burying her face deeper into my poor pillow. 'We had such a good time at the cinema the other night *and* whenever it's just him and me. I thought he really liked me. He kept touching me and flirting with me.'

Jamie flirts with his *teachers*. There was nothing new here.

'Jamie always flirts with girls, but he never took it far with his friends,' I noted. 'Did he hit on you?'

'Yes!' Toni answered. 'Yes, he did…'

I eyed Toni suspiciously as she trailed off. There was something she wasn't telling me, but she didn't need to. I didn't have to be psychic to know whose advances had been stronger out of the two of them. I couldn't help myself at this point. 'I told you that friends getting together was a bad idea.'

'Yes, I know!' she said shortly. 'But clearly I didn't listen, and now I've found out he's dating Abby! Do you know her?'

'Not well,' I replied. All I knew was that she was most likely a redhead with big boobs.

'Abby McTram,' Toni spat. 'Abby *McTramp* more like, if she's already sleeping with Jamie.'

It took all my effort and copious amounts of restraint I didn't even know I possessed to not mention to Toni that at least Abby slept with Jamie *whilst* in a relationship with him, as opposed to what she had done.

'Aren't you going to say anything?'

'Oh, I'm…I'm so sorry, Toni,' I tried. 'Maybe, you know…'

'What?'

'Maybe…maybe after dating Abby, he'll realise how much better for him you are…maybe.'

'Please!' she snorted. 'As if I'd give him a second chance.'

I heard her mind think the exact opposite before I blocked her out.

'But…I do suppose, if he realises sooner…I wouldn't, you know, rule him out of anything. Do you think…maybe you could talk to him?' she asked me, lifting her head to look at me imploringly.

'No,' I replied instantly; I didn't even need to think on it. 'No, I can't.'

'Why not?' she practically shrieked. 'Ava, he's perfect for me! Not to mention we're already friends! How would the relationship not work?'

Because it hadn't already?

'Because he's a massive flirt?' I asked instead.

'Yes, but maybe he'll change for me,' she said. 'I just *know* he will, and that's why all you need to do is talk to him.'

219

No, all I have to do is figure out a way to save Hayven. Obviously, I'd rather face Toni's problems, but it didn't seem I was being provided with the choice.

'Look, Toni, I feel...*bad* for you, I honestly do,' I said, 'but I can't. Jamie and I aren't as close as we once were and I don't think I would've been comfortable speaking to him about something like this even when we *were* close. Ask Susie.'

'I already did. She said she didn't want to get involved! Can you believe that?' she questioned, clearly offended. 'It's because she's friends with Abby.'

So Toni could accept Susie's refusal but not mine, and I knew why. Because she thought me a push over and in her defence, I've done nothing to make her believe otherwise. Well, not anymore; I had more pressing matters to deal with.

'Well Toni, that's unfortunate, but I can't talk to Jamie. I just can't.'

'But you have to try!' she shrieked. 'For me!'

How is it only now I'm realising Toni might be crazy? The things guys made us girls feel...

'Toni, I played with his friend's feelings, Jamie doesn't like me very much.'

'And how do you know that?' she asked, not bothering to tell me I was wrong – how considerate of her.

'I just know.'

'I still think, as a friend to *me*, you should try.'

'No,' I said finally.

'How can you just say no?' she barked. 'Can't you see how miserable I am?'

Yes. Definitely crazy.

'Toni, I'm sorry you feel —'

'I don't need your pity, Ava.'

Unfortunately, pity was all I had available to give, so I kept silent hoping she'd storm out, but she just continued to lie on my bed.

'Aren't you going to say anything?' she asked me again.

'I don't know what to say,' I said.

'You don't know what to say? You have nothing to say about the fact that my life is over?' she cried.

Wow.

'That's a bit of an exaggeration,' I said, well-used to Toni's tendency to be over-dramatic. She should try putting herself in my shoes. I was currently dealing with a potential world threat when six months ago, all I could think about was whether I could afford those skinny jeans I'd seen in the town centre window.

I gazed at the picture of Madrina on the wall. Her cold eyes, her even colder demeanour. The power I knew she had. The heart I knew she didn't. I suddenly transferred all the pity I had ready to spend on Toni, to myself. How was I going to save Hayven? I was only Ava; I was only Avery Charlotte Gray. You wouldn't think of me as anything special if you walked past me on the street. I'd doubt you'd notice me at all.

'Is it?!' Toni cried shrilly, bringing my attention back to her. Her high pitched voice was really starting to bother me. 'I don't see how! It's so easy for you! All you do is lock yourself in your room and paint on the walls like some kind of psycho!'

It took a lot to surprise me lately, what with all the extraterrestrial stuff I had discovered over the past seven months, and so I was indifferent to Toni's hurtful outburst. I used to make up excuses for her and call it 'speaking without thinking', but as I was in no mood to deal with her crap, I now called it 'bratty and annoying'.

'Please leave, Toni.'

It clearly didn't take much to shock Toni as she whipped her neck around to look up at me, her elbows propped up on my bed, her eyes drunk with disbelief. 'You're throwing me out?'

'No, I'm asking you nicely. I don't have the upper body strength to actually throw you out,' I replied.

'Oh, wow. You really have changed. Jamie kept telling me you have but I always defended you and never believed it until now. I don't know what's happened to you, but breaking an innocent boy's heart, keeping to yourself, dropping all your friends, and drawing on walls isn't the Ava I know. Some friend you are,' she spat ferociously before leaving.

I closed the door firmly behind her. At least she'd left. I didn't have time to care, not anymore. I had given her advice and she had refused to take it; I had been a real life example with Alfie and she'd ignored that too. I know I'm a good friend, just to people who deserve it.

I straightened my bed covers, placed the stained pillow on the floor, sat down with my back to the wall, and stared at the drawing of Madrina and her Cliders. They looked a lot more vicious now that I had heard what they were capable of. I'd had no more time to question Theo some more because he'd had a shift at *Hayven Books*. To be honest, there was nothing more for me to ask him. He'd kept his word and told me everything he knew. The Cliders were back, but the question was, where were they? Do we wait for them to show up or do we go looking for them? How did you destroy a Clider? How did you destroy anyone? Was it possible that Madrina had already somehow returned to Hayven? I looked towards my window to watch the darkening sky. Was there a way to ensure that she didn't?

The only person I knew of who could possibly answer any of these questions was now dead and it turns out that even Theo hadn't been trusted with the entire story. I looked upon Madrina again, truly focusing on her. Her orange hair flickered around her like wild flames, almost bringing her to life; her pale sapphire eyes glittered in a way I hadn't noticed when I'd been drawing her, and her lips were plump and red. She was beautiful, in a very strange way.

I'd never known an evil person before. I've always thought that people liked to use the word evil too loosely nowadays. 'Evil' was my version of Theo's 'impossible', too frequently used. Someone who stole your boyfriend wasn't evil, someone who took innocent lives for fun, was. Apparently, the world is full of evil people these days; people you can't trust and should never associate with. I don't think I've ever met such a person. You could say I've led a very sheltered life, but I wasn't naïve. I knew these kinds of people existed, and looking at Madrina now, I could see what evil really looked like. It was never about the face; you can't tell most things about a person by looking at their face. Looks can be deceiving, after all. It was all about the eyes. Not the colour or the shape, but the story they told when you looked deep enough. I had only drawn Madrina's eyes from a mental image, but in my dream I'd looked into them. I'd looked into them for only a second, but that had been enough. Her eyes had managed to tell me shocking stories and terrifying tales; her eyes told me there was an empty space in her body, as dark as her cloak, where her soul should have been. Her eyes told me what she was capable of and how much she was determined not to fail the second time around. And if there is anything you should fear or revere in a person, it's determination.

***

'So what you're saying is that the Cliders have returned. Madrina too,' Baleigh said, popping a fried chip into her mouth.

'Yes,' Theo and I replied simultaneously.

It was now a couple of days after Theo and I had walked through Mysteria Park and we were all gathered in *Gordon's* for lunch: Theo, Baleigh, Lucas, Faye, Peyton, Oliver-Raine and me.

'And you're sure?' Oliver-Raine asked.

Oliver-Raine I hadn't met until recently. He'd been away from Naveya with his family for a year, travelling across Europe. When he'd returned the group had ran towards him all in a desperate bid to greet him first, shouting, 'Ollie's back!' I soon found out why.

I was now in love with Oliver-Raine Gardens – platonically. He was a mixed race of Cuban and Puerto Rican, which gave him light brown skin, incredible light brown eyes, a chiselled jawline, and an infectiously warm smile. He had one of those cool urban haircuts with clean cut sideburns, and he wore square hipster glasses that suited the shape of his face. He also wore an orange leather bracelet with a metal clasp in the middle, just like the others.

He was very handsome, and he had the personality to back it up too. He had Theo's laid-back attitude and Lucas's sense of humour, but Oliver-Raine was more into books than ladies. Not to mention his gift was atmokinesis – *weather control*. It had been about to rain when he'd returned to Hayven, but he'd simply swept his hand across the sky, and the sun reappeared whilst the grey clouds disappeared.

'Yes,' Theo and I said simultaneously again but with less conviction in our voices.

The reaction we got from everyone wasn't what I had been expecting. I'd been expecting panic, fear, and maybe so far as a hysterical scream, but I didn't get any of those. I didn't know whether to be glad or annoyed.

'Well, we're *quite* sure,' Theo said.

'Quite?' Lucas repeated.

'The thing is, we don't have any *proof* so to speak, only that Sidra said it was going to happen,' I paused and looked up at my new friends. 'Is happening,' I corrected.

'Sidra Calix was also said to be slightly mad,' Lucas pointed out.

'Ava saw it happen in the future,' Theo explained.

'But the future is subject to change. It's never guaranteed,' Peyton voiced apologetically.

This wasn't going well at all. My mum had once told me that fear makes people believe only what they want to believe, whether it's the obvious truth or not. Was that the case with my friends? I looked around the booth at everyone's faces. Theo looked stern and ready to argue back. Baleigh appeared unmoved and was currently more interested in her milkshake than in our conversation. Lucas seemed just as unconcerned and was now eating the fried chips from

Baleigh's plate. Faye had looked petrified when we'd first spoken about Madrina and the Cliders, but she seemed more collected now, and Peyton looked her usual dreamy self. Oliver-Raine was the only one who paid us any real attention. He listened intently and it was clear he was gathering all the facts before he made his decision.

'Look, we just thought we should tell you what we thought,' Theo said.

'Madrina isn't coming back,' Baleigh said. 'Not now, not ever.' She sounded so confident I felt myself starting to believe her, but how could I? How could I after everything? Sidra's murder, Sidra's warnings, the mental images of an empty, dark night sky and burning cities, the vision of Madrina and her Cliders and of Mysteria Park on fire; the shadow in Huxton Park, the shard of glass, they couldn't mean nothing.

'Bales is right,' Lucas added. 'If Madrina was coming back, we'd know it.'

'How?' I asked.

'Well, according to what Sidra told Theo, Madrina's power is dependent on the stars and the sky hasn't gotten any darker. In fact, it's only gotten lighter.'

There was no escaping that fact. It was almost summer in Hayven and that meant longer days and shorter nights, and that hadn't changed.

'And Madrina would need the orb,' Faye pointed out.

'*If* it even still exists,' Baleigh added.

'Exactly,' Lucas said. 'Relax, guys. If she was coming back, we'd know it.'

As Theo continued to plead our case, I stared out of the window onto the street and the grassy patch of land. The streets were empty of people for long periods of time until a boy would run past, or a woman would walk by. It was eight in the evening and *Gordon's* was full as it usually is at this time of day. Something about the open fire, the clusters of hanging pendent lights, and the loud, warm atmosphere made the restaurant the perfect place to have dinner either by yourself, with someone else, or with a group.

Maybe everyone was right and Madrina wasn't returning, not yet anyway. Maybe Sidra *was* mentally insane. Maybe my dreams of Madrina and her Cliders were only that – dreams. Maybe the shard of glass I found was nothing special. Maybe the shadow at Huxton Park was...*the shadow*. It was back.

I slowly sat up.

'Ava? You okay?' Lucas asked.

The shadow was back. Across the street, hiding amongst the trees on the patch of land. I got up, stepped over Baleigh's feet, and walked slowly towards the door. The roaring fire suddenly went out, and the hanging lights began to flicker, one after the other, before they turned off completely, plunging us all into darkness. Concerned voices replaced peaceful chatter, but I continued to stare out of the window, refusing to lose sight of the figure moving in and out of the darkness until a line of glowing, green liquid stole my attention. It started at the very edge of the grassy land and ran down, down, down, until a line of lime green separated the grass from the pavement. My hand reached for the door handle when the grass caught fire and I was thrown back by the impact as tiny pieces of glass from the windows fell all around me. My head hit the wooden floor first and the last thing I felt was a scratch on my face. The last thing I saw was a piece of glass bounce on the floor, a thin line of my blood coating its jagged edge. The last thing I heard was someone shouting my name.

CHAPTER TWENTY

I came to, large circles of light dancing in front of my eyes. When my vision finally focused, the circles of light turned out to be the restaurant's ceiling spotlights. The hanging pendent light bulbs had been blown to pieces and I was lying on my back in one of the grey leather booths. I tried to sit up, but lost my balance and slid back down. A hand shot out to steady me and I looked up to find it belonged to Theo, who was sat beside my head.

'I got you,' he said, helping me sit up. 'Easy now. You hit your head hard so you might have a concussion.'

'I'm fine,' I said, noticing Lucas, Ollie, Faye and Baleigh also sitting in the booth. 'Where's Peyton?'

'Getting a cut looked at,' Baleigh answered, pointing to Peyton sat at a corner table, her curly hair piled on top of her head, whilst a woman attended the scratch on her forehead. Peyton saw me and gave a small smile before breathing deeply and pressing her lips into a firm line.

'She's not the biggest fan of blood,' Ollie revealed.

'What exactly happened here?' I asked. Pieces of glass still lay in certain areas of the restaurant, visible from the way they sparkled in the light. A soft wind blew in from the glassless windows, and it hadn't looked like anybody had left yet – the restaurant was still as full as it had been when we'd entered. 'I remember seeing green.'

'Something akin to a forest fire is most people's guess,' Lucas said.

'A *green* forest fire?' I questioned. 'Did anyone else see green or was it just me?'

'No, it wasn't just you,' Theo responded. 'One second, everything was fine. You got up and started walking towards the door, the lights went out, and then a burst of green. Next followed the explosion that shattered all the windows, then…chaos. You were closest to the door so you got the full force of the impact and hit the ground. I was too busy checking if you were still breathing to notice anything else.'

'Nothing much happened after that,' Faye added. 'We were all instructed to stay here whilst the fire was seen to.'

I saw beyond the window that the innocent area of land had been destroyed. The ground, once covered in luscious green grass was bare and brown. Trees were missing and large patches dotted the naked earth where they had once stood. For at least half a mile, it was desolate land. Firemen and policemen surrounded the area; I almost laughed out loud. They looked so normal and normal didn't belong here.

'What are you thinking?' Theo asked me.

'I'm thinking, green is a very unusual colour for fire,' I answered.

'Very unusual,' Ollie said. 'You might say, rare, even.'

'Rare?' I repeated.

'Extremely rare,' Ollie said.

The others shifted uneasily in their seats.

'Don't frighten her, Ollie,' Theo whispered to him.

'What are *you* thinking, Ollie?' I asked.

'Ollie,' Theo warned.

'I'm thinking,' Ollie began, ignoring Theo completely, 'that although green flames are rare, they've been sighted before. Especially flames like that,' he said, pointing behind him to the glassless windows. 'Flames that were not just green, but orange and red, with flecks of blue too. I call fires like this rare because the last time a fire like this was seen was over a thousand years ago.'

'I see.'

That was the last thing I said at that moment. Nobody had any follow up so we sat in silence until Faye could no longer keep it in.

'Wildfire.'

CHAPTER TWENTY-ONE

Wildfire. Wildfire. Wildfire. Wildfire.

We were finally allowed to leave at midnight. We walked pass the singed area that had been cordoned off with the classic yellow and black checked tape. After Theo had dropped me off in my room, I took off my coat and waited for the very last indigo blue dot to disappear before putting it back on. I faltered, though and paced my room. An hour later and my mind was made up. I travelled back to Hayven and materialised in front of the yellow and black barrier before slipping underneath it. I almost expected an alarm to sound as soon as my foot hit the barren land, but none did. I walked into the area the wildfire hadn't touched. I'd returned here to find an answer or a clue. Anything that would either explain what was going on or tell me what to do next.

'Silly of you to come back here alone, Avery.'

I whipped around at the sound of a female voice and saw *someone* in the shadows a few metres away, again only an outline, a shadow, but a familiar shadow.

'Who are you?' I asked, slowly stepping backwards until my back hit a tree. The contact knocked the breath out of me. Yet the woman stayed right where she was.

'Who am I?' she said, as if asking herself, or as if wondering which identity to give me. 'Who am I? If I tell you, I'd be cruelly robbing you of the opportunity to discover that out for yourself.'

Her voice was very soft and tranquil, it almost put me at ease. I subtly looked around the area, trying to figure out the best way to get out and maybe alert someone, but it was past one in the morning, hardly anybody was about. I ignored the feeling that my heart had grown thorns and repeatedly told myself that she couldn't hear my heart beating.

'Did you start the fire?'

'No,' she answered.

'Have you been the one following me?' I asked, mentally deciding on running to the left before heading to the right to reach the checked tape. I didn't dare travel. From what I've seen, if a person is close enough, they can mix their colour with yours and travel with you.

'Yes,' she answered. She stepped forward, melted into a shadow and appeared as part of another, but never came any closer.

I'd been about to propel to the left, but her frankness stopped me. 'Why?' I asked. 'What is it you want from me?'

'What do I want?' she asked.

'Yes, what do you want?' I repeated. 'Whoever you are. What is it you want?'

'Only your lives,' she answered.

'Lives?'

'Yes,' she replied. 'Yours, Theodore's, Baleigh's, Lucas's, Faye's, Peyton-Jane's and Oliver-Raine's. Keep going down the road you are now and they will be mine soon enough.' She laughed and the sound resembled claws on a chalkboard. 'Patience,' she continued, 'is something you and I have in common, Avery Charlotte Gray. Patience is a virtue we both do not have.'

233

I started at the paraphrased mention of my own words, blinked and lost her shape. That's when I ran.

***

I'd attempted to get some sleep, but it was no use; I just ended up tangled in my bedsheets from the effort. Her words ran circles in my head and each time it repeated, a drop of sweat rolled down my back. My heart hadn't returned to its regular rhythm since I'd gotten back.

I turned to my drawing on the wall. I lay with one side of my head pressed on my pillow and focused on each Clider in turn. Who had I spoken to? Which one produced wildfire? Immediately, my eyes zoomed in to the shortest Clider who stood at about five-feet, four-inches, but the short height was all I could tell of the person as, just like all the other Cliders, I had drawn the hoods covering their faces. Though, by the delicate detailing of the hands, I thought it might be a woman. If what that shadow had said was true and she hadn't started the fire, I could rule this Clider out. Unless they'd both been there…

Who the shadow could be was all I could think of. It was all I thought of when I finally dragged myself out of bed. It was all I thought of whilst I brushed my teeth, then showered, the heat of the water stinging my skin. It was what I had still been thinking about when I'd finally made a decision. Fresh out of the bathroom, I went over to my desk and opened the second drawer, usually only home to my socks and underwear. I delved into the back and grabbed hold of the glass. The temperature in my room dropped a few degrees, but I could blame that on the fact that I had nothing on but a large white towel. I sat on my bed and lifted the shard of glass to my eye line. Nothing had changed; it was still an ordinary, thick piece of glass with an extraordinary wisp of smoke floating inside it. It was time to show it to someone, and I knew just the person.

**

I knocked three times on his door. Luckily for me, he was the one to answer it.

'Hey, Ava,' Ollie said. 'Is everything okay?'

'Everything's fine,' I answered. 'Do you have a minute? Or thirty?'

'Sure. Do you want to come in?'

'Is anyone at home?'

'My dad and little sister,' he replied.

I hesitated whilst Ollie waited for a reply. He stared at me inquiringly before asking, 'Coffee?'

'Coffee,' I answered with a nod and he took his jacket from the back of the door, keys from the table, threw a goodbye up the stairs, and followed me outside.

We decided on the coffee shop ten minutes away from Ollie's house. When I'd found out that Ollie lived only twenty minutes away a few weeks ago, we'd gone to the same coffee shop on Albert Street then as well. Ten minutes later, we were sat in a secluded corner at a two person table. Ollie sat with a peppermint tea in front of him, I sat with a hot chocolate in front of me. A plate of biscotti sat in the middle of the table.

'I forgot to mention before, nice jumper,' I said, nodding to his chest. Ollie was wearing a woolly, knitted jumper that matched his travelling colour: orange. Not many guys, or girls for that fact, could pull of orange, but Ollie, with his light brown skin, square glasses, and clean hair-cut, easily could.

Ollie laughed. 'My nana made it for me! It's so comfortable, but, yes, very…orange,' he said. 'In my defence, I only ever wear it around the house and you didn't look like you'd wait for me to change jumpers.'

'You're right,' I agreed, 'I wouldn't have waited because I desperately wanted to show you…this.' I took the shard of glass out from my cardigan pocket and handed it to Ollie. 'And tell you what happened to me last night.'

Ollie adjusted his glasses in the way that only people who wear glasses can understand, and examined the glass. 'Fascinating,' he breathed. 'What's that inside?' He tapped the glass.

'I have no idea,' I answered honestly.

'Where did you get it?'

'Do you know the "forest" area of Huxton Park?'

'The bit that's always dark, with all the trees? Yes.'

'Well…' And I told Ollie about the day I'd found the glass, and then about what happened when I'd returned to the street opposite *Gordon's* last night. Once I'd finished, I reached for a biscotti and Ollie sank back into his seat.

'I'm sure I don't have to tell you that going back to the scene of a recent spontaneous wildfire occurrence in the early hours of the morning wasn't a good idea.'

'No, you don't.'

'Good, we can brush that to the side then,' he said.

I smiled before I remembered the question I'd been meaning to ask him. 'Ollie, are you one hundred per cent sure that fire last night was indeed wildfire?'

'It's my best guess,' Ollie answered. 'I would never say I was one hundred per cent certain of anything, but I'd say I'm ninety-eight per cent sure about this. Why do you ask?'

'I ask because, what I've heard about wildfire is that it consumes everything in its path, which it did, but—'

'Some of the land still remains untouched?' Ollie finished. I nodded.

'Yes, that is what's stopping me from being ninety-nine per cent sure,' Ollie admitted. 'But there is a way for that to happen, and that's if the gifter, or…Clider, stopped the wildfire themselves.'

'A person can do that?'

'Well, I've read about one person who can do that – *control* wildfire. Kindle McKay.'

'How tall was she?'

'History books say she was five-feet, four-inches,' Ollie answered. 'Always identified as the shortest Clider.'

'Right…'

'Why do you ask?'

'I thought it might have been her. Who saw me last night. But the shadow hinted at a person a little taller.' I hunched over our table and whispered, 'Madrina?'

'I did think that when you told me, but it couldn't have been her,' Ollie said. 'Madrina is no longer gifted, meaning she cannot return to Hayven. Theo told us the entire Sidra and Madrina story when we were waiting for you to regain consciousness.'

'That explains the look of unease on all of your faces last night.'

Ollie nodded gravely. 'Yeah, well, when you hear Naveya's most dangerous gifter in recorded history isn't actually dead, unease is one of the many things one feels. But that's not to say that whoever is following you isn't as dangerous. Especially if we're on her hit list for no apparent reason.'

'That's what's getting to me,' I confessed. 'That's what makes me think, you know, maybe this is just some crazed stalker. If they really wanted to kill me, why not have done it already? They had the perfect opportunity last night, yet here I still am. And it's like you said, the person has no reason to want all of us dead, we can't all have offended the same person.'

'I'm not so sure…'

'What do you mean?'

Ollie took a deep breath. 'What happened when you met Sidra Calix, Ava?'

I missed a beat and looked away.

Ollie nodded slowly. 'I thought so.'

'What is it you think?'

'I think there's something you're not telling me, Ava, but I'm not one to pry. Nonetheless, since we're on the subject, it's my guess that Sidra gave you her gift because she wants you to do something with it. Just nod if I'm right.'

I nodded.

'Okay, then it's also my guess that you're not telling me the entire truth, not because you don't trust me, but because you think I'm really smart, and if I give you another explanation that fits and makes sense, you'll abandon your

238

original explanation and convince yourself that my explanation is the one you should go with.'

I stared at Ollie, the smartest guy I knew.

'After Sidra grabbed my wrist and gave me her gift, she told me that I had to do what she failed to do before, rid Hayven of Madrina, or darkness would engulf the city,' I said. 'She knew my name, Ollie. She was waiting for me.'

Ollie listened sympathetically until I'd said my last sentence, to which he looked upon me with naked confusion.

'You believe she was waiting for you?' he asked.

'Yes, otherwise how else would she know my name?'

'The same way you know people's names when you touch them?'

I opened my mouth to speak, but said nothing.

'Forgive me, Ava. I've just always assumed Sidra gave you that gift.'

'No, no, you might be right,' I said. 'I thought she just gave me telepathy. I thought the name thing was my additional gift, but Theo told me Sidra had two gifts. That's probably the two gifts she had and gave to me. I can't believe this. Ollie, I wasn't *born* to save Hayven, I was just in the wrong place at the wrong time.'

Ollie smiled. 'I wouldn't go that far.'

'No?'

'No. Ava, I believe that life presents us with many life-changing choices that we may not even consider life-changing at the time,' Ollie said. 'Whether it be walking the dog in a different park or choosing the train over the bus, our futures change every day because of the decisions we make. When faced with an option, when we choose one thing, chances are, we've either missed or avoided something the other option may have provided. So, no, I would say Hayven has no chosen one; you are free to walk out of this coffee shop, avoid Hayven, cut all ties, and never have to hear of Madrina again. Or you can stay and accept whatever fate comes with that choice. It's entirely up to you.'

CHAPTER TWENTY-TWO

I walked into *The Sandwich Bar*, determined to eat a proper lunch, and the first table I saw was my old one, where Toni, Susie, Alfie and Jamie now sat, eating their lunch in silence. I hadn't spoken to any of them since Toni and I had fallen out three weeks ago, except for Susie, who I'd been texting and secretly meeting up with for coffee. I was about to turn back and find somewhere else to have lunch when Toni caught me staring. Susie, Alfie and Jamie caught on and looked in my direction too. Only Susie smiled.

It was too late to run out now, so instead I joined the queue and settled on a chicken rice bowl, a slice of chocolate cake, a fruit pot and a bottle of orange juice. There was an unoccupied seat at Toni's table, but I knew I wouldn't be welcomed by at least two of its occupants.

The Sandwich Bar was usually busy, but today it was practically full. Only two tables were free; a four-seater table I'd have to pass Toni's table to get to and a five-seater table right in front of me. I opted for the latter and sat in the seat closest to the wall. I'd never eaten alone before and usually got food to take back to my room. That had been my plan that afternoon, but after having Toni clock me, I didn't want it to seem as if I was too intimidated to sit on my own two tables down from her.

I opened my rice bowl and at that exact moment a sudden hush swept over the room. The change in sound was impossible to ignore as the bar was always quite loud, full of students ordering food and chatting with friends, music playing from the suspended TVs, the scraping of chairs and tables, and not to mention the noise from the outside world whenever the door was opened. I looked up from my lunch to find the cause of the silence when I noticed literally everybody in the room staring motionless in the direction of the restaurant entrance. And for good reason.

I copied literally everybody else in the room and sat gawking at their arrival as they stood in a neat line in front of the door. The boys all wore T-shirts and jeans, but Ollie had on a long, dark camel trench coat, left unbuttoned, Lucas wore a black, quilted bomber jacket, and Theo a navy hooded parka. Baleigh wore a plain T-shirt dress with an oversized flannel shirt with the sleeves rolled up, and military boots tied to the top. Peyton wore a cardigan and skirt so similar in colour and length that it was hard to tell where her cardigan ended and her skirt began, and Faye wore a hooded jumper over her dungarees.

Theo, Baleigh, Lucas, Faye, Ollie and Peyton were good-looking people, and good-looking people hardly ever went unnoticed, but out of Hayven, especially at that very moment, they looked to be from another world.

They all stood, searching the room until Baleigh's brown eyes found mine. She pointed to me, letting the others know, and everyone else in the room know, where I was. As they walked past Toni's table, one behind the other, I noticed Ollie look back at Susie, and she blushed peony pink in response to his light brown gaze.

Once they'd reached my table, all the boys and Faye sat down. Ollie got up to offer his seat to either Baleigh or Peyton, but Peyton stopped him.

'That's alright, Ollie,' she said, and her tranquil, drawling voice brought about a wave of nostalgia. 'I can sit on Ava's lap, if you don't mind.'

She was now speaking to me, but I was still in shock from their surprise appearance and could only nod my head. Lucas, who had taken the seat opposite me, patted his thigh jovially and smiled at Baleigh. She sighed and sat on his lap.

'Urmm, what are you guys doing here?' I asked.

As the shock settled down, I couldn't ignore the way my heart thudded at the sight of them all. Something warm hit my chest and swam to my stomach; I was so happy to see them. Ollie radiating calm, Faye in her ever-present dungarees, Peyton with her curly hair and multiple bracelets, Lucas with his nonchalance and ability to make me smile just by looking at him, Baleigh and her carefree attitude, and Theo. Theo with his relaxed smile and warm eyes. My heart beat even faster.

'Well,' Ollie said, 'me saying that the choice was yours to never return to Hayven appears to have caused a misunderstanding. I didn't really mean you could leave.'

I was well aware that people from nearby tables, including Toni's, were straining their ears in order to listen to our conversation. The sound in the bar had picked up again slightly, but not nearly as much as before. Luckily, we were in the furthest corner.

'Yeah,' Lucas chimed in, sliding my chocolate cake his way. 'We're emotionally invested in you now, Ava.'

'We don't like not having you around,' Faye said. 'We notice that something isn't right when you're not there.'

'Baleigh,' I said, 'do you feel the same?'

Baleigh looked up from the cake she was now sharing with Lucas. 'Don't start,' she answered. 'I'm here, aren't I?'

'That means yes,' Theo said. 'I've missed you too. We all have.'

Peyton turned her attention away from my fruit pot she'd managed to finish half of and rested her hazel eyes on me. 'I know things look a bit daunting with the prospect of Madrina returning, but I meant what I said in *Gordon's* about the future being subject to change and I still mean it today.' I'd almost forgotten she was sat on my lap; she didn't weigh a thing. 'You don't have to do this alone,' she continued, 'and we had no intention of letting you do so. I know you feel like it's your battle because Sidra made it seem that way, but that isn't the case. It's all of ours too.'

'So, please don't leave Hayven forever,' Faye added.

I looked around the table at the six people I'd known for less than a year and felt I could never live without.

'You guys thought I was leaving Hayven?'

'Well, yeah,' Lucas said. 'You haven't been back for almost a month. Theo kept telling us you were just taking some time out to figure out what to do next, but even he was starting to worry.'

I smiled. 'Theo was right,' I said. 'I was just taking some time off to think. I did often say to myself that I wouldn't return to Hayven, but I never believed it. I'm emotionally invested in you guys too, and I can't just sit by and let Madrina burn Hayven to the ground. So I've been thinking—'

'Hold on,' Baleigh interjected, 'if you were going to return all along, why not tell any of us?'

'Where's the fun in that?' I asked.

Baleigh's scowl turned upside down. 'True.'

'Besides, hanging out with you guys in Hayven distracts me,' I added.

'That's easy to understand,' Lucas said. 'We are a hoot.'

Ollie chuckled. 'So what have you been thinking, Ava?'

'With Sidra knowing Madrina was still alive, chances are, she knew Madrina would return. I'd like to think she wasn't sitting idly in her chair waiting for that day to come. Also, I've been thinking a lot about the day she died. Why was she alone in *Hayven Books* after closing hours? What was she doing there? And if Cliders were the ones who murdered her, how did they know where she'd be? Long story short, I want to talk to Gaige.'

'Sidra's husband?' Faye clarified. 'You think he knows something?'

'Subconsciously, perhaps,' I answered. 'Sidra may have said something to him that may not have struck him as important at the time. I'll look into what he's thinking when I ask him, if he hasn't learnt how to close his mind, and see if he's hiding anything. If he admits nothing and says nothing then we find somebody else close to Sidra. Somebody knows something.'

'And any piece of information is useful information,' Ollie finished, taking a sip from my orange juice. 'Good idea. By the way, Ava, who's the blonde on that table?' he asked, subtly jerking his head in Toni's direction.

We all turned to look at Susie, who like everybody else in the room, was still staring. She jumped at having been caught and spilled her water all over the table. She now flushed beetroot.

'She's what you would call a mortal,' I answered, drawing their attention back. 'Why?'

Ollie shrugged. 'Just wondering.'

'It's not often a girl catches Ollie's eye,' Lucas said.

Ollie rolled his eyes. 'Alright, I have a lecture.'

Faye, Lucas and Peyton chorused, 'Me too.'

'Just out of curiosity,' I said, addressing the group, 'how did you find me here?'

'We went to your room first, but you weren't there. Then we saw a lot of people heading in this direction so we decided to follow them and see if you were here, and you were,' Theo answered.

'But you need key cards to enter this part of the building,' I pointed out.

'So?' Baleigh questioned simply. 'We once got onto a plane without tickets, and you think a key card machine could stop us? Anyway, my lecture's in an hour,' Baleigh said to Theo and me. 'Want to check out this Gaige guy now?'

'Yeah, good idea,' Theo said. 'I have his address and I'm free for the rest of the day.'

'Me too,' I said, inwardly noting to ask Baleigh about that plane story in the future. 'Let's go.' I closed my rice bowl and planned to deposit it in my fridge and have it for dinner instead. As we left, Ollie cast a quick glance over his shoulder at Susie who was still mopping up the mess she'd made.

I prodded Ollie in the back. 'Eyes forward, Gardens.' And we left, with all eyes still on us.

***

247

'Gaige lives *here*?' I asked.

'Yup, number twenty-seven,' Theo replied.

Baleigh, Theo and I stood outside a tall glass building, not far from Mysteria Park, located in front of a river that shimmered and rippled when the sun's rays bounced off it and a soft wind blew across it. Surrounding the building were acres of grass, bordered by granite stone. The place reminded me of those sleek modern apartments in London that only wealthy people could afford to reside in, but the golden glow of Hayven made it differently beautiful and somehow more homely.

Inside was just as modern as the outside; the lobby had laminated hardwood floors, expensive framed paintings hung on the walls, and the occupiers could either take the lift or the stairs to their own apartments. We walked up to the second floor and then down the corridor.

'Number twenty-seven,' Theo announced as he stopped outside a dark green door. It was the only door I had seen with a sticker that read, *no junk mail*. Theo raised his left eyebrow at us before knocking three times. Not long after, the door opened a tiny crack and an angered grey eye appeared.

'Who is it?' a gruff voice demanded.

'Mr Calix? Hello, it's me, Theodore-James Connors,' Theo introduced himself politely. 'I don't know if you remember me. Years ago, I came with —'

'I remember you, I'm not senile,' the man unjustly admonished. 'What is it you want?'

'We just wondered if we could come in and talk to you about Sidra,' Theo persevered undeterred.

'Why?' Gaige questioned, the door still open only a fraction. 'I don't know what happened to her!'

'We know that,' Theo continued. 'It isn't about how she died, it's more to do with *why* she died.'

'Oh, right,' he relented. 'I suppose you can come in then,' he said, his voice slightly less defensive, and he opened the door wider to permit us entrance.

The door opened straight into a living room decorated in an odd combination of beige and grey, where there was nothing but a table, a television box and a few chairs. I clocked a fat cigar, a few wisps of smoke escaping from its burnt end, and a folded newspaper on the table. That explains why he had been so short with us at the door; we must have interrupted his reading time. I looked closer at the newspaper; it was an English tabloid, folded to reveal the sports section.

'Who are they?' Gaige asked Theo, pointing to Baleigh and me in turn, the hard edge back in his voice.

I looked up to get a better look at Gaige Calix, the second husband of a revered gifter. He was an old man with a full head of grey-white hair that he had combed back. He had a round belly that stretched against his navy woollen jumper, grey eyes that looked to be made of matte glass and a grey bushy moustache to match his grey thick eyebrows. He wore corduroy trousers, along with what seemed to be, guessing from the deep lines at the corners of his mouth, a permanent scowl.

I was randomly reminded of the warning my mother used to tell me whenever I'd grimaced: *'If the wind changes, your face will stay like that.'*

'My name is Avery Gray, sir,' I answered for Theo. My mother had raised me well after all.

His cold eyes looked me up and down. 'No. That name means nothing to me.' He walked over and sat heavily in his armchair. 'You don't look like much so that's probably why I don't remember you. Sit down then,' he finished, pointing to the sofa on the opposite side of his chair. 'What about you?' Baleigh's turn.

'A friendly stranger,' she replied.

'I don't like strangers,' he riposted.

'And yet, you just let two into your home,' Baleigh said.

Gaige narrowed his eyes at her before turning back to Theo. 'What is it you three want? I'm busy.'

'Oh, yes,' Theo said, 'we just wanted to know if Sidra had any relatives who might still be alive. Anyone she may have been particularly close to?'

Gaige's mind was silent. I'd suspected Sidra had taught him how to close of his mind to those who might try to hear it.

'That's a nosey request,' Gaige stated. 'What do you want to know that for? If Sid had wanted you to know something like that, she would have told you herself when she was alive.'

'We want to know so we can speak to one of them,' Theo answered.

'Because?' Gaige prompted impatiently.

Theo turned to look at me.

'Because Madrina is planning to return. Soon.'

Gaige's eyes widened at my words. 'I knew you three would be trouble! That's all you kids are nowadays. Glad I never had any myself! Don't you go spreading those vicious

250

rumours around town, making people nervous. You troublesome lot need to learn to leave the elderly in peace. It's time you were going now and I don't want to see you back here neither!'

He spat unpleasantly throughout his rant and the darkening shade of puce his face had turned was a slightly worrying sight to behold. But we couldn't leave without any answers now that it was established we wouldn't be allowed to return.

'Mr Calix, please, calm down,' I pleaded. 'Honestly, we're not here to cause trouble. We're not exactly thrilled by the news either!'

I had gone from wary to irritated in a matter of seconds. Is this how every person I told was going to react? If so, Hayven would descend into a state of pandemonium, all set for Madrina to lay claim. All this man had to do was provide information; *I* was the one who had to deal with everything afterwards.

'Listen to me, Sidra had valuable information that I now need, and you *are* going to help me or you'll be wishing you had when Madrina does return. Not *if*, *when*. So just tell us what you know and then we'll leave.'

Gaige clenched his jaw and bristled in silent indignation. I couldn't break eye contact with him long enough to turn towards Theo, but I sensed he was shocked by my little outburst, and to be honest, so was I. I may not always be calm, but I hardly ever snapped at anyone, let alone a stranger. Baleigh on the other hand radiated pride.

'Sid had a half-sister she was fond of – Jane Hartleigh,' Gaige replied after moments of silence. He looked at us each in turn, considering something deeply before he heaved himself up and wandered over to a desk beside the window. We watched as he took out a small white card and quickly wrote something on it.

'This is her last known address,' he said, handing it to Theo and ignoring me completely. 'I'm not sure if she lives there anymore, but you could always check.'

'Thank you so much, Mr Calix,' Theo said, safely tucking the paper into his shirt pocket. 'You have no idea how much we appreciate this. We'll leave you in peace now.'

'Thank you,' I said, and he nodded curtly in reply.

As we reached the door, Gaige asked, 'You're a future-seer?'

I nodded.

'So you saw Madrina return? With her...*followers*?'

'Yes.'

An expression flitted across Gaige's face that I recognised all too well. Fear. From what I was slowly gathering, it seemed the Cliders were to be as feared as much as Madrina herself. The notion didn't fill me with hope.

'The future is not always guaranteed,' Gaige said, unknowingly repeating Peyton's words. 'You can change it.'

'That is what I aim to do, sir,' I said.

Theo had once said he could only imagine what it was like to live during Madrina's rule. It's easy to feel pity and sympathy towards people who have gone through a tough time, but you can never say you understand. Not unless you've lived through it yourself. That's why I couldn't relate to Gaige. I was scared of Madrina because of what I've been told about her, but I couldn't *fear* someone I've never met before, it would make no sense if I did. That's why my heart didn't slam so hard against my chest at the thought of

Madrina, like I knew Gaige's was doing now. That's why I couldn't fully comprehend why he'd reacted so harshly towards us when I'd told him of her pending return. And that's why I couldn't understand the terror that coursed through his veins at the thought of Madrina and her Cliders, because I hadn't experienced the horror first hand. One look at Gaige and a wave of pity hit me in the stomach for those who did. It was enough for me to realise that I couldn't allow the people of Hayven to suffer through it again.

'I will stop her,' I said, surprised by my own confidence. 'Or I'll die trying.'

Gaige looked up at me with something in his eyes that hinted at respect.

'She always said, "She's coming back".'

'Who did, Mr Calix?' Theo asked.

'Sidra, my Sid. Almost every morning, she'd whisper, "She's coming back" to herself over a cup of some herbal tea she'd only drink when she'd had a bad dream. Whenever I'd asked her who, she'd shake her head and say nothing.'

'Mr Calix, may I use your bathroom?' Baleigh asked.

'Baleigh, can't you wait?' Theo asked, obviously desperate to leave.

'No, I can't,' Baleigh replied. 'I can't wait much longer.'

Gaige pointed a beefy finger towards the darkened corridor.

'Thank you,' Baleigh said.

She was gone for the longest two minutes of my life.

'I never would have guessed that...*Madrina*...still alive...' Gaige continued as if Baleigh hadn't left.

'Mr Calix,' Theo said, 'we assure you, we'll do all that we can.'

'I'm sure you will. Now, please, just leave,' he begged, turning his back on us.

And so we did.

*****

'I didn't think he'd be so emotional,' I said as we exited the building.

'Terrible memories bring up terrible emotions,' Theo voiced. 'At least it wasn't a wasted trip used to upset an old man for nothing. We got Jane's address.'

'And something else,' Baleigh said, fishing two tea bags out of her pocket.

'What's that?' I asked her.

'Don't you remember Gaige saying something about Sidra drinking some kind of herbal tea whenever she'd a bad dream?'

Theo and I both nodded.

'Well, on my way to the toilet, a destination I never actually intended to reach, I went snooping in the kitchen cabinets. These were the only tea-bags I found. They were in an unnamed box and they smell really strong.'

'You think there's something in them?' Theo asked.

'Could be,' Baleigh answered. 'If not, no harm done, right? I'll give it to Ollie to examine. See if he can find anything strange in them. Right, if I don't leave now I might be late. You two are on your own.'

'Wait,' Theo said, stopping Baleigh in her tracks. 'Do you know this address?'

Baleigh took the paper Gaige had written on and studied it for a few seconds before handing back. 'Nope. Good luck.'

'You've lived in Naveya all your life and you don't know this place?' I questioned.

'What do you want from me?' Baleigh shrugged. 'Just...follow the yellow brick road.' She left with a smile, her violet specks of being dancing across the river.

'Let me have a look at the address,' I said in a bid to be helpful. I don't know why I bothered; all it did was earn me a chuckle from deep within Theo's throat.

'What's so funny?' I asked, nudging him with my elbow.

'Nothing,' he said, shielding his ribs. 'It's just, well, if I don't know this place, you definitely won't!'

Then he actually *snorted*.

'Hey! I've been here a while. I know a few places.'

I looked down at Gaige's surprisingly neat handwriting. Damn, Theo was right. The address was not a familiar one.

Jane Hartleigh
9 Greenweir Close
Laydon

'Well?' Theo asked.

I knew *of* Laydon, it was a small town on the edge of Hayven, but that was as far as my knowledge of the place went.

'We'll just have to ask around,' Theo suggested smugly once I'd failed to provide directions.

It wasn't until the fourth person was asked that we were eventually pointed in the right direction. Greenweir Close was a lovely area that looked very much like a village; it had such a rural country feel to it. It was odd that there existed a place so different from all the other parts of Hayven I had

255

visited, but then again, all my friends here were city kids and only took me to places in the city, so that was all I ever saw. Only Peyton knew of the countryside, but whenever she suggested we go there, she was outnumbered, four against three.

The village appeared separate from the rest of Hayven, like a close-knit community where everybody knew each other. There were vast fields, a few shops selling local produce, and cottages with thatched roofs and flower beds, instead of congested roads, huge supermarkets, and grand houses alongside shiny apartments. *I like it here*, I thought to myself as Theo and I walked up the cobblestone street. It was so quiet and peaceful, almost like Huxton, but without the buzz of the university and town centre.

This would be a nice place to live when I'm older. When life had run its course and I had seen all I needed to see and had heard all that was to be heard, I would come here to settle down and remember. To settle down and grow old.

'Okay, number five…seven…and…nine, here it is. Nine Greenweir Close,' Theo announced as he opened the white picket fence that guarded the house.

I couldn't help but allow a small bubble of hope to rise in my chest. Jane Hartleigh seemed as if she'd be genial if her cottage was anything to go by. It was wide sized, but short in height, which gave the impression that there must only be one floor, but judging by the number of windows, there were plenty of rooms. The red and brown bricks sat firmly in place, protected by a large thatched roof decorated abundantly with green vines and wiry lines of ivy, snaking their way down from the roof and onto the cottage, wrapping and binding itself to the house forever.

Jane was obviously a keen gardener, and a good one too, as the front of the house had rows of potted flowers and neatly trimmed bushes. A pair of red breasted robins sat upon a bird feeder that hung from the top of the porch area, chirping softly and pecking at their free food.

'Here goes,' Theo said before knocking on the dark red door, ignoring the heavy wrought iron knocker. Nobody answered. After knocking again and getting the same response, he rang the doorbell and a light trilling sound that reminded me of an unnamed nursery rhyme filled the house.

'One moment,' came a female voice. We heard a light jingle of keys and then the door opened.

Jane looked a lot like her half-sister, Sidra; whichever parent they shared clearly had the dominant genes. In fact, Sidra and Jane could have been twins if it were not for the different coloured eyes. Sidra's had been a dark, duck-egg blue that hinted of a past filled with adventure, spontaneity and excitement, whilst Jane's brown eyes reflected a more calm and sensible nature.

'Hello dears, Theo, is it?' she smiled, and the wrinkles on either side of her eyes creased further, giving her a very warm and friendly appearance. I sighed with relief. After our earlier interaction with Gaige, I'd been holding my breath since Theo had spotted Jane's house. Jane's silver hair was tied back with a few curly strands decorating her ears. She was dressed in a light brown dress that fell to the floor and she had wrapped a silver shawl across her shoulders.

'You know me?' Theo asked surprised. 'Sorry, have we met before?'

'You were at Sidra's funeral but unfortunately, the only mutual friend we had was Sidra so we were not formally

257

introduced. However, whenever she visited me she spoke fondly of you. And who is this? I'm sad to say you and I have not met before.'

I hadn't been paying much attention to the conversation after the bit where Jane had said, 'whenever she visited me'. Because that meant Jane and Sidra must have been quite close, implying that Jane might have answers.

'This is Avery Gray, Mrs Hartleigh,' Theo introduced on my behalf.

'It's Miss Hartleigh dear, I never married,' she said with a sad smile. 'But, hello, Avery Gray.' Jane looked up at the sky and nodded before looking back at us. 'Please do come in, I've just made some tea.'

Jane had not only made tea, but for us, she also lay out a selection of biscuits, a plate of lemon cake slices and a tray of mini chocolates on her coffee table as we all took a seat in her large and inviting living room. The room was simple enough, with an unlit brick fireplace built into the wall and two armchairs facing it, dressed with white and lilac scatter cushions. To the side sat a single, cream-coloured armchair opposite a wooden-paned window with drawn cream lace curtains; a pendent light hung from the white painted ceiling and a set of French doors led to the expansive garden. Every now and again, I'd spot an interesting artefact that I knew must be from a different country, placed carefully upon a shelf or on another smooth surface. Jane sat in the single armchair facing the window whilst Theo and I sank deliciously into the two pressed together.

'So, how may I help you both?' she asked.

It was comforting to know Jane was not only polite, but welcoming too. It was hard to imagine why she had never married; she seemed such a loving and attentive woman. I suddenly felt my head start to swim. The room was so warm, my chair so soft, my tea so sweet, and the cottage smelt of countryside air and freshly baked biscuits. I hadn't slept properly in a while, I realised, and I sunk deeper into my chair.

'We don't mean to be a bother —' Theo started.

'Oh, don't be silly!' Jane reprimanded gently. 'This village can get fairly dull from time to time so it is rather wonderful to see some new and young faces.'

I watched Theo smile warmly at Jane; he could probably see Sidra in her too.

'This may sound a bit odd, but we just wanted to know if Sidra ever spoke to you about…the future,' Theo said.

'Oh yes, my memory is quite remarkable,' she said, tapping her temple. 'Sidra was all for living in the present, but nearing her death, she occasionally brought up what was to come.'

I felt my sleepiness melt away as my ears pricked and I leaned forward in my seat. 'What did she say?'

'That Madrina would return,' Jane answered.

'Do you…' I could sense Theo treading lightly. '…Do you also believe Madrina will return?'

'Yes, I do.'

'How is it you know?' I asked. 'Have you seen it happen too?'

'Oh no, dear,' Jane said. 'No, my gift is memory, astonishing memory. I can remember the day I was born, the look on my mother's face, the smell of the hospital, and the sound of my wailing.' She chuckled softly at the old thought. 'I did not see Madrina return, but Sidra believed she would

259

and she informed me, perhaps because I was the only one likely to believe her. Yet, everybody knows it deep down, they just refuse to admit it, as if keeping it in will prevent it from coming true. Fear is a funny thing, especially if you've experienced all its horrors first hand. It has the ability to make you see, hear, and believe only what you wish to.'

'You seem very *composed*,' Theo pointed out, obviously thinking back to Gaige's earlier reaction.

'You know, I used to worry a lot, too much you might say,' Jane said with a smile. 'I'd worry about school, friends, boyfriends, family, love, life, death, you name it. But then one day, my father gave me some rather valuable advice: worrying about something you can change is necessary, but worrying about the inevitable is a waste of time. Madrina's return is inevitable because she did not die. There was always the possibility of her returning, and those who were there when she took over know how determined she was to rule, and that one day she will build on that possibility and make it an opportunity. Once she has that opportunity, she will not hesitate to grasp it with both hands. I believe that is what we must all do in our short lives,' she finished.

'Is there anything you know or anything Sidra told you that could help us?' Theo asked.

'Hmm, let me think,' Jane replied. 'I'm afraid to say Sidra often preferred to speak in riddles, even as a child she was enigmatic. There exists three years between us you see, me being the eldest, and I will always remember the day our parents came home with her from the hospital. Our mother had married my father and not long after, Sidra arrived. Such a fascinating baby, as quiet as a mouse and always looked to be deep in thought. As she grew older, she became more vocal of course, but even so, she was always thinking. One thing I can say for sure is that she was very clever. Not in the way others expect you to be – intelligent, witty, and concise, but in the way people *should* be – creative and consistent.

'Anything cryptic she'd say always had a reason behind it. She would not always tell you the reason, but you'd find it in the end, whether in a few hours, days, weeks, months, or even years – you were guaranteed to find it. On one of the occasions she spoke of Madrina's return, she elaborated. I have no idea what she meant by it mind you and I doubt you will either, I did say she was fond of speaking in riddles, so try not to worry yourselves about it too much, but I feel it is perhaps something I should share.'

'What was it?' I asked.

'She said to me, "If anyone on our side was ever to visit you, use your judgment and tell them all you know. Tell them to trust only a few and to look out for the rainbow at the end.".'

CHAPTER TWENTY-THREE

'The rainbow at the end?' Faye asked us as we all sat sprawled on the grass surrounding Fulton the next day. 'What could she have meant by that?'

We all turned to Ollie for an answer.

He heaved a playful, exasperated sigh and said, 'I'm *guessing* Sidra meant that the sign that will signify when Madrina is well and truly destroyed and Hayven is restored, is by the formation of a rainbow.'

'Can't you just make a rainbow?' Baleigh asked.

Ollie shook his head. 'Nope,' he said. 'I can make the sun shine and open the clouds so that it rains at the same time, but a rainbow won't appear. I've tried it before. I suppose it has to be natural.'

'Alright, there's going to be a rainbow, good for us,' Baleigh said. 'Anything else?'

'No, that was it,' Theo said before turning away to look off into the distance.

Something had happened to Theo ever since we had left Jane's cottage yesterday. He'd been quiet and slightly...*off*, which was unusual for him. Perhaps he was downhearted about the fact that we hadn't found anything that could really help us. Out of all of us, Theo seemed to be effected by this the most, maybe because Sidra's stories haunted him. The rest of us could only imagine what could happen to Hayven and to the lives of its citizens, but Theo had the best idea of what was to come if we didn't stop the Cliders soon.

He was agitated and tension practically radiated off him. But surprisingly, he was the only one. Everyone else appeared to be completely relaxed. Baleigh and Faye were slowly flicking through a magazine. Lucas and Ollie were discussing home renovations, as they and Theo were moving in together later this month. Peyton was sunbathing on her back, whilst I lounged with my back up against a tree. *Was* Theo the only one taking this seriously?

'So what do we do now?' I asked the group.

'Who knows? Sidra didn't exactly make this easy for us,' Baleigh said, lazily looking up from under her enormous black sun hat. 'It's either Sidra had no idea what she was doing or we're missing something she thought would be obvious.'

Theo's eyes widened slightly, but nobody had caught it but me.

'Guys, I'm going to take a walk,' he said. He stood up abruptly, brushed away stray blades of grass from his jeans, and took off.

'What's up with him?' Lucas asked, lifting his head off Baleigh's back where it has been resting before Theo's departure.

'Only one way to find out,' I said.

Theo hadn't gotten far and I was able to catch up with him within seconds.

'Something's wrong, Theo, what is it?' I asked stopping him in his tracks.

'It's what Jane said,' Theo answered, 'about there being a reason behind anything cryptic Sidra said. What if she told me something important, but I hadn't listened closely enough? She gave me a clue, Ava, I just know it. But how am I going to find it? I can't remember everything!'

'Theo, calm down. You can't beat yourself up about it,' I said, resting my hand on his arm. 'If Sidra has left you with something, it'll come to you in time.'

'We don't have time!'

I took a step back.

Theo inhaled deeply and looked away. 'Ava, I'm sorry, I hadn't meant to shout.'

'I know,' I said, ignoring the heat in my cheeks.

'It's just…everyone is *too* chilled,' he continued. 'No one is taking things seriously enough. *This*, right now, is the calm before the storm, and storms destroy everything in their paths and wipe out lives. Hayven faces a major threat *again*, which we have to stop, which *only* we can stop because for some cruel reason, fate chose us. What if we don't? What if we can't? How many lives are going to be lost? Men, women and innocent children, all dead or dying. And why? Because the people with the ability to stop it didn't take it seriously enough at the time it mattered most.

'Part of me wants to find Kindle McKay and the others, but a part of me doesn't because what happens when we do find them? We kill them?' Theo asked, his eyes so sad and so empty. The spark had fizzed out and the brightness had died, all washed away by thoughts of the past and the future. 'How do we kill them? I don't know how to kill a mortal, let alone a Clider. It's not something I've ever imagined myself doing.'

I wanted to tell Theo how much I understood how he felt, but I couldn't bring myself to do it. If I said the words aloud, I'd crumble; my resolve would weaken. I didn't want to kill anyone, not even a Clider, but it seemed I had to; Sidra had made that much clear.

'I wish I could make it easier for you, Theo, I really do. But don't forget, I'm in the same boat.'

'Oh, Ava,' he sighed, as he pulled me into a tight hug and rested his cheek on my head. 'It's just...hard.'

I let myself collapse into his chest. 'Trust me, I know.'

***

I hated returning to Huxton. I felt helpless, alone and useless, all at the same time, with the drawing on my wall serving as a constant reminder as to why I felt all those things. What Theo had said stuck in my brain. What had he missed? Had *I* missed anything?

How was I going to kill Madrina, or any Clider for that matter? Did gifters die as easily and quickly as humans did, or was it as slow a process as our ageing?

It was four in the morning when a smattering of indigo blue dots formed Theo in the centre of my room, his face flushed with excitement.

'Come with me,' he said, holding out his hand.

As I learnt never to question Baleigh in fear of getting my head bitten off, I had also learnt not to question Theo when he asked me to follow him. I took his hand and let him take me to a dark and deserted lane – it was almost midnight in Hayven.

'Where are we?'

'Shush!' Theo's eyes enlarged to twice their size. 'We have to be quiet here,' he whispered, pulling me closer to him.

Silently, I shadowed him as he walked up a concrete pathway. Although his hand was hot in mine, it did nothing to warm the place we had just landed in.

On either side of us were large houses that had been beautiful and grand once upon a time. Now most had their roofs slanted, hanging off the edge of the house as if in a desperate bid to escape, whilst other houses had no roof at all. Windows were either broken or boarded up, and doors were either rotting or dangling off their hinges. Despite knowing we were still in Naveya, I felt as if we had stepped over to a dark world, hidden beyond our own. I wanted to go back home. I didn't belong here. As long as my heart was beating and warm blood was flowing, I didn't belong here.

The town was so still and so quiet, nothing could be heard but the cruel jibe of the harsh wind. The further we walked the stronger and icier the wind became until it began to snatch at my clothes, seizing and grabbing frantically for warm skin; racking its fingers through my hair, clawing at my throat, growling, hissing and nipping at the tips of my ears; sneaking up my back and causing me to shiver violently. Yet still, Theo persevered, deeper into the never-ending darkness with my hand firmly in his. He knew where he was going and I trusted him enough to keep following.

The trees towered menacingly over us, canopies and top branches hunched as if protecting from the bitter cold. But there was no escaping the air's icy fingers; they were everywhere. The trees here were nothing like the ones in Hayven, full of leaves, petals, fruit and life. Instead, these trees were filled with grief, sorrow and death – the petals long gone, its fruits shrivelled, its life ended and its branches naked. This was truly a haunted lane.

But we soon came across a tree that stood different to the rest. It was an odd but entrancing tree. Its trunk was brown and gnarled; it stood strong and proud, its roots buried deeply and stubbornly inside the earth. The tree made me think that whilst the ground it stood on lay dead and rotting, underneath, within the earth and soil, life was thriving. The tree's branches worked into complicated knots, long, winding, tangled and *hidden*. All the branches were covered and smothered with the darkest black leaves, the dark colour managing to separate itself from the dark night. The wild wind continued to blow and whilst the branches followed the steps of the familiar dance, the leaves remained motionless – unsettlingly undisturbed.

Suddenly, a pair of yellow buttons appeared amidst the leaves, followed by two more pairs, then five more pairs. Pair after pair these dim lights appeared whilst others disappeared, just to reappear having brought a friend or two. *Eyes.* They weren't leaves, but crows and ravens.

I stopped to stare.

'If I know anything about birds, any kinds of birds, it's if you don't bother them, they won't bother you.' And with this, Theo pulled me gently from the spot I thought I'd never be able to move from again and we resumed walking.

Finally, he stopped and pulled us both behind a brick wall that guarded an empty house, similar to all the rest.

'This is Murmmers Lane,' Theo whispered to me. 'This is where most of the fighting happened when Madrina took over.'

I looked around the place again, through the dense darkness, and saw more closely what I had missed before.

The houses that stood, defeated and crumbling, were not just empty, they were abandoned. The remaining grass in front of the sad houses were not darkened by the absence of light, but burnt and singed from a thousand years ago, unable to grow back since. The roads and pathways were not dirty or badly constructed, but neglected, upheaved and ignored.

Spirits of those both good and evil floated aimlessly and harmlessly in and out of houses, and through and around the trees. I could not see them, but I could *feel* them, and I considered that to be worse. I heard their yells, their screams and their curses; I heard the voices that had died here with them on this very street more than a thousand years ago. I pulled my jacket tighter around my body in an attempt to trap any heat cruel enough to escape.

'Is it always so dark and cold here?' I asked.

'Yes,' Theo replied. 'The sun doesn't visit dead places.'

'Why are we here?'

'Do you remember the story I told you in Mysteria Park? About Madrina giving Sidra an address, but every time she visited she only found a warehouse?'

'An abandoned warehouse, yes,' I answered, remembering clearly.

'That's the clue, Ava,' he whispered, his words so quiet the wind almost stole them. 'The *warehouse*. Sidra mentioned it to me not once but twice, for a reason.' His brown eyes were wide and full of energy and I could feel mine take a life of their own and imitate. 'This lane is famous, or rather infamous depending on your viewpoint, so everybody knows where it is, but nobody ever comes here. Why would you?' He stretched his legs slightly and lifted his head slowly over the brick wall. '*That* is the warehouse.'

He pointed to an old and dilapidated building directly opposite the house whose wall we were currently crouched down behind. I peered over the top to get a better look. The warehouse was like every other building on the lane, aged and deteriorating, but different in the fact that it took up vast amounts of land due to its long length and was so tall it appeared to graze the dark heavens. I couldn't begin to imagine how many floors the warehouse was home to. Apart from the height and width, it was too dark to see any more features of the building, but that was probably for the best.

'How do you know?' I asked Theo.

'I asked Mrs Castel,' he answered, 'and a few other teachers to make sure, and they all said the same thing. That this is the only warehouse located on Murmmers Lane.'

I looked back at the warehouse. This was it, wasn't it? This was our chance...but our chance to do what exactly?

'Do we go in?' I asked, feeling a shiver that had nothing to do with the cold air.

'I have no idea, Ava,' he answered. 'Who knows what we'll find in there. Will we find dusty shelves and rats, or will we find a roomful of Cliders?'

If it were a choice between Cliders and rats, I'd be a fool with a death wish not to insist on the rats.

Suddenly there was a shift in the air. Theo had felt it too, and he brought us lower down, gripping my arm tightly in response. It had gotten remarkably colder so quickly I half expected to see Ollie beside me, but I'd seen Ollie use his gift enough times to know that even he couldn't work that fast. No, Ollie wasn't here, but somebody else certainly was.

Something moved near the warehouse where shadows appeared to morph and emerge into other shadows, as still and silent as the dark, thick air.

Theo pressed his index finger to his lips to indicate for me to stay silent. He needn't have bothered; I had lost my voice. Soundlessly, we gradually lifted our heads to peek over the brick wall. It was unnaturally dark, but luckily the moon seemed to be on our side. The glow momentarily landed on two cloaked figures that had been the cause of the sudden shift in atmosphere.

Cliders.

My heart accelerated to a speed that was likely to prove fatal, and a trail of sweat made its way, slowly down the back of my neck. *They are real.*

I wanted to scream and run for my life, but I didn't; I didn't move because I didn't dare make a sound. I sat, hunched, and felt my legs begin to ache and burn. Watching.

I noticed instantly that one Clider was shorter than the other, much shorter – Kindle McKay. She had her hand on the proffered arm of the other Clider, who stood taller than six feet, and together, floating in and out of the shadows as if walking on air, they strode up to the warehouse and stepped through it.

I blinked rapidly, unsure of what had just happened.

'Intangibility,' Theo whispered.

'What?'

But before I could be given an answer, the two Cliders returned again, the same way they had gone. Theo pulled me down and with a complete lack of self-control I hadn't suffered in weeks, my mind switched on through its own accord. One Clider had heard something across the street and was curious.

'They're going to come,' I mouthed to Theo in panic. 'We need to leave.'

Theo grabbed my arm just as I was about to travel. 'They might see your colour!' he mouthed back. He tightened his grip on my arm and we shifted back to my room where I finally allowed myself to breathe, slow, short, greedy gulps of air. I watched Theo do the same as he regained his breath quicker.

Once graced with the ability to stand straight on questionably shaky legs, I grabbed a pencil off my desk and above the shortest Clider wrote: *Kindle McKay – Wildfire*. Then moved onto the leader: *Madrina – Absorption*.

When Theo grasped what I had done, he nodded solemnly. 'Just nine more to go,' he said.

***

Baleigh had once said that once you saw a Clider, you didn't live for very long afterwards. I had taken that to mean that if you saw a Clider's face, that meant that they had seen *yours*, and if by some stroke of short-lived luck you managed to escape, they would find you before you did them, and kill you. I was certain this was just a tale, as I knew someone who had lived more than a thousand years later after having seen a Clider and although she was dead now, I was certain she wasn't the only one. What we needed was someone who had seen, and could still remember, everything.

'I remember the look, gift and colour of each and every Clider,' Jane said, setting out tea and biscuits onto the coffee table before sitting down.

'Really? How?' Theo asked.

Jane laughed a strong laugh that did not reflect her age. 'Sidra was not the only one to fight that war and survive. There were many survivors, never forget that. Some people joined Madrina, others fought; I had partaken in the latter.'

It was difficult to imagine sweet, old Jane in any kind of fight, especially one against such ruthless monsters.

'Will you tell us everything you know?' I asked.

'That will not be a problem,' Jane said. 'Ah, Madrina and her eleven Cliders,' she murmured to herself. 'Now, of course Madrina had many followers, even she could not take over Hayven with only eleven. Unfortunately, Madrina is a smart woman and was well aware that many of her followers had joined out of fear and not loyalty, because of that, she named her most trusted followers, "Cliders". That is not to say that there were only eleven people true to Madrina's cause, oh no, far from that. There were thousands upon thousands of people who truly believed in Madrina and wanted nothing more than to gain her trust, prove themselves to her and become a Clider. But Madrina liked to keep things close to her chest and so trusted in only eleven. It is sad that you saw a vision of Madrina returning with all eleven of her Cliders, Ava, because that means they have been alive all this time, not one of them destroyed, only scattered.' Jane gave a long and dissatisfied sigh before she continued.

'Madrina had, or rather *has*, long red Pre-Raphaelite-like hair and piercing blue eyes that you will never forget. I do not know how she walks without making a sound. I do not know how her eyes show no emotion. I do not know how she survives without a heart or soul. Her gift is absorption – the ability to take another's gift and make it her own for a short period of time, a gift Madrina used to the best of her ability. Surprisingly, her colour is a magnificent silver, almost invisible in sunlight. I always wondered, and still do wonder, how such a woman was born with such a lovely colour.

'Sia Valour, Madrina's closest Clider, has waist-length black hair and skin so pale she'd be lost in snow; her gift is flight and her colour is a suitable dull grey. She is second in command, if you will. You do not want to come across her almost as much as you do not want to come across Madrina. They're both two peas from the same decaying pod. Then there is Nyx Orian, who has brown skin and extraordinary golden eyes – you won't be able to miss them and, like Madrina's, you will never be able to forget them either. His gift is speed, he is unnaturally fast. You blink once and he is gone; his colour is cyan – a green-blue. Next is Phoebe Bridgewell, she has blonde hair and big blue eyes; her gift is Petra – the ability to turn people into stone, and her colour is a soft pink.'

I'd noticed the way Jane's voice had adopted a gentler tone when speaking of Phoebe, but I did not want to ask anything that might break her stride.

'Now, who else? Oh yes, Damien Conrad,' Jane continued. 'A man with short black hair, blue eyes, and a muscular physique. He is ashamedly very handsome and his gift is strength beyond any of ours; his colour is a moss green. Hayden Links is and has always been a mystery. Hayden uses her brown hair to conceal her pointed ears; her gift is merely agility, she is nothing more than light on her feet; her colour is a dark purple. For some reason, Madrina seems to value her enough to keep her close, but after all these years I have not been able to figure out why, and so I believe there is some importance surrounding her. It would perhaps be best not to underestimate her. Thulin Dolan is blond with brown eyes and an immeasurable level of arrogance; his gift is heightened senses – he is able to see, hear, and smell things from miles and miles away. He is known for being the most merciless Clider, often surpassing Madrina, which is not a simple feat. He is quick and rash in his desire to kill, whilst Madrina and Sia are more cunning; they would rather calculate your worth before killing you. Thulin's colour is an apt crimson red. Ember Jace has a cold smile that can cause the acid in your stomach to bubble; his gift is the ability to generate electricity from within his body, his preferred method of torture is electrocution.'

I felt the bile from my stomach rise to my throat.

'His colour is jet black and some used to say his colour was an accurate representation for the colour of his soul. Dain Copper wears a permanent scowl that I don't believe even he can change; his gift is telepathy and his colour a burnt orange. Corbin Samuels, whom you will be able to identify as the tallest Clider, has brown hair and hazel eyes, and his gift is intangibility – the ability to walk through solid matter. His colour is a pale yellow.'

So that was who we had seen with Kindle McKay on Murmmers Lane.

'Eris Malva is a blonde clone of Sia; however, they are in no way related. Her gift is invisibility. She *was* considered the most dangerous Clider because you never knew where she would come from, but it was soon learnt that she could not project her invisibility to cover others. I believe Madrina would rather somebody who could do more with their gift than Eris could, but obviously she was unable to discover such a person so had to make do with what she could find. Her colour is a coffee brown. And lastly, Kindle McKay.'

I shifted in my seat and waited for the tightness in my chest to cease.

'Kindle McKay is a woman no taller than five-feet, four-inches, with short hair and a sharp face; her gift is wildfire and her colour an off white, almost like the colour of cream. Kindle McKay is the most notorious Clider as discretion was never her way of dealing with things. She always left destruction in her wake, setting almost everything she saw and touched on long-lasting fire.'

Jane shook her head sadly as I was reminded of Murmmers Lane, which once must have been a lovely looking area, perhaps not so dissimilar to Greenweir Close judging by the corpses of the old houses. The name even hinted at a peaceful town, but now it was nothing but dried ash, crumbling bricks and stray spirits.

'You say you fought them?' I asked quietly.

'Yes, dear,' Jane replied.

'How did you kill them?'

Seeing the Cliders yesterday had been a wake-up call. Ever since I realised what Sidra wanted me to do, what Hayven needed me to do, I still coasted. Because if I couldn't see a Clider, they were still fictional. Something out of a horror story that came to life centuries before I was even born. Now I'd seen two. They were real, they were alive, and they wanted Madrina back. From what I've heard about them, they'd kill for it.

I watched Jane's eyes fill with sympathy and regret. She attempted to reach out to me, but I sat too far away. She placed her small hand back onto the arm of her chair.

'They die such as mortals do. A twist of the neck, a stab in the chest, a pillow over our mouth and nose, and we die, each and every one of us. No gifter has the gift of immortality. Phoebe Bridgewell is perhaps the most important Clider for you; with her ability to turn people into stone, all you need do is smash them to pieces afterwards with your natural strength, which is perhaps the *easiest* way.' Jane sighed. 'It will by no means be easy, Ava, I can promise you that. But there is another thing I can promise you; you end those lives, you save thousands more. I am not as young as I was back then: my joints are stiff, my bones ache, and I struggle to open a jar of jam. I am no use in a fight, but I am useful for advice, so allow me to give you some.'

As she leaned forward in her chair, Theo and I mirrored her action.

'You *need* Phoebe on your side. You must find her and convert her to your cause. She must be on the right side once more.'

'Once more?' Theo repeated.

Jane leaned back into her chair and sighed, her brown eyes glazed over from a past memory. 'Phoebe was a lovely girl. Young, carefree and rosy cheeked, always wearing gingham dresses and plucking up daisies. As she grew older, her manners and politeness never left her. Such a lovely girl indeed.'

'How did she become a Clider?' I asked.

276

'It was either join or die,' Jane said with deep sadness. 'Madrina had a knack for finding those with useful gifts and coercing them to join, no doubt so she could absorb the gifts herself whenever she needed. When talk of Phoebe's gift reached her ears, Madrina personally hunted her down and in exchange for the safety of her family, Phoebe became a Clider.'

'You really think she'll help us?' I asked.

'I admit it is unlikely as last I heard she still has children to protect, but then again, she bares no true love for Madrina. Nonetheless, you must try; you must find her and convince her, it is the only way to make your lives easier. One less Clider is always better than one more.'

'Anyone else we can look to?' Theo asked.

'I'm afraid there is hardly anyone, as no one will believe you when you tell them Madrina will return unless they see it with their own eyes and by that time it will be far too late, but like Phoebe, there are people that you *need*. Three in particular: Giselle Clementine, Everett Stone and Ivy Lamont. Giselle Clementine is a healer, she has the gift of being able to mend broken bones, stitch wounds and sometimes restart a silent heartbeat with nothing more than a touch. Everett Stone has the gift of intelligence, he is the smartest man alive, and Ivy Lamont has a different kind of intangibility to Corbin Samuels. Her gift allows her to not only walk through solid matter, but breathe under water, run through treacherous storms, and walk calmly through fire.'

'Even wildfire?' Theo asked.

'Even wildfire,' Jane confirmed with a nod. 'I'm sure you can see how beneficial they are and no doubt Madrina will see them the same way. Reach them before she does because once she does, you have lost.'

'Where can we find them?'

'Alas, Ava, I do not know. Madrina was last hunting for Everett Stone, but whether she found him or not, I am unaware.' She sighed deeply. 'Those who knew of Madrina's likeliness to find those she deemed valuable went into hiding. I would not be surprised if in over a thousand years they have not come back out. Nobody will be able to describe how horrendous a time it was in Madrina's day.'

'Do you know how Sidra turned Madrina mortal or where the silver orb—?'

Jane shook her head before I had finished my question. 'I'm afraid not, I doubt Sidra told anyone,' she said, and she glanced to Theo for validation, to which he shook his head to say that she was correct.

'Rather silly of her to keep such valuable information to herself, God rest her soul. Still, information like that was perhaps too risky to share with anyone. I do not know the workings of the silver orb or understand the power and knowledge contained within the stars, but I'll bet every last penny I have that Everett Stone does.'

CHAPTER TWENTY-FOUR

'Everett Stone? Yeah, I've heard of him. Smartest guy in recorded history,' Ollie said. 'He's also my dinner guest.'

'Dinner guest?' I asked.

'Yeah, you know, when people ask you, if you could invite anyone to dinner, dead or alive, who would it be? My choice would be Everett Stone.'

'Oh. Mine would have to be Roald Dahl,' I said.

'Mine would be Martin Luther King,' Theo added.

'Good choice,' Ollie said.

'Really?' I asked Theo. I didn't know why I was surprised, I just was.

'Absolutely,' Theo answered. 'A man as inspirational as him has to be a great conversationalist.'

I smiled and turned back to Ollie. 'So do you know where this Everett Stone is?'

'Definitely not.' Ollie shook his head. 'Nobody does. Nobody has seen him in such a long time; people question whether he's still alive. People say he disappeared; I like to think he's just keeping to himself. He could be in Hayven, he could be elsewhere. With a gift like that, he could fit in anywhere. He could always play his intelligence down and people would think he was just a normal guy with an extremely high IQ.'

'So he could be anywhere?' I asked.

'He could be anywhere,' Ollie answered gravely.

We'd come down to Fulton University Library in hopes that Ollie would know anything about Everett Stone that could help us.

'Jane's piece of advice was a good one,' Ollie said. 'We could use Everett. I have so many questions that I can't figure out or even *find* the answers to.'

'Like what?' Theo asked.

'Well, for starters, surely you can't just *pick* the stars from the sky, or else what's stopping everybody from doing it? I need to know how Madrina does it as that's the only way for me to figure out how to, in a sense, reverse it. Also, I've been doing some additional reading...' and he patted the top of a towering stack of books piled on the table we were currently sitting at, '...on many things, but more specifically on turning gifters into mortals. I thought that could help us too.'

'Find anything interesting?' Theo asked as he picked up and flicked through the thinnest book in Ollie's pile, which still managed to be at least three hundred pages long.

'Sort of...it's not entirely clear.'

The frustration emanating from Ollie was palpable. On the day Theo had walked off, feeling frustrated himself, I'd given the guys a good telling off. Since then, they'd all taken things a lot more seriously, but no one more so than Ollie. Since he was the brains of the group, I think he saw it as his responsibility to be able to provide answers to all of the questions we might ask, so he had spent day after day reading books in the library and pestering teachers for extra information without giving anything vital away. Oliver-Raine was a naturally clever guy, so it was no surprise to me that he got incredibly annoyed when he couldn't find an answer he was looking for.

'I'd love to find out if Everett knows – he must,' Ollie continued. 'The thing is, mortals can't travel to Hayven because of the invisible barrier between Hayven and the rest of the world. Meaning, *technically*, Madrina shouldn't be able to return to Hayven, but since she can age as a gifter and has gifted blood...'

I immediately saw his point. 'So, there's a chance Madrina won't be able to get through?'

'There *should* be, but in your vision you saw her return, therefore there must be a way of her getting into Hayven, but I'm assuming it can't be easy, so maybe we can make it harder. It's all very confusing,' Ollie said, rubbing his forehead. 'Gifters being made into mortals isn't a common occurrence so there's hardly anything written about it in these books. I asked my History Studies teacher, Professor O'Brian, but he thinks the same thing I do: that there *is* a way for someone who is mortal with gifted blood to get into Hayven, but he doesn't know *how*.'

'Seems like finding this Everett Stone will be the answer to a lot of our problems,' Theo stated.

'Perhaps we could have a look through old school records and trace the surname Stone, see if we can find a member of his family. It's a long shot, but we've got nothing to lose,' Ollie suggested.

'It's worth a try,' I encouraged.

'Right, I'll print the names off the school system,' Ollie said, getting up from his chair.

'I've got a shift at the bookstore; I'll catch up with you two later,' Theo said, and with a nod to Ollie and a soft touch on the back of the neck for me, he was gone.

'That's a lot of Stones you've got there,' I said, as Ollie returned from the printer with a thick wodge of paper with names on them.

'You can say that again,' Ollie replied. 'Can you believe that this isn't even all of them? The printer ran out of paper before I could print the rest. Now, I couldn't print out their pictures, but I could print out what courses they take and even better, I recognise a few of these names.'

For three days we searched for a Stone related to Everett, but as it was a very common surname, and over twenty thousand students attended Fulton University, it was proving to be quite a difficult and daunting task. Fortunately, we got a break one Thursday afternoon when Ollie and I were heading to the science department to find Emily Stone. My shoulder bag strap had managed to slide down my arm and when I'd lifted my arm to put it back in place, my exposed skin accidentally brushed against the hand of a passing boy. The touch was so feather light he hadn't noticed and I wouldn't have either if his name hadn't flashed in my head, *Thomas Noah Everett Stone*.

When searching for Stones I kept my mind open in order to gather whether it was truth or lies hidden within their denial, and thankfully I had kept my mind open since we had spoken to Casper Stone mere moments ago. I grabbed Ollie by the back of his shirt.

'I found him,' I said to Ollie. 'Thomas Stone!' I shouted in the direction the boy was walking in.

'Yes?' he said, turning around, bemused.

Thomas Noah Everett Stone was a skinny guy, no older than twenty, with a mop of brown curls and glasses that brushed his nose. He wore brown corduroy trousers, a lime green woollen jumper, despite the heat in Hayven, and a heavy looking rucksack on his back. But there was something else about him, something about his curly hair... Then it hit me. He was the boy, or rather young man, I'd seen that night I'd found Sidra in *Hayven Books*. When Sidra had taken hold of my wrist, images had flickered through the forefront of my brain, and one of those images had been of this young man – Thomas Stone.

What could that possibly mean?

'Hello,' I said, suddenly unaware of how to proceed. Usually Ollie or I would ask the standard question: do you know Everett Stone? But since I knew this boy must, it seemed rather futile. I also didn't want to scare him off by mentioning that I had seen him in some sort of freaky vision months ago. 'My name is Ava and this is my friend, Ollie.' I gestured to Ollie, who gave Thomas a friendly smile.

'Oh, urm, hello,' Thomas replied, trepidation heavy in his voice.

I chose to forget about the vision for now and focus on why we'd been looking for Thomas in the first place. 'I know this is going to sound odd, but do you have a moment to talk to us?' I asked.

He looked questioningly at Ollie and I before he decided it was safe. 'Sure, okay,' he said, and the three of us headed towards the exit.

'How do you know it's him?' Ollie whispered as we walked behind Thomas.

'His name flashed in my head,' I answered. 'Thomas Noah *Everett* Stone.'

Ollie's eyebrows shot up. 'Man, I should have brought dinner.'

'How can I help you?' Thomas asked politely once we had all taken a seat on a bench under a shady tree.

'We just wanted to know, do you know Everett Stone?' I asked.

His face betrayed nothing, a complete mask. 'No, I'm afraid I don't,' he said.

'Yes you do,' Ollie said.

'No, I don't.' *How does he know? Don't say anything, Tom. Just excuse yourself and get up.* 'I have to —'

'Your name is Thomas Noah Everett Stone,' I said.

Thomas slowly sank back into his seat. 'How do you know that?' he asked.

'It's…part of my gift,' I answered truthfully.

'Whatever it is you both want, I can't help you,' he said, making another motion to get up and leave.

'Seriously, Tom, would you just relax?' Ollie scolded gently. 'Do we look like trouble?'

Thomas looked to us both in turn and for the second time, sank slowly back into his seat.

'I suppose not…'

'Do you know Everett Stone?' I asked again.

I could sense his internal struggle as his gaze swivelled from Ollie to me and back again countless times.

Should I tell her? She seems friendly and harmless enough. Don't know if I can say the same about her friend though…but she does seem nice.

I smiled a warm yet pleading smile.

'Yes,' he said finally, before adding, 'he's my great-grandfather.'

'Is he still alive?' I asked hopefully.

'Yes.'

Relief flooded through me. 'Do you know where he is?'

'Can I lie to you?'

'I'd rather you didn't,' I admitted.

'But can I? As in, will you know I'm lying?'

'Yes.'

Thomas heaved a soft sigh. 'Then yes, I do.'

'Are you allowed to tell people where he is?' Ollie asked.

'He's advised me not to,' Thomas answered. 'He lives a quiet life and has done so for…a long time. He's always preferred his own company, but being who he is, people always want to talk to him and ask him questions about things he'd rather not discuss. Which I'm guessing is what you both want to do?'

Ollie and I nodded shamelessly.

'Why?' Thomas asked.

'What's your gift?' I asked him.

'Invisibility.'

My blood ran cold. I'd never experienced that feeling before and it was like everything functioning in my body just stopped, frozen by ice.

No two gifters were the same. Jane had said that Eris Malva could not project her invisibility and Madrina kept her close because she could not find somebody who could, no doubt because he hadn't been born yet…

'Ollie's a weather changer,' I said, noting the tremor in my voice but making sure not to betray my thoughts in any other way. Thomas looked to Ollie with awe. 'And

I'm…well, I don't really know for sure what I am, but simply put, I…*specialise* in telepathy and precognition.'

His look of awe transferred to me.

'You have *two* gifts?'

'Yes,' I replied. *Although, technically, one of them isn't really mine.*

'Did you say precognition?' Thomas asked. 'So, you're a future-seer… you can see the future?'

'Yes.'

Thomas drew back. 'Did you see my grandfather?'

'I thought he was your *great*-grandfather?' Ollie said.

'He is, but I call him grandfather because calling him great-grandfather all the time sounds odd,' Thomas explained before turning back to me. 'So did you see him?'

'No…I saw Madrina —'

Thomas recoiled sharply.

'— and her Cliders,' I finished.

'It's not possible.' He exhaled slowly.

'Nothing is impossible,' I said with a wry smile at the thought and mention of Theo's words. 'I saw Madrina return with her eleven Cliders. I can't stop the future, but I can change it.'

'How?' he asked.

I was uncertain on how much to divulge. I had hoped to live by Sidra's advice, seeing as it was about all she had really given me, by keeping important details between only me and my six close friends. But I couldn't ignore having seen Thomas in a vision, so he had to be important. What I had to decide for myself was whether he was important in a good way or a bad way. I couldn't afford to mess up, but I needed Thomas's help, and to get it, the truth needed to be told.

'I see the future,' I said, 'we are currently in the present. Madrina has not returned *yet*, but she will, unless she doesn't have all her Cliders, but that part isn't necessary for you.' I looked to Ollie for help.

'Madrina wasn't destroyed,' Ollie explained, 'she was turned mortal. However, in Ava's vision, Madrina returns to full power in Hayven. As we all know, mortals can't travel to Hayven, but somehow Madrina manages it, whether it is because of her gifted blood or the power she'll get from the silver orb, we don't know, but we think your great-grandfather will.'

'So ...you *just* want to speak to him?' Thomas clarified.

'What else would we want?' I asked.

Thomas gave a hesitant look.

Ollie laughed. 'We're not *recruiting* and we wouldn't expect your great-grandfather to join our cause even if we were. You however, may be a different story.'

Terror flashed in Thomas's eyes. He obviously wasn't sure if Ollie was joking or not. Neither was I.

'We *just* want to speak to Everett, that's all,' Ollie repeated.

'The Cliders wanted him before…when they return, they'll want him again…he's so old,' Thomas said, sympathy etched deep on his young face.

'*If* they return,' I rectified.

'Talking to my grandfather might stop their return,' he said, more so to himself than to us, but Ollie and I nodded anyway.

Thomas looked at me, his glasses unable to conceal the indecision and anxiety that flooded his hazel eyes. He took a deep breath and said, 'Okay.'

'Okay?'

'I'll take you to see him.'

Thomas took us to Gaige's apartment block and went to the very top floor where there were three cream coloured doors…or so we thought.

Thomas walked to the very end of the corridor where there was nothing but empty wall space. He grabbed at thin air, gripped *something*, and pulled whatever it was to the side, causing the air to ripple.

'Woah,' Ollie gasped.

I had been right about Thomas being able to project his invisibility. Whatever Thomas had pulled away, revealed a door, cream coloured like the rest. The scene chilled me. After speaking with Everett, I could haul Thomas in no further. If I failed, and there was always the possibility of that, Madrina would somehow find out about Thomas and his gift. The more distance I put between him and me, the safer he'd most likely be.

Thomas smiled shyly at Ollie's approval as he pulled keys out of his pocket. 'It's sort of an invisibility shield,' he said by way of explanation.

'Can he walk through it?' Ollie asked intrigued.

'No,' Thomas answered, 'but he doesn't need to, he hardly goes out.'

'How many people know of your gift, Thomas?' I asked.

'Aside from my family? Not many,' he replied.

'Promise me something?'

'What?'

'Make sure you keep it that way.'

'Why?' he asked.

'What you can do,' I said, pointing at the door, 'no one else can. That's very valuable, and I won't be the only person to think that.'

Thomas instantly grasped what I meant and nodded bashfully, and as he opened the front door, the smell of old books and potpourri floated out to greet us.

'Thomas?' came a weak croak. 'Is that you?'

As we walked through the corridor, I found books covering every single surface. We were definitely in the right place. In the living room were more books, so many more books. It was difficult to imagine so many books in one room without the house itself being a library.

The flames from the fireplace cast light and shadows, revealing books of every size and colour. Books with black spines and purple faces, and books with white edges and brown pages. Books stood with their spines facing out from sturdy bookshelves, their neighbours aged, their charismatic covers probably filled with wrinkled, tea-stained pages that crackled with every open and close of the book and turn of a page. Books filled with action-packed adventures and haunting historical horrors, poignant poetry and powerful prose, sung songs and quiet thoughts, hidden knowledge and spoken truths, tragic tales and nonsensical words – each story breathing life into the reader until the last page was read and another book was lifted, allowing another life to begin.

There had to be all sorts of different books in the room. Books with crinkled, creased, and peeling spines, and supple leather bound books. Educational books read by scholars during the day, and guilty pleasures read at midnight; stories for young children and fables for all ages. I thought of dog-eared corners and forgotten bookmarks poking out of books left behind, clutching promises that their reader would return. I thought of memorable manuscripts and self-published works, young paperbacks and ancient hardbacks, piled on top of one another. Small handbooks leaned against large volumes, and known publications sat beside anonymous titles, causing the tables it sat on to teeter precariously, but never to wobble. Filled exercise books with short-lived ideas, used reference books, and thumbed-through guides all jumbled onto another shelf. The smell of potpourri somewhat masked the smell of this library, but the smell of books was always apparent to me no matter how subtle the scent; the quaint musty smell never escaped me. It also smelt of hardly dried ink on fresh paper. It smelt of years and years of moments spent in front of a dancing fire, turning pages, and often peering up to notice the rain droplets on windows.

An old man, whose face I couldn't see due to his chair facing away from the entrance door, sat in front of an electric fire. It blazed cheerily, sending its warmth and light across the room, permitting the actual room lights to remain switched off. Next to the chair was a long black sofa. In between the chairs and fireplace, a glass coffee table stood with only a wooden bowl on it, filled with sweets. Apart from the grand piano in the back, if it were not for all the books and furniture, the room would be empty. As I stepped further in, carefully navigating around scattered book piles, I was taken aback. I hadn't thought people in Hayven could arrive at an age so...*old*.

Everett Stone was a very thin man, even in a thick purple robe. He had wrinkles, lines and creases covering every inch of his skin, reminding him and telling others of the joys and miseries, the trials and tribulations, he had encountered throughout his long life. His remaining hair was wispy and white, his lips thin, and his sagging eyes a watery pale blue. But there was such a kindness on his face you could not look away from.

'Of course it's me, little guy,' Thomas said, smiling warmly down at Everett.

'Nice to see you too, big guy,' Everett replied slowly, smiling up at Thomas.

'And it is nice to meet you two,' he said, looking to Ollie and me. He spoke very softly and very slowly, as if each word was an effort to speak, it was almost impossible to hear him – *almost*.

'I can't believe I didn't bring dinner,' Ollie whispered to me before facing Everett. 'Hello, Mr Stone. Please don't be angry with Thomas for bringing us here, we just —'

Everett interrupted Ollie's apology with a deep, shaky chuckle. 'Angry?' he repeated. 'How could I be angry? If only you knew how nice it is to see new faces. Thomas is very protective and hardly brings anyone round, so your visit is most welcome and must be important. Please, sit.

'Would you like a sweet?' he asked, pointing a thin finger to the bowl on the glass table.

Before Ollie and I could answer, Thomas picked up the bowl and offered it firstly to Everett who gratefully took one, unwrapped it and popped it into his mouth with measured and practised fingers, sighing softly at the taste.

291

Thomas then took one for himself before offering the bowl to us, and Ollie and I each took one. 'These are his favourites,' Thomas said, throwing his into his mouth.

'Would you like something to drink?' Everett asked.

'No, thank you, sir.' I was quite thirsty, but didn't want to be a burden to such a lovely old man.

I unwrapped my sweet to reveal a hard boiled, dark purple jewel. I searched the pastel purple wrapper to find that there was no name or brand mark. I popped it into my mouth and was about to address Everett when my mouth began to water uncontrollably. I could hear Ollie beside me, desperately trying to control the amount of saliva in his mouth as well, whilst Thomas and Everett sucked expertly on their sweets.

The taste was *delicious*. There was simply no other way to describe it. It tasted of dark purple grapes that carried both sour acidity and sweet fruit juice. Even though the juice ran from the sweet and spilt all over my taste buds making them tingle, it didn't seem to decrease in size. How odd…

'How is school, Thomas?' Everett asked.

'It's going well,' Thomas answered. 'How is your chest? Any better?'

'I am an old man, Thomas, my chest is as good as it is ever going to get,' Everett replied with a smile. 'Now, how may I be of assistance to your friends?'

'To tell you the truth, I've only just met them,' he replied. 'This is Ava and this is Ollie.'

'Sir, it is a privilege to meet you, sincerely,' Ollie said. *What a nerd.* I smiled.

'Thank you, young man. It is kind of you to say so,' Everett said.

'Sir, we came because...well, we need to pick your brain,' I said.

Everett chuckled softly; it was a contagious sound that reminded me of babbling brooks. 'What an odd expression, but I understand what it is you mean. What is it you wish to know?'

I let Ollie explain Madrina and the barrier to Hayven.

Everett's face stilled. 'Why do you ask such a question?' he whispered.

Ollie and I hesitated. Upsetting Everett wasn't part of the plan. I wanted to leave the man in peace and try to figure it all out by myself, but we had all tried to do that and had come up with nothing.

'Ava is a future-seer,' Thomas said. 'She saw Madrina return.' Thomas looked to Everett for confirmation, as if to say that if Everett denied it, he would too.

I didn't know whether to expect a reaction similar to Gaige or similar to Jane. We thankfully received the latter.

Everett nodded gravely, the folds under his eyes sagging deeper. 'I see.'

'You're not surprised?' I asked.

'Only the people that know Madrina did not die will not be surprised when they hear your words, afraid, yes, but not surprised,' Everett said. 'I am deeply saddened to say that you're at the starting line of a very long and difficult race when it is time for you to tell others.'

'Who else knows Madrina didn't die?' asked Ollie.

'Only those Sidra told, which I am assuming is only a few.'

'Were you close with Sidra, sir?' I asked.

'I suppose you could say so. I wouldn't say we forged a particularly strong friendship, but we were both in the same situation; both prisoners of Madrina.'

'You were captured?' I asked astonished. 'She found you?'

'Yes,' he replied gravely at the memory. 'She found everyone she wanted to find; you could not hide from Madrina. Being a prisoner of Madrina consisted of months of uncertainty and never ending darkness, unaware of whether the sun has set or if it has risen. I only managed to escape with the help of Sidra.'

'How?' I enquired, knowing the information would one day come in handy.

'She knew a courageous shifter who was able to shift in and take us with her on her way out,' Everett answered. 'You dare not travel. Many times prisoners and captives attempted to escape through means of travel and it never ended well. All a Clider need do was travel in the same spot you did, mix their colours with yours, and they would land wherever you did.' Everett's frail bones shuddered and I feared the vigorous action would disconnect them. 'Too many a wretched time did I witness a Clider travel with an attempted escapee and return with nothing but a smile on their face. Such terrible times they were.'

'What did Madrina want with you?' I asked.

'My intelligence,' he replied. 'She wished to know the true power of the stars.'

'How did she get the stars?' Ollie questioned, leaning forward in his seat.

'With her gift,' Everett answered. 'You see, it was me who realised that Madrina's gift wasn't simply the ability to absorb other gifts; she was given the ability to absorb *power*. I refused to tell her such a thing of course, knowing what trouble it would cause, so I kept it to myself. Alas, one night she absorbed my gift of knowledge and found the answer herself.'

Everett fell into silence and we dared not talk him out of it. If Madrina hadn't absorbed Everett's gift, she would never have found out about the stars and the silver orb would be what most people believed it was – a myth. I hoped Everett didn't blame himself, as he had tried his best to conceal the truth, but in the end like many other gifters, he'd had no choice.

'Oh, young man, I do apologise; I failed to answer your first question,' Everett said suddenly. 'I am afraid there are ways for Madrina to return to Hayven. Though she is mortal, gifted blood still runs free through her veins. For the sake of making this simpler, let us say she is half mortal and half gifted. The invisible barrier between Naveya and the rest of the world only allows the fully gifted to pass through it. Therefore, whilst Madrina cannot easily make it through, the barrier is *weaker* in her case. The barrier will be somewhat *confused* if you please, at the mortal with the gifted blood. And so a confused and weak barrier…is a destroyable one.'

'She means to break the barrier?' Thomas asked. I had almost forgotten he was here.

'I do not think she will break the barrier completely, rather she will break through it. Or she will go with her only other option – the silver orb. The orb will be capable of restoring Madrina's gift. Therefore, if the silver orb exists here in Naveya, all one would need do is to deliver it to wherever

Madrina now resides. Then, once gifted again, she can re-enter Hayven,' Everett explained.

'How am I to stop her?'

'It shall not be easy, Ava, not in the slightest, so it is important you prepare yourself for this grim journey ahead. You must not go into war unprepared.' Everett took a moment to restore his breathing. 'Hayven will grow darker and people will die. People before you made the mistake of thinking this war between them and Madrina was a game, easy to conquer, and they suffered immensely for that mind-set. Many talented and strong gifters went against Madrina and her eleven most valued Cliders and the simple fact that *all* Cliders remain alive…well, that, as you kids say, speaks volumes, does it not? With the stars on her side Madrina is almost all-powerful; you must not allow it to get that far this time. Your fight will seem futile and unmanageable at times; your days harder, longer, and much darker, but you must always remember that nothing in this world is impossible if you are willing to fight for it.

'Madrina is not your main concern at the moment, it is her Cliders, as she is nothing without them,' he said. 'You finish them, you finish Madrina.'

I nodded soberly, this I knew.

'Might I suggest something?'

'Of course,' Ollie and I both said.

'There is one Clider whom you would most benefit from having on your side.'

'Phoebe Bridgewell?'

'Who?' Ollie and Thomas asked in unison.

'Yes,' Everett answered. 'You know of Miss Bridgewell?'

'Yes,' I said. 'I met Sidra's half-sister, Jane Hartleigh, a few days ago. She informed us of Phoebe Bridgewell and her gift. How she was the most reluctant Clider and there was a chance we could get her to work with us.'

Everett chortled warmly. 'Ah yes, lovely Jane. Phoebe would indeed be very beneficial because of her gift. Also, her heart is not as dedicated to Madrina's cause as the other Cliders are. She was a good friend of Sidra's, so there is always that small hope that she may seek retribution for what happened to her. Not forgetting of course, that she will have information on Madrina and the Cliders that can prove useful.'

'What is Phoebe's gift?' Ollie asked.

'She can turn people into stone,' I answered.

Everett nodded approvingly at me. 'The more you know of your enemies, the easier it is to destroy them,' he said. 'If your endeavour to persuade Phoebe Bridgewell proves unsuccessful, your next, if not only, course of action is to find the silver orb before the Cliders do, and destroy it. I do not know where it is, I could not even provide a guess, but I do believe it still exists,' he finished, following with an unintentional yawn that caused his jowls to quiver.

'You must be tired, sir,' Ollie stated. 'We should leave you to rest. Thank you so much for everything. Is it alright if we were to have any more questions we could ask Thomas to pass them onto you?'

'Of course, young man, I am at your service; feel free to drop by yourselves,' Everett said with a kind smile. 'But I warn you, I am not long for this world, not long at all.'

I saw Thomas sadden immediately. He knew it was true.

'So any questions you may have, I advise you to ask soon, sooner rather than later because you're right, Ava. As sure as I am that there are still bones in my body, Madrina will return.' He turned back to stare into the fire. 'I can feel it.'

We made to leave before something occurred to me.

'Sir, just one more question.'

'Yes?'

'When you were captured, where did they take you?'

Everett quivered gently at the thought, his frail body not allowing him to exert himself more than that. 'A very cold and dark place. A place with no windows or doors. A warehouse I believe it was. On Murmmers Lane.'

'Thank you, sir.'

We left, still sucking on our purple sweets.

CHAPTER TWENTY-FIVE

'It all keeps coming back to Phoebe Bridgewell,' Theo said once I'd filled him in on our findings later on in the week. 'Kindle McKay and Corbin Samuels are the only Cliders reunited so far...hopefully. So who knows where she is?' he continued. 'If what Jane and Everett say about her not wanting to be a Clider is true – and I highly doubt it's not – then she's most likely in hiding so Madrina won't be able to easily find her.'

'But how does she know Madrina will come back?' I asked.

'Maybe she's not been out of hiding since,' he replied. 'Maybe it's like what Everett and Jane both said, those who know Madrina didn't die, know she'll return.'

He threw his empty milkshake cup into a bin. 'Are you going to finish that?' he asked, pointing to my chocolate milkshake. I handed it over and rolled my eyes with a smile. 'Thanks.' He grinned and took a long, grateful sip.

'Do you think we can find her?' I asked.

'Who knows?' he replied. 'Ollie informed me that in school records Thomas is only recorded as Thomas Noah Stone, so without the "Everett" people won't make the link. No doubt any family members of Phoebe Bridgewell have done the same thing and that's if they even attend Fulton, which is unlikely. But on the off chance that one of her relatives *does*, then the only way you're likely to find them is by going around and touching everyone until their real names flash in your head.'

'Sounds time consuming,' I opined.

Theo laughed. 'So, do you think the silver orb still exists?'

'Yes,' I answered. 'Everett believes it does and I trust his judgement. Not to mention it explains Sidra's death. Chances are that was what the Cliders were looking for when they murdered her. Either she refused to tell them its location or, she actually didn't know. I think she just refused because according to the story so far, the last person in possession of the silver orb had to be Sidra herself. Madrina is still alive, that's now a fact, meaning the orb hasn't been destroyed. So maybe it's hidden?'

'Most likely,' Theo said with a nod. 'It's either hidden somewhere or hidden with someone. Although, I'm leaning more towards the idea of it being hidden somewhere. I can't think of anyone Sidra would trust with it, except maybe Jane, but she said she didn't know where it was,' he concluded. He reached up and pulled my ponytail.

'What was that for?' I asked.

'I actually have no idea,' he said, his facial expression as nonplussed as mine. 'Impulsive decision we can call it.'

'You seem to be getting stranger every day, Theo,' I stated, fixing my hair. 'It worries me sometimes.'

He snorted. 'It worries me too. Anyway, back to the silver orb. Maybe we should concentrate on finding that over Phoebe because if we have the silver orb...then it's over before it has even started. I mean, the Cliders would most definitely seek revenge, but I'd rather deal with them than deal with them as well as Madrina.'

'I like the way you think, Theodore,' I said. 'Just one *tiny* problem. Nobody knows where the silver orb is.'

Theo laughed. 'That in no way means we can't find it! We just have to think of all the possible places Sidra may have hidden it. Then rip those places apart in order to uncover it.'

Just then, Theo's phone began to ring. When he fished it out of his pocket, the name Abbey flashed on the screen. 'Oh balls,' he murmured, reading the name. 'I forgot I signed up for late-night stock take.' He answered the phone call from his colleague and told her he'd be right there.

'What's so funny?' he asked, addressing my smile once he'd hung up.

'I didn't know you used "balls" as a substitute for a swear word, too.'

'Oh yeah,' Theo said. 'I love saying "balls" now.'

I did a double take.

Theo slowly turned to face me. 'Okay, that part of the conversation never happened,' he said.

'I beg to differ.'

'I'm leaving now,' he announced, beginning to travel.

'Doesn't mean you didn't say it,' I shouted at his indigo blue dots.

I swear I'd *felt* him smile.

I decided to make my way to Baleigh's house to catch her up on the latest events; it was almost nine at night so I figured she'd be home now. I'd been to her house enough times that not only did Baleigh call it my third home – after my home in London and room in Huxton – but I could easily travel there too. Yet I decided to walk; it was only fifteen minutes away and it was a warm night.

It was probably imprudent of me to feel so calm about things concerning Madrina, but that's something I've always done. Life was too short to worry about danger that wasn't staring you in the face at the minute, although it's likely your life would be cut even shorter if you waited long enough for danger to find you. But that wasn't the case. I was moving forward. I no longer felt like someone was watching me, there'd been no more spontaneous wildfire occurrences, no disappearing stars by my reckoning, and with the discovery of Phoebe Bridgewell, finding a way to inhibit Madrina's return looked almost possible. I'm not naïve enough to believe that getting Phoebe on board would be the easiest thing, but given her track record with Madrina, perhaps it wouldn't be the hardest.

'Oh. Ava.'

I'd been so wrapped up in my own thoughts I hadn't noticed myself walk straight up to Summer.

Oh, what fresh hell is this?

Summer hated me. I had no idea why, but I knew she did and she made it undeniably clear whenever we were together by either ignoring me completely or feigning a yawn whenever I spoke. At least she didn't say what she thought of me out loud and I'd now made it a rule to block her thoughts out whenever I was near her.

I took a deep breath and forced a smile. 'Hello, Summer. What can I do for you today?'

She rolled her eyes at my spurious politeness. 'Have you seen Theo?' she asked. 'I'm sure you have.'

There was an unmistakable edge to her voice; this was all I needed.

'No, I haven't,' I replied and made to carry on in my path, but she grabbed me by my arm.

'Wait, I haven't finished yet,' she simpered sickly. 'I'm glad I ran into you today. I've been meaning to tell you something,' she stopped to look me directly in my eyes, and hers were blue glass. 'Stay away from Theo.'

I blanched as if she'd raised her hand to slap me. Summer usually threw me dirty looks whenever she found me with Theo, but her boorishness shocked me nonetheless. Then again, I should always remember that even the cutest kittens have claws.

'You need to stay away from my boyfriend, Ava,' she continued, true menace in her eyes. 'You're always hanging on around him. Can't you get your own boyfriend? Is that why you're always sniffing around *mine*?'

'Watch it, Summer,' I warned. 'Take your hand off my arm.'

As she did so, her face contorted to illustrate she was disgusted at the thought of having touched me for so long.

'I mean it, Ava,' she said. 'I won't tell you again. Do yourself a favour and go for someone more in your league.'

'My *league*?'

'Yes,' Summer said. 'Someone who would…*suit* you better. And that someone isn't Theo. You're fat, bland and not his type.'

I slapped her across the face and her right cheek glowed pink before switching up to red.

'Are you insane?' she spat. 'Just wait until I tell Theo about this. He'll get rid of you himself.'

'When you see him tell him I said hi, and that this afternoon was fun,' I shouted after her as she walked away.

I stood where I was until she disappeared around a corner, and my smile fell. *Don't let what she said get to you. Don't let it get to you.* I shook myself off and carried on to Baleigh's house.

'Oh, hey,' Baleigh said upon opening the door. 'What's up with your face? You're bright red.'

I must have looked a disaster. The rain had announced itself suddenly before I'd arrived at Baleigh's. My hair was wet and hung limp in its ponytail, my clothes were plastered to my skin, and my face was painted red after replaying Summer's comments in my head for so long. However, the sight before me was a much more *interesting* one to say the least.

Baleigh was wearing pastel pink flannel pyjamas with *cupcakes* on them, and slippers in the shape of fuzzy bears covered her feet and ankles. Her hair was tied up, a few strands free, she wore not a single scrap of make-up, and she held a giant tub of ice cream with a silver spoon sticking out of it. A small chuckle escaped my lips and I'd had to wipe my nose with the back of my hand.

'What's so funny?' she asked.

'It's not even 9 p.m.,' I answered.

'So?' Baleigh shrugged, a hint of a smile playing on her lips. 'A girl has to get her beauty sleep. Besides, Faye got me these pyjamas, so I'm obligated to wear them every now and again. Come in, you're letting the warm air out.'

I gratefully shuffled in and closed the door behind me before Baleigh made her way up the stairs that led to the second landing where her bedroom was.

'So what happened?' she asked.

'I slapped Summer across the face.'

'Hey, that's not fair. I've been dying to do that for ages.'

'Bales? Who was it at the door?' I heard Mrs Castel ask.

'It's Ava.'

'Ah,' Mrs Castel said, entering from the kitchen. 'Ava, are you alright? You look rather upset.'

'I'm fine, Mrs Castel, thank you.'

'Alright, if you're sure,' she said. 'However, you must change out of those clothes immediately or you'll catch a cold.'

'I've got it covered,' Baleigh said. 'Come, Ava.'

I smiled at Mrs Castel before following Baleigh up the stairs. I was glad I had decided to come, I felt better already; I was still soaking wet and dripping on the carpet, but better.

Baleigh threw me some dry clothes and a towel for my hair before she sat on her bed to finish her ice cream whilst I changed. I loved Baleigh's room because it really showed off her softer side and I was all for that. I'd been in here numerous times, but the effect never wore off. Her walls were painted the same soft pastel violet colour she melted into when she travelled, and she'd gotten giant star-shaped stencils and traced them in black paint so that neat and thin black stars were dotted spaciously on her violet sky. Her four poster bed was next to the window and her desk was up against the opposite wall, leaving the middle of her room a cream-coloured, carpeted space. Her walk-in wardrobe and her en suite bathroom were hidden behind two white doors on the opposite side of the entrance door with the words *bathroom* and *wardrobe* imprinted on them in black italics. The bathroom was decorated tastefully in black and white with a few violet coloured towels and flowers, and her wardrobe was almost the size of my room in Huxton; carpeted and bright, filled neatly with clothes and shoes.

'What's with the ice cream?' I asked. I pushed her large lavender club chair near the bedside table across from Baleigh once I'd changed. It was by far my favourite chair to curl up in, and today was no exception.

Baleigh looked up at me from the tub. 'I like ice cream,' she answered with a baffled expression. 'Bit of a silly question.'

I rolled my eyes. 'Baleigh, I know this will be difficult for you, but could you try and be, oh, I don't know, *comforting* right now?'

'I could *try*,' she replied, 'but I've tried before and it didn't end very well. Nevertheless, I'll give it a go. What's wrong, Ava?'

'Well, Summer said some rude things to me today.'

Baleigh laughed. 'You sound like a child tattling on their sister.'

'*Baleigh.*'

'I told you I was no good at this!' Baleigh retorted. 'Okay, I'll try a different approach. Why did you slap Summer? What exactly did she say to you?'

'Basically that I should stay away from Theo because I'm fat, bland and not his type,' I answered.

Baleigh laughed again. 'Of course she called you fat. It's a petty girl's go-to with anyone over a size ten.'

'You don't think I am, do you?'

'No, I don't,' she answered, 'and if I did, I'd tell you.'

'And you don't think I'm bland-looking, do you?'

'I do not.'

306

'You'd date me, right?'

Baleigh slowly turned to look at me. 'I fear this conversation has taken a turn for the worse. Where are you going with this, Ava?'

'What?'

'It sounds like you're coming onto me.'

'What? No!'

She propped herself up on her elbows. 'Now, don't take it personally. I think you're great and everything, but you're just not my type.'

I paused. 'You could do a lot worse,' I declared. 'And why aren't I your type?' I asked, suddenly offended. First guys and now girls were closing their doors to me. 'What's wrong with me?'

'Well, for starters you have boobs and various other lady parts that I'm not interested in. I shoot my arrows in straight lines, if you know what I mean.'

'You'd be lucky to land a girl like me,' I said.

'Would I?'

'Yes, you would! I can cook,' I said, 'and I'm very clean because I shower twice a day.'

'That's quite a list you've got there,' Baleigh said. 'How are you in the bedroom?'

'*Baleigh*!' I blushed bright red and looked away.

'What?' she asked. 'If you want to be my girlfriend these are the kind of things I'll have to know!'

'I don't want to be your girlfriend,' I mumbled.

'You're blushing so I'm going to have to disagree,' she riposted.

'Okay, let's change topic, please.'

'Fine, but it's the twenty-first century, Ava. *Embrace* your sexuality,' she whispered.

'I've officially stopped listening to you, now,' I announced.

'Look, don't worry about Summer,' Baleigh advised. 'Theo will come to his senses soon enough; he can't remain stupid forever. He'll wake up one morning and realise how much of a fake bitch she is, and she really is. She creeps me out; I don't trust two-faced people. All adorable and breathy one minute, then as soon as Theo's back is turned, the exact opposite. Oh, and concerning the "stay away from Theo" speech? Definitely don't worry about that, I've heard it before.'

'Really?'

'Yes, really. She thinks girls and guys can't be best friends, so I'm obviously after something. I had been all set to pounce on her, but Ollie dragged me away before I got my chance. But perhaps Santa's decided to give me a break and Christmas has come early.'

It was June.

'What are you talking about, Baleigh?' I asked warily.

'Calling you fat is unacceptable and I've suddenly decided I won't stand for it,' Baleigh said. 'It's time for her to go, and if Theo hasn't got the balls to do it then it's my duty as his friend to do what must be done.'

'Which is?' I asked, wondering if this was something I needed to warn Theo about.

'I don't know yet.' There was an unmistakable gleam in her brown eyes. 'I've found that the best acts are always improvised, but I can promise you one thing, it won't be pleasant for her. That evil troll, who does she think she is?'

'Your best friend's girlfriend?' I ventured.

'Your point?' Baleigh asked. 'Theo's told me countless times how self-obsessed and clingy she is and if he isn't that fond of her, I don't see why I should be.'

'Wait,' I said, 'if Theo isn't *fond* of Summer, why are they still together?'

'This thing he calls a "conscious",' Baleigh responded. 'Theo was Summer's *first time* and they only started dating a couple of months ago. If he just drops her now, admittedly, it'll look like he was only after one thing from the start. He may not like her personality one hundred per cent of the time, but Theo has too much of a big heart; he cares about her. So he's selflessly shackled himself to her for all eternity.'

'If he doesn't like her then why did he sleep with her?' I asked.

'Oh, trust me. This side of Summer didn't come out until after they'd spent the night together,' Baleigh replied. 'She's clever. She knew how to act long enough for Theo to actually believe she's a nice girl before letting her true personality show. Worst part is, I can't even blame Theo for falling for it. I fell for it too.'

'You did?'

'Come on, of course I did. We all did,' Baleigh said. 'I mean, Summer looks like Lewis Carroll wrote *Alice in Wonderland* just so she could play the part of Alice. It's not until she opens her mouth that you think maybe she's more suited to play the Queen of Hearts.'

Just then, the doorbell rang.

'Why do you people insist on disturbing me at this time of night?' Baleigh rhetorically asked, handing me the tub of ice cream.

I heard her skip down the stairs and softly padded after her, but remained on the second landing, leaning on the bannister with a good view of the front door.

Now, I've always thought it best to ask who it is at the door before answering it, or better yet, look through the peephole, but assuming it would be one of us, she opened the door without doing either. She'd presumed right, it was one of us.

'Hey, Bales. I was just —'

I took in Lucas's nonchalant expression before *he* took in Baleigh's appearance. I could only see the back of her head, but I'd guessed she was perhaps too shocked to move, due to the instant rigidity of her body. Lucas looked Baleigh up and down, glee and amusement written on his face.

'Marry me?' he asked.

Somehow, I don't think getting the door slammed in his face was the answer Lucas was hoping for.

***

I woke up to the sun streaming in through the window and the smell of freshly made pancakes. I had fallen asleep in the clothes Baleigh had given to me last night, but thankfully, she had laid out a new set of clothes, a dry towel and a new toothbrush for me.

After my shower, I shuffled downstairs and managed to slip on one step, which resulted in me thudding down the remaining stairs on my bum. I heard a cackle drift from the dining room and walked in to find Baleigh alone at the oak dining table, drinking a cup of tea with a stack of pancakes and an array of breakfast goods spread out over the table in front of her.

'I heard that,' she said, recalling my trip down the stairs.

'I don't know what you're talking about.' I rubbed my bum and sat down opposite her. 'Is that millionaire's shortbread?' I asked, pointing to a plate on the right stacked high with shortbread, Jenga-style.

'Yes,' Baleigh answered. 'It's my favourite.'

'I thought vanilla cheesecake was your favourite.'

'No, I like vanilla cheesecake a lot, but get sick of it sometimes. I never tire of millionaire shortbread,' Baleigh explained. 'It's my kryptonite, if you will. Mum only makes it for me when she wants me to be nice to someone and I'm guessing that someone is you. So this is me being nice: how are you feeling today?'

'Feeling about what?' I asked, pouring myself some tea and starting the day with chocolate and biscuit.

'Are you over your fat girl complex, then?' Baleigh asked.

'My what?'

'Your fat girl complex,' Baleigh replied.

'What's a fat girl complex?' I asked.

'It's when a girl who's not fat, thinks she is, so her self-esteem is so low she manages to subconsciously convince herself she's ugly and unworthy of any remotely good-looking guy,' Baleigh explained, biting into a croissant. 'There's a skinny girl complex too, but it's rare.'

'I don't think I'm fat,' I said, pulling the pile of pancakes my way.

'Yes, you do,' she replied, pulling the plate right back.

'And what makes you think that?' I asked, going for the toast instead.

'Ava.'

'Yes, Baleigh?'

'Fine,' she conceded. 'Don't admit it to me, but at least admit it to yourself. I may have known you for only less than a year, but I *know* you. Summer's comment last night hurt your feelings. Something's happened with you, in your past, and I'm guessing it had something to do with your weight and a guy. Which is why you keep Theo at such a distance.'

'What has Theo got to do with any of this?'

'Oh please,' Baleigh sighed. 'You two are crazy about one another.'

I almost chocked on my tea. 'Baleigh, what are you talking about?'

'Summer's hesitance towards you isn't completely unjustified because it's so obvious Theo has feelings for you,' Baleigh explained. 'Summer doesn't hang around you that often so she can't see as well as the rest of us can, that you like him too. I've noticed you guard yourself when you're around him. You try not to get too close. Why? I don't know. Maybe you've got it into your head that he'll never go for you. Just my observation.'

I paid attention to my plate of toast. 'You're wrong, Baleigh.'

'I'm sorry, are you speaking to me or your toast?'

I looked up. 'To you.'

We stared at one another, both of us as stubborn as the other.

The doorbell rang.

'The doorbell seems to be interrupting us a lot lately,' Baleigh commented. She got up to answer it and shortly after I was joined by herself and Theo.

'So, I heard you slapped my girlfriend,' Theo said taking Baleigh's vacated seat and helping himself to her pancakes. 'I think that's a bit unfair seeing as Baleigh called dibs months ago.'

'That's what I said!' Baleigh shrieked from the doorway. 'I'll give you guys some privacy.'

I watched her leave and go upstairs before facing Theo again.

'You're not angry?' I asked him.

'It depends,' he said. 'I get the feeling Summer wasn't telling me the whole truth when she said she accidentally bumped into you and you slapped her for getting in your way.'

'Wow,' I exhaled. 'I knew she would lie, but I was hoping for something a bit more creative than that.'

Theo gave a small smile. 'What happened last night, Ava?'

I opened my mouth to tell him exactly what I had told Baleigh last night – the truth, but something stopped me and I couldn't form the words. I didn't want to tell him. Thankfully, Baleigh had gone upstairs, otherwise I would have had to admit that she was right. I did guard myself when Theo was concerned. I didn't want to tell Theo the truth anymore, in case he noticed. In case he noticed that I was...*bigger* than the girls he's used to being around.

'She told me to stay away from you,' I finally answered, disclosing half the truth. 'I believe she thinks we're getting too close.'

Theo let out a breath of air. 'It's her problem with Baleigh all over again,' he muttered to himself. 'Okay, I'll speak to her. Are you sure that's all she said?' he asked, his eyebrows fighting to touch. 'Doesn't seem like enough for you to slap her over. You're usually pretty chilled.'

'What can I say? She caught me at the...wrong time of the month.'

'*Oh*. Right, I get it,' he said, understanding gathering in his eyes. 'Nonetheless, please try to refrain from hitting my girlfriend. It feels weird telling you off. Baleigh I'm used to, but not you.'

'No problem,' I said. 'If it helps you out you can tell her I'm sorry.'

'Are you sorry?'

'Sure.' I shrugged.

Theo fought another smile before he said, 'Can I tell you something?'

'Of course,' I replied.

'But you can't ask me what I mean by it,' he said. 'I just want to say it.'

'Alright, go ahead.'

He leaned forward, his arms crossed on the table. He was close enough for me to smell him.

'Sometimes,' he said, 'I look at you and I think to myself: it's not you, it's not me, it's timing.'

He fell slowly back into his seat and his face gave nothing away until he caught sight of the plate of shortbread.

'Who does Baleigh have to be nice to?' he asked.

CHAPTER TWENTY-SIX

Phoebe Bridgewell was proving extremely difficult to find, and school records were proving extremely useless. I could only touch so many people without arousing suspicion; I didn't want to get a reputation at a university I didn't even attend. The more we searched, the more likely it seemed that Phoebe was no longer a resident of Hayven, but I couldn't exactly trawl all one hundred and ninety-seven countries in the world.

I was beginning to live in a state of constant agitation. After our visit with Everett, things were slowing down. It had been weeks since Theo and I had seen Kindle McKay and Corbin Samuels on Murmmers Lane and we hadn't returned since. I'd contemplated returning to that haunted lane, but what good could possibly come out of that? I'd either see what I had already seen or end up *being* seen.

'Is anybody else panicking like I am?' I enquired.

Once again, we were sat on a patch of grass outside Fulton University, but it was only me and the girls.

'Yes, but there doesn't seem to be anything we can do,' Baleigh answered. 'Finding this Phoebe woman is our next step, but she seems to be hiding underground, and we've not found anyone who knows where she might be.'

'It's like we've hit a dead-end,' Faye added.

I rested my head on the tree trunk I was sat up against.

'Hey, Peyton,' a young man called out with a winked as he passed.

'Who was that?' I asked, watching the rather cute brown-haired guy swagger past.

Peyton rolled her hazel eyes. 'Just a boy in my class who thinks he's quite something. And Summer's ex-boyfriend.'

I couldn't see how you could go from that to Theo; seemed a bit of a leap, personality wise, but each to their own.

'That's Liam,' Baleigh elucidated. 'One of the world's biggest pigs, one who openly brags about all the girls he's slept with.'

'Last year was terrible,' Peyton continued. 'He used to go on and on about him and Summer in our classes. It didn't help that he would go into such *detail*.' She shifted uncomfortably. 'It was worse because we had to then spend far too much time with her ever since she started dating Theo, and sometimes your mind wanders…' She shuddered again.

'Wait. What?'

'What?' Peyton asked Baleigh.

'He's slept with Summer?' she questioned.

'Yes,' Peyton nodded, 'or so he says. If not, his gift is lying; he was quite explicit. Why do you ask?'

I weighed in and shook my head. 'He is lying. Theo was Summer's first, so he has to be lying or…'

Faye gasped and then there was silence.

'Or…*she's* the liar,' Baleigh concluded, her brown eyes wide. She went mute as she considered something. Suddenly, she sat up. 'I'm telling Theo,' she announced, before she jumped up and ran across the grass. She moved so fast you'd think someone had announced they were giving away real diamonds on the other side.

'No!' I yelled after her, my heart thumping as I scrabbled to my feet and chased after her.

I managed to catch up, but because she still wouldn't slow down I had no choice but to tackle her to the ground.

'Baleigh, are you crazy? You can't tell Theo!'

'Oh yeah? Says who?' she said, squirming beneath me. 'Get off!'

'Baleigh! Imagine how much trouble you'll cause, and most importantly, I know you're going to drag me down with you. I really don't like public confrontation.'

'Too bad,' she squealed breathlessly. 'I told you that I would get rid of her and this is how I plan to do so. There's nothing you can say or do to stop me. She's such a little liar! She's not getting away with this one!'

'Think about this logically,' I whined. 'You don't know whether Liam is telling the truth or not!'

'I'll take my chances. Get off!'

'Promise you won't say anything!'

'Never!'

'What are you two doing?'

I looked up to see Theo and Summer holding hands and staring down at us; Theo with an amused look on his face and Summer with a mildly disgusted look on hers.

'Are you two kissing or something?' Summer snubbed.

My cheeks went aflame as I lifted myself off the ground, but Baleigh remained perfectly calm, *dangerously* calm. 'Open your mind,' she whispered in a voice so low only I could hear as we were both bent over, dusting blades of grass off our clothes.

'No, we weren't kissing,' Baleigh said once she was stood straight. 'Ava and I have already discussed it; she's not my type.'

Theo's eyes narrowed as his gaze swivelled between us both accusingly. I looked down at the ground and did as Baleigh bid and freed my gift from the confines of my mind. I soon regretted it.

I can't stand these two. I don't get why Theo's always around them.

Either Theo hadn't told Summer what my gift was or she simply didn't care.

'We were discussing something else actually,' Baleigh continued, her voice cool but clear, her eyes never leaving Summer's. 'Well, truthfully, we were fighting over something, and since we don't seem likely to settle it, maybe you two would like to weigh in,' she said.

'Urm, Baleigh —'

'So basically,' Baleigh started, ignoring my plea, 'Ava has this friend in Huxton, well she's not really a friend, is she?' she asked turning to me, but didn't wait for my answer. 'No, Ava is more friends with her boyfriend.'

'Oh, Ava seems to enjoy hanging out with other girls' boyfriends, doesn't she?' Summer remarked.

My palm twitched, eager to meet her other cheek. I couldn't help but think, *I could take her.* But Baleigh could take me and she probably would if I took away her chance to bring down Summer. Theo looked down at his girlfriend with a hard expression on his face and subtly unlocked his hand from hers to scratch his neck before he folded his arms. Baleigh, on the other hand, had a smile on her face.

'Anyway, this girl told her boyfriend that she was his first...' Baleigh turned to look at Theo and he cocked his eyebrows, suddenly very interested.

I yanked on the back of Baleigh's top, growing redder and redder; couldn't she at least be more subtle?

'...kiss,' Baleigh finished. It wasn't subtlety personified, but I'd take it. She had stepped back slightly due to the rough pull I had given her top, but her eyes never left Theo's, until she turned her unnerving gaze to Summer, and I caught Summer begin to squirm.

Despite my constant pulling of her T-shirt, Baleigh wasn't going anywhere and I let go, thinking furiously of another tactic.

'But Ava has just found out that she *lied* because this other boy claims to have been her first. Kiss. Oh, what was his name, Ava?' she turned to me, pretending to think deeply. 'Liam, wasn't it?'

Summer's eyes became doll-like and her lips thinned as she pressed down on them tightly. *She doesn't know. They don't know. Liam said he wouldn't tell. She's obviously talking about someone else, but then why does she keep looking at me?*

'Theo, can we go to lunch now?' Summer asked him, but from the corner of my eye I could tell he was too busy staring at me to answer her, and I was too busy staring at Baleigh, who was still staring at Summer.

'Wait!' Baleigh said with an innocent giggle that reflected her personality in no way whatsoever. 'We haven't gotten your advice on the matter yet!'

I didn't dare avert my eyes from Baleigh to Theo, not when my face screamed *guilty*. When would the ground ever do what I asked it to and just swallow me up? Perhaps I could talk to Peyton about setting something up…

'We don't have time to give you advice,' Summer snapped. 'Figure out your own problems.'

It seemed rather stupid of Summer to add fuel to Baleigh's already roaring fire.

'No,' Theo said, halting Summer's attempts in pulling him away. 'I want to hear this. What sort of advice do you need?' I didn't have to look up to tell his jaw was clenched. He knows. Or does he? I couldn't concentrate with Summer swearing and cursing in her head. I shut my mind off and the silence was more welcomed than ever.

'Theo, I am so glad you asked,' Baleigh said.

'Listen,' Summer growled, 'we don't have time for this, I —' But Baleigh was already speaking over her.

'Ava doesn't know whether to tell the girl's boyfriend who, don't forget, is also her very good friend.'

'What's the girl's name?' Theo asked through gritted teeth. 'Maybe I've seen her around Huxton.'

'No, you haven't,' I said, keeping my eyes firmly on Baleigh, too much of a coward to turn my head. Maybe if I pulled her hair she'd follow me…or beat me up. It would definitely be the latter, but I was growing desperate. 'Baleigh, we should —'

'Autumn,' Baleigh said. 'Her name is Autumn.'

I heard Theo take a sharp and menacing intake of breath. I winced and closed my eyes. *Just leave, Ava.* Baleigh wasn't going to budge until she had taken Summer down to a point of no return, so I should just save myself and walk away. My feet stayed rooted to the floor.

'So, Theo,' Baleigh went on regardless of *all* our physical discomforts. 'Do *you* think Ava should tell Autumn's boyfriend?'

'It depends,' Theo said, threateningly quiet. The tone in his voice frightened me and I looked to see Summer turning a dangerous shade of red. 'How close is Ava to…*Autumn's* boyfriend?'

He definitely knows.

'Very close,' Baleigh answered. 'They're *really* good friends. Like you and Ava.'

'Then yes, she should,' he replied, his gaze hot on me and I couldn't avoid him any longer. 'He has a right to know.'

I couldn't read him; his face was so still and his eyes empty of any emotion. It was worse than seeing him hurt, upset, or angry – much worse. Yet, I couldn't look away.

Baleigh clapped, jogging my reverie. '*That's* what *I* said!' she announced. I wondered if Mr and Mrs Castel would miss their only child. 'Right! Now that that's settled, we'll leave you two to your lunch date. I'm sure you have lots to discuss. Come, Ava.' She dragged me off by my upper arm and thank goodness she had because I wouldn't have been able to move otherwise.

'Ava? Are you alright? You look very distressed. What happened?' Faye asked as we re-joined her and Peyton.

'I had hardly said a word and yet *my* life just got a lot more complicated,' I answered. 'That's what happened.'

CHAPTER TWENTY-SEVEN

Despite everything concerning Madrina and her Cliders, everybody still had lectures and classes to attend, and so did I. It had been three days since the Baleigh and Summer incident and I'd not heard from either Baleigh nor Theo. Although, that was probably because Theo was ignoring me and I was ignoring Baleigh.

On my way to what my teacher had called a 'mandatory lecture', I thought about what I could possibly say to Theo when I saw him next. Then I remembered I'd left my books on my bed in an effort to make it to the lecture on time.

You know when you have enough on your plate that even the smallest things can tip you over the edge? I was standing precariously close to that edge at the moment, and it seemed that all it was going to take was something little, like me running out of bread, to push me over.

I slapped the palm of my hand repeatedly against my forehead, ignoring the questioning looks I was attracting from students, before I heaved a laborious sigh and turned back the way I had come. It wasn't until I was slowly trudging up the stairs that I suddenly felt my temperature spike and I stumbled, but managed to grab onto the stair railing in time. Seconds later my shoes were filled with cement and my head began to swim. Soon I was crawling on all fours to my bedroom, unable to stand up straight, sweat dripping onto the floor and my pulse out of control. No one was walking down the corridor to notice me and I couldn't decide whether that was for the best or not. I was able to fit the key into the lock and amazingly made it to the middle of my room before my eyes glazed over and I collapsed.

I was thrown into a dark abyss that I began to think had no end until I landed painlessly on my back in the middle of an empty room. It was cold and dark, the walls were grey, and there was not enough light. I turned my head to find that I was not alone. Five people were sitting around a circular table metres away from where I'd landed. Around the table were seven empty chairs, one of the empty chairs was much bigger than the others. The five people were dressed in black robes and their faces were covered with their hoods.

Cliders.

They were discussing something, but I couldn't hear what they were saying. The only way I knew they were speaking was because every now and again, their chins would lift and I'd see their mouths open and close in mid-speech. They couldn't see me or maybe they just couldn't hear me. Or both.

I stood before I took a shaky step forward and fell into a dark empty space again. The drop took me by surprise and I screamed, but no sound came out. I woke with a start, tangled in between my bed sheets. How I had gotten into my bed was beyond me, but I didn't have time to think about that just then. Instead, I got out of bed and ran.

I ran and ran until I reached *Hayven Books* and I didn't even stop there. I burst through the door at full speed and ran right into an unsuspecting Theo, and we both toppled to the marble floor.

'First Baleigh and now me,' he said. 'What's with the constant need to tackle people?'

He wasn't angry with me? His eyes were warm, his voice gentle. Wasn't he angry with me? Why wasn't he angry with me?

'Urm, are you both alright?' asked a woman with a concerned look on her face.

I had taken Theo down to the ground so hard he was now flat on his back and I was now lying flat on top of him. I had been staring at him ever since we had fallen, wondering why he wasn't furious with me over the entire Baleigh and Summer situation. My hands were pressed flat on the floor on either side of his head and his hands were on my waist where he had placed them in an attempt to stop me barrelling into him when I'd arrived. I hastily stood up, ignoring the heat spreading in my cheeks and *everywhere* else.

'Yes, thank you,' Theo replied to the woman. She gave us a curious smile before walking towards the exit, stopping every now and again to look back at us with the same bemused expression she'd first given us.

'I'm so sorry, Theo,' I said as the crowd around us started to disperse.

'For what?' he asked, helping me pick up the books he had dropped. 'For bumping into me and knocking me over, or for not telling me about Summer?'

If I had been pink before, I was beetroot now.

'For knocking you…over,' I stumbled. 'And for the Summer thing…I had…I had just found out.'

'I know, Baleigh told me. Were you going to tell me though?' he asked.

I looked down at the books in my hands. 'I don't know,' I answered truthfully. 'I didn't think it would have been my place to get involved in your relationship.'

'My *past* relationship,' he corrected and I felt my pulse pick up. 'And Baleigh seemed fine with it.' Thankfully, his tone was still warm and there was a hint of amusement hidden in there. It was hard for him to stay mad at Baleigh. I hoped the same applied to me.

'Yes, but she's Baleigh,' I explained, finally looking up at him. 'She's your best friend aside from Lucas.'

'And what are you?' he asked.

'Your...I'm your friend.'

His lips formed a line and eventually he nodded. 'So, what's up?'

I suddenly remembered why I had high-tailed it here in the first place. 'Three more Cliders have joined Kindle McKay and Corbin Samuels. Theo, there's five now! And they're waiting for the others,' I finished, remembering the seven empty chairs clearly reserved for Madrina and her six remaining Cliders.

Theo stilled. 'Abby,' he said to the girl with the blonde pigtails behind the counter. 'I'm going on my break.' And before she could answer, Theo pulled me outside.

'How do you know?' he questioned.

'I saw it,' I answered. 'Well...I dreamt it, I suppose. I felt ill...I mean, I *was* ill; I don't really know what happened. I was on my way to a lecture when I realised I'd forgotten my books, and on my way back to my room my temperature suddenly spiked, then I couldn't walk, and then I collapsed on the floor of my bedroom and after the dream I was in my bed. The dream couldn't have lasted more than two minutes.'

'And what happened in the dream?'

'I fell down a black hole and landed in a cold room. It was empty except for a round table with chairs studded all around it,' I explained, trying my best to remember. 'The five Cliders had their faces covered with their hoods and they were talking, but I couldn't hear them and they couldn't hear or see me. There were seven empty chairs around the table and one was the biggest of them all.'

Theo took a deep breath, having understood the significance of the chair and who those five Cliders intended to have sit in it.

'So, there are five now. Five out of eleven isn't bad, but it isn't great either,' he said, dragging his hand through his thick hair.

Out of nowhere, both of our phones beeped twice to indicate we had a message.

'Message from Baleigh,' I said. 'Cinema invite.'

'Same,' Theo said. 'She says everyone's going and it just so happens we need to speak to everyone.'

I nodded. 'Shall I meet you after work?'

'No, we can't wait any longer,' Theo said. 'I'm taking the rest of the day off.'

***

'Change of plans, guys,' Theo said as we arrived at the cinema to meet everyone.

'Why, what's happened?' Ollie asked.

'Kindle McKay and Corbin Samuels have company,' Theo answered. 'Three more members of company.'

'Theo and I need to show you something,' I said.

326

A few seconds later, all seven of us were crouched down behind a familiar brick wall on Murmmers Lane.

Faye went to stand up, but I caught her in time and pulled her back down. 'No!' I whispered. 'You have to stay down and make sure you're quiet.'

Despite the looks of deep confusion, they all obeyed.

'Where are we?' Baleigh whispered. 'What is this place?'

'Murmmers Lane,' Theo answered as I observed recognition sweep across their faces.

'This is where Madrina…'

'…died? Yes,' Theo finished for Lucas.

'I don't understand,' Faye said, rubbing the goose bumps that had appeared on her arms. 'It's four in the afternoon in Hayven, why is it so dark and cold?'

'It's always dark and cold here,' I answered, repeating Theo's words. 'The sun doesn't visit Murmmers Lane, not anymore.'

'Why are we hiding?' Lucas questioned. 'What's here that we should be afraid of?'

'Slowly peer over the edge of the wall…not too much!' Theo instructed. 'You see that warehouse right in front?'

'Yes,' Ollie answered as the rest nodded.

'That's where the Cliders meet, that's where Everett was captured and taken to, and that's where Ava saw the five Cliders in her dream.'

'It's so dark,' Baleigh said. 'I can't see a door.'

'There isn't one,' I answered. 'Everett said as much.'

'Then how do we get in?' Baleigh questioned.

'We don't go in. Not yet anyway,' I said. 'Theo and I just wanted to show you the warehouse.'

'Guys, I know this isn't the best time, but before I forget,' Ollie said, 'you know the tea-bags you took from Gaige's house? In them I found —'

'Oh my—'

I clapped my hand across Baleigh's mouth to keep her quiet. Three Cliders had emerged through the wall of the building, just like Theo and I had seen Kindle McKay and Corbin Samuels do on our last visit.

Two of them I recognised by their height, it was Kindle McKay and Corbin Samuels, just as before, but now they had brought a friend. I couldn't recognise the third Clider as their hoods were still up and it was pitch black, but then the moon, always on our side whenever we were here, glowed and I caught sight of waist-length jet black hair.

It was Sia Valour, Madrina's right hand. The Clider I feared the most. I felt my back freeze and my throat constrict. She was there. She was real. It was her who would stop at nothing to make sure Madrina returned to Hayven. It was her who was our biggest threat. I couldn't take my eyes off her silhouette, and then suddenly she turned and her eyes were on *me*.

I ducked back down behind the wall, but it was too late. In my haste to get down I knocked into Baleigh who then caused a domino effect, causing Peyton, who was at the very end, to topple over and out of the area the brick wall protected.

'Who is that?' said a male voice, which could only have belonged to Corbin Samuels.

'Shall we found out?' replied a sharp female voice and seconds later the brick wall burst into orange, red and green flames.

I rolled away from the burning heat of the wildfire, clumsily got to my feet and watched the others do the same. We were now in open space and within clear view of the Cliders thanks to the bright flames consuming the brick wall. I could hear my pulse drum in my ears threatening to deafen me and my legs grew soft and weak. *What was next? What should I do next?*

'They're children!' Corbin Samuels laughed. He pulled his hood down and revealed his short spiralled hair and brown skin. What was it they said happens when you see a Cliders' face?

I pressed my hands to my ears in an attempt to steady the vibration.

'They're children who have seen where we meet,' said Sia Valour. Her voice was a slow and cold drawl that sent icy fingers down my spine. 'They cannot leave,' she finished, turning away.

With a nod of understanding from Corbin Samuels, he began to walk our way.

We couldn't travel, he was close enough to mix with us and I couldn't bear the thought of bringing him to the sunny side of Hayven. He belonged here, among the cold and the dead.

I was frozen to the spot and Corbin Samuels was getting closer, towering over six feet tall, his shadow almost as menacing as he was, until he stopped in his tracks due to a circle of orange fire Lucas had thrown around him.

'Oh!' Kindle McKay shrieked, cackling shrilly, like a witch who'd just learnt a new game. 'You want to play with fire do you?' After shaking off her hood to reveal a face as sharp and pointed as her voice, and a grin that turned my insides to ash, she cupped her small hands, released a rotating globe of fire and blew it in our direction.

The ball swivelled in the air as it came directly towards me, mesmerizingly beautiful as it swam through the air, spinning colours of red, green, and orange. Ollie, who stood closest to me, made a dragging motion with his hand and a sudden wind blew the swivelling ball of wildfire away from me. Instead, it landed in front of us before it spread and set the ground ablaze. The impact it made with the ground when released from its circular cage knocked us each off our feet and left us sprawled on the dead earth. There was dirt in my eyes and an even louder ringing in my ears, mixed together with the palpitations of my heart, I was all set and ready to pass out.

This couldn't be how it ended, it couldn't be. I had to save Hayven, we had to save Hayven. How could we do that if we were all dead? I spat dirt out from inside my mouth. The dirt was mixed with blood.

'Guys!' Theo coughed. 'Grab my hands!'

I had landed awkwardly on my left leg and whilst I knew no bones were broken, I knew a purple bruise had formed and it hurt too much to lift it. Instead, I crawled with my arms, coughing and spitting blood, dragging my legs to get to one of Theo's out-stretched arms. Then I heard Peyton scream and turned on my back to look up.

A Clider was in the air, floating and melting in the shadows, her whereabouts betrayed only by her purple rope belt – Sia Valour. She had the gift of flight, I reminded myself too late.

She was bearing down on us before she hit a slab of invisible air and was thrown backwards. I looked closely to see we were all encased in an invisible dome – a shield.

Faye had now fallen on her knees from the effort it had taken to cast a protective shield so wide to cover all scattered seven of us.

'Guys! To me! Now!' Theo shouted as I watched Sia Valour recover from the shock. My mind was all over the place and I found that when my mind was lost it was also open. The anger resonating off Sia begged for spilt blood; she had underestimated us before, but it would not happen again.

Theo was now standing and I forced myself on my feet; I forced myself to ignore the pain that shot up through me and hurtled towards him for the second time that day. Soon I was joined by Ollie, Baleigh, Lucas and then Faye.

'Where's Peyton?' Theo asked frantically.

Peyton, who had been knocked the furthest back, was now running towards us.

'Peyton!' I shouted as I kept one hand firmly on Theo and the other out-stretched to her. 'Hurry!'

She was so close, but now so was Sia Valour. Even closer was Kindle McKay, laughing manically into the darkness.

Whilst running, Peyton turned back, flicked her wrist upwards and a pile of earth created a mini hill, blocking Kindle's path. I felt Peyton make the lightest contact before shouting, 'Theo, now!'

I screamed as we hung in mid-air as Peyton careered into us. At that moment, Theo began to shift and next there was nothing before we were thrown onto grassy ground. Baleigh and Ollie rolled past me and stopped. We had landed in front of Fulton University…and a lot of its students.

The sun and warmth was back and for once the bright Hayven sun burnt my eyes. Students stood around us, gaping at the seven people who had just hurtled out of thin air.

Lucas spat out blood from where he had bitten his tongue and Baleigh groaned from the fierce impact she had made on the ground. Peyton was breathing heavily, clutching grass strands, whilst Ollie slowly pulled himself up. Faye wiped the blood from a red scratch above her eyebrow, and Theo helped me to my feet, having been the first one of us to land.

We were all back – alive.

I looked up at the clear bright sky and then in the direction we had just come falling out of, past the students milling around and continuing to stare; my chest heaving, my leg and cheek sore.

Theo came up behind me. 'It's not over, is it?' he asked.

'No,' I answered. 'This is just the beginning.'

About the Author

J.A. George is the author of the four part series, GIFTED - THE HAYVEN SERIES. She spent years of her life reading book after book before sitting on her bed one morning, opening her laptop and typing Chapter One into a Word document. Now, not only does she read book after book, she writes book after book too. Usually with a large bar of chocolate by her side.

Want to know more about the upcoming sequel, *The Silver Orb*? Follow her blog and twitter for updates.

Feel free to contact her in the following ways:

Email: jess.george@hotmail.co.uk

Twitter: @JGeorgie_

Blog: www.thejourneyofgifted.co.uk

She loves hearing from readers!

Made in the USA
Charleston, SC
02 June 2016